TIME PAST

A Time Travel Novel

Elyse Douglas

Broadback

Copyright © 2023 Elyse Douglas

All rights reserved

Cover design by: Carl Master
Library of Congress Control Number: 2018675309
Printed in the United States of America

ISBN: 9798375119779

For Bingo Brady and his 1969 dinged-up truck out under the stars.

"The past beats inside me like a second heart."
—John Banville

"The universe is under no obligation to make sense to you."
—Neil deGrasse Tyson

More Time Travel Books

by Elyse Douglas

❉ ❉ ❉

Time Visitor

Speakeasy

Time Stranger

Time Sensitive

Time Change

Time Shutter

The Christmas Eve Series

The Christmas Town

Time With Norma Jeanc

The Lost Mata Hari Ring

❉ ❉ ❉

www.elysedouglas.com

Join Us For Updates!

ELYSE DOUGLAS

TIME PAST

PART 1

CHAPTER 1

May 2022

Seventy-four-year-old Kate Clarke Cunningham pushed through the glass revolving doors of Macy's Department Store and stepped out onto 34th Street. Her purse hung over her left arm; her right hand clutched the rope handle of a heavy shopping bag containing an aqua enameled steel tea kettle she'd just purchased on sale.

As hectic shoppers flowed around her, she dodged and weaved and struggled ahead, feeling like a salmon swimming upstream.

On Seventh Avenue, she turned north and joined the next onslaught of pedestrian traffic, craning her neck, searching for a taxi. She saw none, so she stopped near a wall, reached for her cellphone, and called for an Uber.

The late May day was warm, with plenty of hazy sunshine, and she was comfortably dressed in white capris, a short-sleeved blue cotton top, flat sandals, and sunglasses. For only seconds, she was distracted as a police car weaved its way through heavy traffic, its siren screaming. Fumbling purse and bag, Kate raised fingers to her sensitive ears to plug them up. Although she'd recently been diagnosed with a mild hearing loss in both ears, she could hear loud, high-pitched sounds as well as ever.

After looping the shopping bag over her left wrist, Kate touched her hair, still adjusting to the length and feel of the new cut and style. She'd visited a different salon that morning and met Alvita, who hailed from Barbados. The 30s-something hairdresser had artistically styled Kate's silvery, short hair, with plenty of layers to create volume. Kate thought it took five years off her age. Now, if she could just get rid of her belly and spreading hips.

Though she strained through a yoga class twice a week, and she tried to walk the Central Park Reservoir track twice a week, jogging slowly when her back and knee allowed, she couldn't seem to regain her slimmer, younger figure.

"Good hair you've got, Mrs. Cunningham," Alvita had said, in a lilting Caribbean accent. "You're lucky, you know."

"Actually, Alvita, you can call me Ms. Clarke, or just Kate. Clarke was my maiden name and, just this morning, I decided to go back to it."

"All right, Ms. Clarke, but you still have nice hair,

although it *is* thinning a bit here on the top."

"Yes, I've noticed that."

"What color was it when you were young?" Alvita asked.

"Black, and I wore it long at my shoulders, sometimes in a ponytail, tied with a bright scarf. I especially liked yellow or blue."

"Did you grow up in New York?" Alvita asked, as she cut and fingered Kate's hair, studying her work in the full-length mirror.

"No. I'm originally from Ohio, a small town."

"I've never been out that far in this country."

"It was a pleasant little town. I haven't been back in years, not since my parents died."

"And you said you've got two kids?"

"Yes, Ellen is happy in Paris, working in computers, and my son, Greg, is a freelance film editor in L.A. I wish they weren't so far away, but that's life, isn't it?"

"And your husband?"

"My husband died in 2020 during the first wave of COVID."

"Oh, I am so sorry to hear that. COVID was so bad for us all. I lost an aunt and a cousin, and I pray it will not come back to us."

"David, my husband, caught it right away, and he went fast, like so many others with underlying conditions."

"We should talk about happy things," Alvita said, her expression pleasant, her smile warm. "Let's talk about New York in the spring."

"Yes, it's the best time to be in New York. The flowers are so dazzling."

This was how Kate had returned to the world of the living after her husband's death, and after the worst of COVID had passed. She'd reconnected to life in bits and pieces, mostly through conversations with cashiers, restaurant servers, salespeople, her super, and people who waited in line at places like Starbucks, Zabar's, or Mondel Chocolates, famous for their homemade chocolates since 1943.

During the COVID lockdown, Kate had forgotten how wonderful it was to talk to people without fear of catching a potentially lethal virus. Now things were almost back to normal. She'd even returned to volunteer tutoring at the library, teaching English language skills to public school students who were performing below grade level due to the pandemic. Although she still had to sit several feet from the students and wear a mask, she was delighted to be working with children again, doing what she'd done for over thirty years at a private school in Manhattan.

David's death in April of 2020 had brought a cold, visceral shock, which triggered dark loneliness and depression, along with stinging remorse and regrets. Theirs had not been the best of marriages, especially after the children left for college. She had overlooked his two flings with younger women because, through the years, he had overlooked her aloof indifference to their relationship. More than once, he'd told her, "There's a coldness in you, Kate, a place I can't reach. It's like you left me long ago. Can anyone reach you? Maybe the kids... I don't know."

After David died, and as the pandemic raged, Kate sat isolated in her terraced, three-bedroom, East Side apartment, reliving scenes from the past. Isn't that what older, retired widows do when they find themselves alone? Escape into the past, giving themselves permission to ponder what had happened and imagining what might have been?

At first Kate resisted reliving the tragedy, the tragedy that had occurred when she was a college girl; a tragedy that had completely changed her life and her image of herself as a caring, responsible person. She felt guilty of a terrible crime, and she never really forgave herself.

During the first years of her marriage, she'd been able to push it from her mind and move on with her life. But when the children moved away and her relationship with David grew stale, she began to think about Paul Ganic at unexpected times and places: in the grocery store, in Central Park, and by the ocean in Montauk, where she and David had rented a house every August.

She'd remember, in vivid detail, Paul's elegant eyebrow lifting in astonishment or amusement, prompting her to do the same. She heard his soft, deep voice; saw his tanned, handsome face; smelled the manly scent of his neck; felt the spring rain on her face as they kissed at the entrance to the cave where they often met and then made love.

As these memories grew more frequent, she recognized that it was the sadness and the searing pain of loss that had also turned her cold to the marriage. That and the bald truth that her husband, David, had become someone she did not admire. He complained and argued with waiters and managers in restaurants to get free dinners; he cheated his real-estate clients and partners and, finally, he deceived her in thousands of ways while he had his short affairs.

She didn't ask for a divorce because he was the father of her two children, Ellen and Greg, and they loved him, and he, them. Kate felt too old and tired and, sadly, indifferent, to start again as a middle-aged divorcee, so she stayed with him. As Kate's practical father used to say, "Life meets you where you are, and you better be ready to duke it out all day long." That's what she'd done: duked it out in quiet desperation, out of apathy and for financial security.

Now that David had been dead for more than two years, and her marriage of more than forty years was over, she wondered if she was capable of truly loving anyone. Had she loved her children as she should have, or had she been a cold, unfeeling mother? Had she been a distant, unapproachable teacher? These were the questions that now haunted her. She'd wanted to be more empathetic with the students. She'd wanted to be more playful with her children; she'd wanted to hug them freely and spontaneously—but something had stopped her. The past, it seemed, had blunted her emotions.

The past had damaged her. The dark past seemed a live thing that never left her.

Of course, she should have told David what had happened all those years ago, about the tragedy that had shaped her life. Admitting what she'd done might have led to self-forgiveness; it might have released her from torment and self-loathing. Perhaps it would have brought them closer, or at least allowed her to love him and the children more fully.

Once, when they were in their early forties and on vacation, lying in bed after a day of watching the children ride the waves and skip along the beach, she'd almost told him—but she couldn't push out the words. Her memories were too private. Too personal. Too devastating.

In her sixties, Kate had seen a therapist because of depression, but when he probed too deeply into her past, she'd grown uncomfortable and defensive.

"Why should I tell you anything about my past?" she'd said sharply. "Would you tell me, a perfect stranger, any of your personal, buried secrets?"

On Seventh Avenue, traffic snarled, horns honked, and fists jutted out of windows. Kate glanced at her phone and then to the street. Searching for her Uber, which was close by, she stepped off the curb at the same time there was a break in the traffic. For only seconds, she glanced down at her phone. A white SUV lurched ahead, barreling toward her, just as Kate lifted her eyes. Her heart jumped to her throat.

It was too late to dart away. She froze as the SUV rammed into her, sending her tumbling onto the street, her shopping bag and purse scattering. Brakes squealed, horns blared, and women screamed. Kate lay motionless, as a stunned and curious crowd encircled her.

CHAPTER 2

Forty-two-year-old Greg Cunningham and forty-year-old Ellen Cunningham sat next to their mother's hospital bed, where one or both had kept vigil for three days. Kate was lying on her back, covered by a white cotton blanket, IV fluids flowing into her veins. She was pale, there was a scratch on her cheek, and on her forehead was a small bandage.

Kate's sticky eyes fluttered open and, for a moment or two as she stared up into the faces of her grown children, she believed she was dreaming.

"Hello, Mom," Ellen said, jumping up. She was a pert, efficient woman, with short, curly, auburn hair; a round, attractive face; and dark eyes that seemed to search for secrets.

Greg gave his mother a little wave. "Hey there, Mom. How are you feeling?"

Greg had a paunch, and short, crisp hair, graying over the ears. His stooped posture was a testament to Kate's failed campaign, ever since he was ten years old, to get him to stand up straight.

Kate struggled to find her voice. "I'm either dreaming... or I'm in big trouble," she said.

"Not in trouble, Mom," Ellen said, patting her hand. "Some idiot driver hit you near Macy's and almost killed you. Do you remember?"

Kate felt pain in her right leg and left shoulder. "I think so... Everything's fuzzy.... I know I'm in Lenox Hill Hospital, but... How long have I been here?"

"Four days."

Kate's eyes opened a little wider. "That long?"

"Yeah," Greg said, moving toward the bed. "You were in shock. They wanted to make sure you didn't have a heart attack or something. As soon as we heard, I took the redeye and Ellen flew private."

Kate blinked. "Private, all the way from Paris?"

"Philippe insisted," Ellen said, shrugging a shoulder. "Don't worry. He's on his third tech company. He can afford it."

"Why don't you marry him?" Kate asked. Her speech was slow but not slurred. "What are you waiting for?"

"Don't go there, Mom. Not today. We're happy the way things are, and marriage would probably ruin everything. Our relationship is best described as a thicket of stylistic fireworks. So, no, marriage would blow us both to pieces."

Kate shut her eyes and sighed. "Whatever. You're overly dramatic as ever."

"Well, Mom, you were the one who wrote about

marriage in that novel you never finished, saying it was, and I quote, 'a shallow and stumbling affair being played out in a sophisticated and complicated way.'"

Kate smiled weakly. "I'm impressed you remember."

"I remember, all right. I liked what I read. Now that you're retired and are going to be laid up for a while, why don't you finish the thing?"

Kate felt herself heavy on the bed, fighting exhaustion. "Not now. Not ever. I'm too old... and... I don't want to remember those things." She tried to swallow, but her throat was parched. "Can I have some water?"

Ellen reached for a glass of water with a straw, held it close to her mother's lips, and Kate took a few sips.

"So I guess I'll never have grandkids," Kate said, slowly moving her head to look at Greg. "Unless you have some good news for me."

"Nope," Greg said. "Shannon just walked out on me, and thank God she's gone. Not only were we incompatible, but we also grew to despise each other."

Ellen returned to her chair. "So, you probably won't have grandkids, Mom. Greg and I would be the worst parents, anyway. I mean, look at us."

"Hey, speak for yourself," Greg protested.

Ellen laughed. "And do you even want kids, Greg?"

"I don't know. Maybe. I mean, I've thought about it."

After a few seconds of consideration, he shook his head. "No, I don't."

"I rest my case," Ellen said.

They both looked at their mother and instantly realized she was not paying attention to their chatter. Her eyes were fluttering, struggling to stay open.

"You should rest now, Mom," Ellen said softly. "Don't worry about talking. Your voice sounds all scratchy and tired from that tube thing, anyway. You need to rest."

Kate nodded, forcing herself to speak. "But... how am I? I think I talked to some doctor... but I don't really remember much... not since..."

"Paramedics saved your life," Ellen said. "A woman and a man. Both young, and both unsung heroes." She paused, trying to gauge her mother's strength. "Your heart stopped, and they brought you back from the big abyss."

Kate's eyes widened. "I don't remember that."

"I tracked them down and personally thanked them, and I tried to give them each a big tip, but they refused. Anyway, you have cracked ribs, a sprained shoulder, a very bruised leg, and it's a bloody miracle you're alive. That's what Dr. Harris said. Oh, and by the way, she's a woman, originally from the U.K., hence the expression 'bloody miracle.'"

Kate forced a small chuckle. "How nice. Do you like her?"

"Yes," Ellen said.

"I like her, too," Greg tossed in. "We talked movies.

Old movies. And get this: she loves *Two for the Road* with Audrey Hepburn and Albert Finney. And *This Sporting Life* with Richard Harris and Rachel Roberts."

"Maybe you two should get married and give me grandkids. I know I'd be a better grandmother than I was a mother."

Greg shook his head. "Ain't gonna happen. She's already married. Two kids."

"Of course," Kate said. She tried to take a deep breath, but the pain in her ribs made her wince, so she stopped. "How long will I be here?"

"At least two more days," Ellen replied. "You were hit by a car, a very big car, and you're seventy-four years old. They need to keep you under observation a little longer."

"I'm so tired... Why am I so tired?"

Ellen glanced at Greg. "Well, it might be because of the medications... and also because your heart is beating irregularly. They're giving you something for it that I can't pronounce."

"The condition is called arrhythmia," Greg said.

Kate nodded. "I know what that is. Your father had it. It's not good."

"You'll be fine, Mom," Ellen said soberly. "You have good doctors."

Kate fought sleep. "Who hit me?"

"Some young kid about twenty years old. The cops haven't filed any charges."

"... probably my fault," Kate whispered.

Ellen's voice turned sharp. "It was not your fault,

Mom. He hit *you*, didn't he? He was probably texting or something."

"You don't know that," Greg said.

Ellen turned a sassy face to him. "Are you defending him?"

"No, I just think we should wait to find out what happened."

Kate shook her head. "It's okay... I wasn't looking where I was going... I was looking at my cellphone."

"Well, don't tell the cops that, Mom," Ellen demanded. "No way tell them that."

Kate felt her head sink into the pillow. She was so very tired. "My head's okay, though... right?" she asked, softly. "I mean, I know who I am... and who you are."

"No concussion," Greg said. "It really is a miracle."

Kate nodded, finally allowing the wave of exhaustion to overtake her. She closed her eyes and was just on the edge of sleep, when suddenly, she heard the screech of the braking SUV and felt the impact of the car against her body.

She jerked and made a sound of fear. All at once, she was back there, in that other accident, the one she'd been in fifty years ago, her body filled with terror as the car she was driving went crashing through the guard rails of the bridge, and she felt a wave of nauseating panic as the car plunged into the stinging cold water and sank.

In her head she screamed out, *I have to find Paul! I have to find Paul!* She'd struggled to find him, but she couldn't breathe! She had to find a way to breathe!

And then came the awful pain and the screaming when her father told her that Paul had died, and she wanted to scream now. She wanted to scream out the truth; she wanted to tell someone the truth before she died.

"I killed him!" Kate said, stifling sobs, her eyes shut against the world but streaming tears. She couldn't bear to look at her children, but she had to tell them. "I killed him… I killed him."

Ellen's voice was confused. She gently touched her mother's face. "Mom, what's wrong? What are you saying? Why are you crying? Should I get a nurse?"

Kate spoke through choking sobs. "No! No… nurse."

"Mom, what is it?" Ellen pleaded. "Are you in pain?"

Kate fought to control her emotions, struggling to anchor herself in time and place. She opened her eyes, staring up at Ellen and Greg through blurring tears.

Greg moved closer. Ellen hovered, blotting Kate's tears with a tissue, as they stared at her, anxious and troubled.

Kate's breath was uneven, her body quivering. "Before I die… I must tell you…"

"You're not going to die, Mom," Ellen said. "You just need to rest."

Kate turned her face from them. "I'm not the person I wanted to be. I wanted to be… better."

"Don't think so much, Mom," Ellen said. "It's not good to think about things so much."

"Yeah, stop thinking!" Greg said, trying to lighten the mood. "Hey, look at me. I stopped thinking a long time ago." And then his hand shot up before Ellen's face. "Don't say it, Ellen. Just don't say it."

"What?" she shrugged innocently, hoping, like him, to humor their mother. "Say what?"

Kate didn't respond to their banter. She wiped her eyes. "I was … being punished," she said faintly. "I had it coming."

"Had what coming, Mom?" Greg asked. "What are you talking about?"

"It happened so long ago…" A cry almost choked her. "… but I have to tell you," Kate said, her eyes blinking slowly as she fought to stay awake. "I have to get it said once and for all. I can't hold it in anymore."

"What, Mom? Tell us what?" Ellen asked.

Kate gathered all her strength and spoke deliberately, pushing the words out in a rush. "I killed Paul. I killed the love of my life."

Ellen and Greg exchanged startled glances. "What?" they said in unison.

"I killed him," Kate whispered, and then her eyes closed, and just before she lapsed into sleep, she muttered the final words, "And I killed our baby."

CHAPTER 3

T hree days later, Kate sat in her living room, resting in a black leather recliner. She was staring out the 15th floor windows, watching the ship and barge traffic on the East River. A helicopter was taking flight, heading east, toward the sun-glinting towers of Brooklyn.

How did I end up being the woman I am? she thought. And then, *Come on, Kate, you know.*

That one rash act when she was twenty years old had changed her life forever. It had robbed her of the power to become the woman she had wanted and planned to be. The young woman she'd been in the past held her true soul and her happy, soaring spirit. The woman she had become was a stranger to her, and she was frightened of the secrets that lay embedded in her heart's core.

Since the SUV accident, Kate had felt the pressures of the past tightening around her in dreams and in a persistent nostalgia that had become an insatiable longing. She longed to be that young woman again, to stand at the golden dawn of that point in her life again, so she could choose a different course than the one that had swept her away into what, she now believed, was a hijacked destiny.

Although she'd been an attentive and practical mother, raising two successful children, and she'd been an effective teacher—at least her colleagues and supervisors had said so—she'd always felt somewhat like an imposter, as if who she was did not jibe with the aloof, inadequate inner vision she had of herself.

As she sat staring, she realized that her life had fallen into ever-dwindling, narrow options. Perhaps it was time to change that? Perhaps it was time she faced the past? If not now, then when? She should have done it long ago, and then maybe the broken pieces of her life would have mended, and maybe her marriage would have thrived, and maybe she would have thrived.

Confrontation and reconciliation waited for her in the small Ohio town, where her life had taken a tragic turn, and where she had begun to carry the unbearable weight of guilt and regret she'd endured for over fifty years. Did she possess the courage it took to return and face her past?

Greg was in a bedroom on his cellphone making work calls, and Ellen sat on the sofa, her fingers chattering across her laptop keyboard.

"I'm going to be fine, now," Kate said.

Ellen didn't look up from her laptop screen. "I'm not leaving until I'm sure you're okay. I can work remotely, no problem."

"That's sweet," Kate said. "How lucky I am to have such good kids."

Ellen glanced up. "You're the only mom we've got, and we don't want to lose you."

Kate turned her head left to look at Ellen. "Was I a good mother? I know it's a heck of a time to ask, but... I ask just the same."

"Can I be honest?"

Kate frowned. "That bad, huh?"

Ellen shrugged. "Not always."

"And you're always honest, Ellen."

"I know. Philippe hates it, but that's who I am. As I said, not always. You cared for us and protected us, and we knew you loved us. We knew you would do anything for us, and that, mother of mine, got us through lots of growing and family pains."

"So, when wasn't I a good mother?"

Ellen lowered the laptop screen. "When you shut off, which happened often and randomly, and we never knew when that was going to happen. It was as if you flipped a switch and turned the light of yourself from ON to OFF. Just like that."

Kate looked down. "I did that, huh?"

"I always thought it was because you were working on your novel. You were lost in your own world. I guess Dad thought that, too."

"You mean that stupid novel I never finished?"

"But you were always working on it."

Kate leaned back, taking the truth in silence, and Ellen lifted the laptop screen and resumed typing.

Minutes later, Kate said, "Yes, I was... working on that thing. God, for how many years did I work on some version of that damned novel?"

"Do you still have it locked away in a box?"

"Oh yes. I finally gave up on it when your father died."

Ellen paused her typing and fixed her gaze on her mother's profile. "That's an interesting comment."

"Do you think so? I don't know."

"Will you let me read it—all of it—now that it doesn't seem to matter anymore?"

"No."

"No?"

"That's right. No, and I'll never finish it."

"So, it still matters... Why?"

"It's too personal, Ellen. That's probably why I never finished it."

"So, it wasn't really a novel? It was more autobiographical?"

"A mix, I guess."

"Mom, why weren't you and Dad happy together?"

Kate shut her eyes, wishing she didn't have to answer the painful question. "We had happy times. We understood each other."

"I don't think so. Dad confided in me a year or so before he died."

Kate shot Ellen a glance. "Did he? He confided what? A marriage is a personal thing that no one else will ever understand."

"He said you always kept a part of yourself hidden and he didn't know how to reach you."

"Most people keep things hidden. He hid things from me, too."

"I don't hide. I tell it like it is."

"I'm not you, Ellen, but I do admire you for your honesty."

"Why won't you tell Greg and me what happened to that man you said you killed? Right before you fell asleep, back at the hospital, you said he was the love of your life."

Kate's eyes opened fully, and they searched the ceiling, the windows, the outside sky, and the creamy white clouds. "I was on medication. I didn't know what I was saying."

"Forgive me, Mom, but I think you're lying."

"Maybe I am."

"So, there you go again. Withholding and shutting off. It's a little irritating, you know. No, not a little irritating, it's a whole lot irritating."

Kate sighed. "I don't know how to talk about these things. They're buried deep and they hurt deep. What else can I say?"

"You can just let it go, Mom."

Kate massaged her forehead with a hand. "When I'm completely recovered, I'm going to Ohio, back to my old college town."

"That was a quick change of subject."

"Yes... it was. After I return, then maybe we can talk about it. Maybe I can tell you everything. Right now, I can't."

Just then, Greg entered, his cellphone in one hand and a can of soda in the other. "Hey guys. Mom, I'm going to have to leave tonight. This production company I'm working for just bumped up their release date and they want me there to work with this jerk of a director. It's the director who's insisting I return ASAP."

Kate said, "Come over here and turn this chair around, Greg, so I can see you both. I've had enough sky gazing. I want to talk to you both now."

As Greg did so, Ellen closed and stored her laptop beside her on the sofa and turned her full attention to her mother.

"I'm sorry I have to go, Mom," Greg said. "I need the money."

Kate sat up. "Don't be sorry. Go. I'm fine. I'm just so happy that you came. I can't tell you how much I've enjoyed having you both here. It was almost worth getting hit by a car."

"Don't even joke about that," Greg said.

"She's going to visit her old college town in Ohio," Ellen said.

Greg took a sip of his soda. "Okay. Cool, but I don't remember you talking about a college town in Ohio. You graduated from the University of Cincinnati, didn't you?"

"Yes, but I transferred there from Paxton College in Paxton, Ohio. It's a university now. Back then, it was a small, prestigious college, founded in 1825 or 1830, I think. Something like that. It had a lovely campus, with Greek-styled buildings, beautiful gardens, and a stadium with an electric green football field. And I remember the wide, open sky and beautiful hills, with hidden caves."

Ellen rose. "So, why go back to Paxton, Ohio?"

At first, Kate wasn't going to explain, but then she thought better of it, when she considered Ellen's criticism that she was withholding and shutting off again. She didn't want to do that anymore. Not to her kids, whom she loved more than her own life. They deserved more from her—that "more" she'd never been able to give.

"You're not going to tell us, are you?" Ellen said, with an exasperated shake of her head.

Kate didn't meet Ellen's gaze. "Yes, Ellen. I'm going to tell you both what happened because I can't live with myself anymore, holding it all in. I don't have the strength anymore. I can't face the darkness alone anymore."

CHAPTER 4

The silence was loud in the room, and when Kate gave Ellen and Greg a mannequin smile, she sat up a little straighter, bolstering herself with a breath and a lift of her chin.

"I'm going back to Paxton because... not to sound too dramatic, but..." she stopped, cleared her throat, and tried again. "I'm going back because I think a part of me died back there. When I was twenty years old, a few weeks before my twenty-first birthday, something awful happened, and I lost my way. I need to go back, face that awful thing, and see if I can finally move on. I should have done it long ago."

Ellen and Greg were sitting on the sofa, waiting, eyes glued on their mother.

Ellen decided to coax her. "I assume it had something to do with the love of your life?"

Kate averted her eyes. "Yes... Silly as it sounds. I was a silly girl, and I was reckless and rebellious."

"I don't see it," Ellen said. "You've never been silly, reckless, or all that rebellious."

"It was the 1960s," Kate answered. "Your grandfather wanted me to go to college and become the best writer I could be, but your grandma didn't want me to leave her. When I got a half scholarship to Paxton, I never looked back. The summer before I left, I worked at an A&W Root Beer drive-in stand to help pay my college expenses. I still remember the menu: the Papa Burger came with two beef patties, and it was 90 cents. The Mama Burger was 70 cents, and root beer was 15 cents for regular and 30 cents for large. Shakes and malts were 45 cents."

"Okay... I remember the 1960s," Greg said. "I edited a documentary about the 1960s a couple of years ago. Vietnam. Free love, drugs and rock and roll. Bob Dylan. Pink Floyd. Cream. The Byrds. I loved Jefferson Airplane. Oh, and there was Woodstock. Who can forget Woodstock and Joni Mitchell?"

Kate stared into the middle distance, with a ghost of a smile. "Yes, it was another world... a world long gone."

Ellen rose and moved toward the windows. "So, you were saying about being reckless?"

Kate shrugged. "It was a... what do I say? It was a different life, and I was a different person."

"And his name was Paul?" Ellen asked, looking at her mother.

Kate lowered her gaze. "Yes... his name was..." and then she stopped. "Why is it still so hard to say it?"

"Paul what, Mom?" Ellen pressed. "Just say it. Get it out."

"His name was Paul Ganic. He'd been in the service and was in Vietnam for about thirteen months. So he'd started college late and was older than most of us. He was also wiser because of the war, and sometimes he was wild because of what he had seen and experienced over there. And sometimes he was tender and sometimes he wasn't. We met in the fall of my junior year, and I fell in love with him just like that... at first sight, like all the novels and the movies say, and Paul said he felt as though he'd known me before. We dated for only a few weeks before we got married."

The room dropped into stunned silence as Greg and Ellen shared a quick side glance.

Ellen scratched her forehead. "Okay, that was a surprise. Did Dad know you were married before?"

"No... I never told him."

"Awkward," Greg said. "Why didn't you tell him?"

"Because I didn't want to," Kate said firmly. "Because... well, I had my reasons."

"Do you have any photos of the guy?" Greg asked.

Kate shook her head. "No... There was no social media in those days. I suppose we took photos, but I don't remember."

"So, what happened?" Ellen asked.

Kate twisted her hands. "Paul was a contradiction. He loved opera and rock. He dressed well, and didn't wear the usual 1960s clothes—faded jeans and jeans jacket, bell-bottom pants, wide striped shirts and sunburst T-shirts. He was a great auto mechanic, and yet he hated the smog and the acid rain cars produced."

"And acid rain was?" Greg asked. "Basically smog, right?"

"Yes. Paul and I took the only environmental course that was offered in those days, Environmental Studies and Climate Trends. Coal plants were spewing sulfur dioxide and nitrogen oxides into the air, turning the clouds and the rain acidic. It poisoned lakes, and killed trees, and made fish-eating birds sick. Anyway, Paul wanted to help change all that because he had a real love for nature. He also wanted to work with the coal industry to help solve the problems of pollution."

"So he was a forward-looking guy, I guess," Ellen asked.

"Yes, he was, and he also made moonshine, but I never saw him drunk."

Greg's eyes opened wide with pleasure. "Moonshine? Did you drink it?"

Kate gave him a guilty smile. "Oh, yes, and it burned like fire."

When she looked down at her nervous hands, Kate's spirit sank a little. "I know you've heard old people say it, but it truly does seem to have happened a long time ago, and yet a short time ago. I read something once in a magazine article a few years ago and I never forgot it. Basically, it said that sometimes we don't experience time in the 'clock time,' because clock time is false. It doesn't really measure anything. So whenever I think about Paul and those days I often feel as though I can jump into the past and then return to the future, and both seem real and present. Maybe that's why I sometimes tuned out and turned that ON switch to OFF because I truly was in another time and place. Well, anyway, I'm getting distracted."

"Was Paul from that area?" Ellen asked.

"Yes, close by. He didn't live with his parents, though. He lived in a trailer near Cove Lake, and he baked his own bread and grew vegetables."

Ellen laughed. "Are you kidding me? A veteran, a car mechanic and a smart guy, who baked his own bread? He sounds like a female magnet. I bet he had to fight the girls off."

"Yes... he was very handsome, and he could have had any girl he wanted, and a couple of the female adjunct professors were smitten by him, as well. I even heard that his 30s something literature professor made a pass at him one day after class."

"But he chose you," Ellen said.

Kate shifted in the chair. "We fell in love. Yes."

"So, what happened, Mom?" Greg asked.

Kate stared at them, searching for words. "We secretly married in the fall of 1968, at the start of my junior year. Three months later... I was pregnant."

After another long, startled silence, Ellen returned to the sofa and sat, digesting her mother's declaration. She cleared her throat. "Mom... This is like, totally wild. Why didn't you tell us this before? I can't believe you kept this a secret for all these years.

Did you have the baby?"

Kate lowered the recliner and slowly pushed to her feet, reached for her cane, and moved toward the windows, peering out. "No. On March 23, 1969, I was driving in a heavy rain storm. There was lightning, and the windshield wipers could barely slap away the thick drops of rain. Paul had just rebuilt the engine on a light green, 1962 Chevy Bel Air, and he wanted me to drive it. Of course, I wanted to. He was so proud of it. He'd done something to increase the gas milage and minimize the carbon emissions. Well, anyway, I'd had some moonshine, and I was driving too fast. Much too fast, and I shouldn't have been drinking, because I was pregnant, although things were different then. We didn't know as much about things as we know today."

Ellen's breathing was shallow as she waited. Greg's eyes were turned down.

"It happened in a heartbeat. On a tight curve, I lost control of the car, and it went speeding across a wooden bridge, skidding, and bursting through the guard rail, plunging into the lake."

Greg's gaze shot up. Ellen didn't move as she looked at her mother, who was framed in sunlight streaming in from the windows.

Greg saw his mother trembling, and he got up and went to her. "Are you all right, Mom?"

She didn't look at him, her chin quivering, her eyes bold and misty. "I was struggling to hold my breath, and I couldn't find Paul in that cold, murky water. I reached and searched, but... well... I must have lost consciousness. To this day, I don't know how I escaped. A police car just happened to be approaching from the opposite lane and saw the car splash into the lake.

"I don't remember much after that. Even after all these years, I don't remember much except that I screamed a lot in the hospital, and they had to keep giving me something to knock me out. I don't know how long it was before I learned I'd lost the baby."

Tears streamed down Kate's cheeks, but she continued. "Back home with my parents, I roamed the house in a trance, and whenever I looked at myself in the mirror, I saw my large, wet eyes were raw with self-hate, disgust, and fatigue. My parents hadn't known I was married or that I was pregnant. Of course, I should have told them, but I didn't. I don't think they ever really believed I was married. They were terribly embarrassed at the hospital when they were told I'd lost a child that they didn't even know about."

Kate reached into her robe pocket for a tissue and blotted her eyes. "I'd never seen my father so defeated and my mother so fragile, unable to look at me, sometimes unable to even get out of bed. As you both know, your grandfather was a pharmacist, and his drugstore was busy and popular. And he loved that place and he worked so hard. Okay, I'm rambling. For a time, he brought some sort of sleeping powder home for Mom so she could sleep. He didn't give me any or take it himself. I heard him walking the floors at all hours of the night."

Kate turned and looked into her son's eyes, hers wet and sad. "So, now I've told you. Now, I've let it out after all these years. Now, you must know, you must understand, that I have to go back and make peace with it. If I don't, I'll never be able to let go of the sadness and hatred of myself that I've felt for all these years."

Ellen went to her mother and wrapped her in a tight embrace. Greg touched his mother's shoulder.

"I'll go with you, Mom," Ellen said.

"Me, too," Greg added. "I'll tell my boss to get somebody else to edit the thing, and I'll go, too."

Kate pulled back from the embrace, dabbing at her tears. She slowly shook her head. "How sweet you both are. How I love you, more than you'll ever know, but I must go alone. It's my way. The only way. I have to face this alone, as I should have done long ago."

"But what good will it do, Mom?" Ellen asked. "It will just stir it all up again, won't it?"

Kate scratched her cheek. "I don't know, maybe, but I've got to do it. It's time I went back to meet the old ghosts of 1968."

CHAPTER 5

It was Saturday, the second week in October, before Kate felt strong enough to rent a car and set off for the 500-mile drive from Manhattan to Paxton, Ohio. By then, the autumn leaves in Pennsylvania and Ohio blazed, shimmering red, yellow, and orange. Kate felt there was a healing quality to traveling alone on the back, curving roads, listening to the whine of the engine, with her window rolled down and the earthy smells of the country blowing in.

The first day she drove five hours and stayed the night in a sprawling motel, with a yellow, erratically blinking, neon sign that read SHADY SIDE MOTEL. Nearby was a roadside vegetable stand that displayed voluptuous pumpkins, freshly picked apples and containers of apple cider. Inhaling the cool, fresh autumn morning air and browsing the stand were mood lifters, bringing back fond memories—and some trepidation as to what lay ahead.

As she drew close to Paxton, Kate became anxious, trying to summon a courage she wasn't sure she had. Memories flooded back, and fragments of old 1960s songs played in her head: *Magic Carpet Ride* by Steppenwolf, *Lady Madonna* by the Beatles, and *Green River* by Credence Clearwater Revival. She rhythmically tapped the steering wheel and swayed to the beat of the music as she drove the two-lane roads, physically traveling in the present, but mentally drifting back into the past.

Young, hopeful faces appeared in her inner mind, as if looming out of a fog. There was Connie Poe, her sophomore roommate, with her full figure and wide-open eyes that always seemed a little startled. Her voice was soft, and her auburn hair tumbled down her back, and she loved to comb it as she hummed a tuneless song.

Connie had been an artist—and a good one—who'd wanted to please her friends, her teachers, her boyfriends. But despite her beautiful face, she'd been insecure about her broad hips. She often stood in front of the full-length mirror, saying, with a frown, "My mother's hips are so narrow. Look at mine. I keep patting them and telling them, 'Hey hips, you've got the wrong girl. I can't be my mother's daughter.'"

Kate would answer, "Those are child-bearing hips, Connie. And look at your face. Beautiful. Look at your breasts. Big. And, let's face it, guys like good hips and big boobs."

Staring into the mirror, Connie would turn this way and that, keeping her focused eyes on her hips. "Yeah, well, maybe I don't want kids. Do you?"

"Of course you want kids. You're an artist, Connie. You'll have them all finger-painting and drawing on the walls."

And then there was Vicki Allen. She and Kate had shared an apartment during the summer and early fall of 1968, before she married Paul. Vicki had a boyfriend, dreamy Luke Parker, who always seemed to have his head in the clouds, and didn't care if the sun came up or went down. Luke had long, wavy, blonde hair and chopped-off bangs. Whenever possible, he had a beer in his hand, and he drove a dinged-up, green and white Ford pickup, with marijuana decals on the side doors, and a large peace sign stuck on the tailgate.

Vicki played the guitar and sang Joan Baez, Bob Dylan, and Peter, Paul and Mary songs, her favorite being *Blowing in the Wind.* She'd play it over and over again until Kate flung a pillow at her.

Luke and Vicki seemed made for each other, but after their junior year, Luke transferred to Ohio State, because the philosophy department was superior to Paxton's. Vicki disliked big schools and decided not to transfer with him, but she regretted it. Luke soon found another girlfriend, and they began living together off campus.

Vicki grew depressed, left school during her senior year, and got well-paying gigs at Holiday Inn lounges, playing the guitar and singing. Two years later, she married a Holiday Inn manager, and they had two children.

Kate and Vicki had stayed in touch for a while, until Vicki divorced her husband. The last time Kate and Vicki had talked—twenty years ago—she'd confessed that her marriage had been a disaster, her kids were in therapy, and she wished she had transferred to Ohio State with Luke.

And there was her favorite professor, Mr. Conning, a stooped, white-haired, published poet, who'd been at the college for over thirty years. He was quiet, intense, and a little scary. Some days he was mild, and others, he was sweaty and shaky, with a shifting glance.

"You must memorize Shakespeare's Sonnet 30, class," he said one day, out of the blue, with the fervor of an inspired apostle, his arm raised toward the heavens. "Yes, truly you must. It will serve you well in your lives."

Kate *had* memorized it. When she was but ten miles from Paxton, she stared at the unraveling road, divided by a yellow, dotted line, and she allowed the verses to rise from the depths of her soul —because Mr. Conning had been right. Sonnet 30 was the perfect sonnet for her now, at seventy-four years old. She leaned her head back and spoke in a firm, sing-song voice.

"When to the sessions of sweet silent thought
I summon up remembrance of things past,
I sigh the lack of many a thing I sought,

And with old woes new, wail my dear time's waste..."

It was a sun-bright Sunday afternoon when Kate arrived in Paxton. She viewed the area with unbiased eyes, purposely not having looked up the town on the internet to study the changes virtually. She drove across red brick roads and past quaint shops, cafés, and a farmer's market, with its white canopies covering vegetable and fruit stands.

On the village green, she was lucky enough to arrive during a band concert, where children romped on the grass, and students and locals gathered around a white gazebo, some seated in folded chairs, some standing, others seated on the lawn.

In the late 1960s, rock and folk singers took turns performing inside that gazebo, singing protest songs about the war in Vietnam. Long-haired hippies flashed the "peace sign" and wore black armbands, and students, who sported beards and headbands, joined them, and everyone sang along and cheered.

In 1968 and 1969, Kate and Paul had been there. Along with the surging crowd, they'd sung *The Times They Are A-Changin'* and *We Shall Overcome*. The smell of marijuana was everywhere, as people passed joints and shared their highs with complete strangers, who quickly became glassy-eyed friends in the pot-filled haze.

Driving slowly along Main Street, Kate pushed

down emotion as she took in a town that had been greatly transformed since 1969. The Towne Grocery was gone, as well as The Busy Bee Restaurant, both replaced by an upscale, multi-level shopping center, with walkways, small gardens, and popular retail chain stores.

She saw a newly built, A-frame community center and a Starbucks. A modern glass and redbrick fire station stood where the bowling alley and the popular Kip's Bar had once been. The Aurora, the town movie theater, with its flashing, yellow marquis lights, was now a Marshalls. Kate had seen *Planet of the Apes* and *The Graduate* at the Aurora, and she could still remember the smell of popcorn as you entered the thinly carpeted lobby.

It elated her to see that the Greek revival library, where she'd spent hours wandering the aisles, was still there. But the Pizza Place and Mackay's Books, New & Old, the bookshop where she'd worked part time for nearly three years, were both gone, replaced by a health food shop and an AT&T store.

Kate's heart warmed as she remembered the owner of the bookshop, a pony-tailed, crotchety old man named Art Mackay. He sat in his dusty shop, perched on a stool, reading, just waiting for the next person or thing to irritate him. He was an anxious, spare, and vigorous man, who wore overalls, black Keds tennis shoes and wire-rimmed glasses.

But Kate had loved him. He knew every book on every shelf and he'd read most of them. When they first met, he'd growled at her when she interrupted his reading to ask where she could find a certain book.

He'd barked. "Oh, piss off."

She'd barked back. "If you don't want to sell books, then what the hell are you doing here?"

He'd narrowed his eyes on her, scrutinizing her anew, and Kate swore he'd flashed her a quick, feisty grin. He'd lowered the book he was reading, scratched a bushy eyebrow and said, "Have you read *Adam Bede* by George Elliot?"

"No. Never heard of it."

He grunted a curse, squirmed down from his stool, edged past her, down a shadowy aisle, soon returning with the paperback in his hand, a frown creasing his thin lips. He'd thrust it at her. "Here. Read it! It was the first novel by Mary Ann Evans or, as most people know her, George Eliot, published in 1859. That book has remained in print ever since it was published."

Kate took the book and ran a hand along the dust jacket. "What's it about?"

"Eliot described it as, 'A country story full of the breath of cows and scent of hay.' But it's really about a carpenter who's in love with an unmarried woman who bears a child by another man."

Art and Kate became good friends, and now Kate wondered when the bookstore had closed and what had happened to Art. Why hadn't she kept in touch with him? She'd grown to love him like a second father. But then, she knew why she hadn't kept in touch, and she pushed the dark thoughts away, replacing them with the happy memories of the shop's creaky floors, the dust shimmering in the window light, the woody, pipe-smoky smells, and Art's cranky expression.

Kate drove along the far side of town, looking left to see new resident housing and administration buildings, as well as a futuristic-looking glass tower that she speculated had something to do with science.

To her immediate right was a small plaza and a man-made pond with a gushing fountain, surrounded by hedges and benches. That hadn't been there in the 1960s, but the two heavy black cannons, artifacts from the Civil War, were still there. She and Paul had once played on those cannons, she darting around them, he chasing her, baring his teeth, his eyes wild, his hands like claws, ready to seize and gobble her up. And then he had growled out, "Give us a kiss!"

In that instant, she recalled a bit of a conversation she and Paul had shared as they stood next to the cannons, just before she'd told him she was pregnant.

"Did you know, Kate Clarke Ganic, that when Lincoln was assassinated, a five-dollar Confederate bill was found in his pocket? The only cash on him. The Confederate States of America issued it in 1864 and it featured an image of the Confederate White House in Richmond, Virginia, and a portrait of the Confederate President, Jefferson Davis."

Kate ran a hand along the cool barrel of the

cannon, a little distracted by the bombshell she was about to drop. "That seems odd, doesn't it?"

Paul shoved his hands into his jeans pockets and rocked on his heels. "Odd it is, Kate."

"So why did he have the Confederate money?"

"Don't know for sure, but some speculate that Lincoln got the bill when he visited Richmond in the week before his death. He probably picked it up as a souvenir."

"Okay, so why are you telling me this?" Kate had asked.

"Isn't it obvious? It's a good short story for you to write. You could romance it up and have the bill given to him by, say, a Confederate woman admirer who invites him over for tea or something. Now, wouldn't that be a good story, especially if she tells him in confidence that she was really a Union spy?"

"So, maybe you should write it," Kate had said, moving closer to him, ready to tell him that he was going to become a father.

Kate smiled at the memory. Paul had always encouraged her to write, and he was always coming up with ideas for her.

Glancing right, Kate found an empty parking space, stopped, and wiggled in, switching off the engine and sitting in silence. Placing her hands on top of the steering wheel, she blew out a weary sigh, feeling an inner trembling. Feeling displaced and vulnerable.

All around her were ghosts of things and people who had been. Paxton was not the same town she'd known, recalled, and longed to return to. Not at all. It was an entirely different world from the one she'd kept locked up in her mind for over fifty years. Her romantic and tragic Paxton, Ohio, was gone. Vanished. Only a dream in her head, and a distorted one at that.

And gone were her roommates, and professors, and Art Mackay and, most of all, Paul Ganic, her husband, and the baby she had wanted to name Diana.

When the tears came, Kate didn't stop them. She let them trickle down her cheeks and drop. She had never allowed the iceberg of her past emotions to thaw; not during her marriage; not during the birth of her children; not during her retirement; not during the years since her husband's death. Only recently, when she'd finally told her children the truth.

The tears were a long time coming, so she sat stiffly, her damp eyes focused straight ahead. She gripped the sides of the steering wheel, squeezing, until her hands turned white. She wanted to be young again, setting off into the infinite blue ocean of possibilities again, like a brand-new sailboat, sailing away into that glorious dawn of youth.

She shook her head and said to herself. "Stupid... There you are again, wishing, regretting and not facing the life you created for yourself. When are you going to grow up, Kate?"

But the past was an enemy she couldn't ignore, negotiate with, or defeat. The past, her past, was still very much alive within her, and that's why she'd returned to Paxton, Ohio. To confront it, and to face all her buried fears.

CHAPTER 6

The next morning, Kate's hotel room was full of sunshine. She showered; dressed in comfortable jeans, a red and black flannel shirt and sneakers; then she slipped into her brown leather jacket and left the hotel. Down the street, she discovered the Blue Wind Café. It was a cheerful place, with fresh fall flowers in small vases on blue tabletops, and there were white chairs, and soft classical music coming from an unseen speaker.

The friendly waitress was a junior at the university, majoring in business, who said she was from Columbus. The maple-flavored oatmeal was delicious, the seven-grain toast was served with unsalted butter and apricot jam, and the coffee was bold and hot.

Outside, Kate drove a mile out of town, far from the lake where she'd had the accident in 1969. She'd face that later, when she'd built up enough courage.

She parked the car in the lot of an office building that stood where the old train station used to be. This was where she'd frequently taken the train from Paxton to Walton, her hometown. The train station had been replaced by a two-story, blond brick building with large windows and office signs for doctors, lawyers, and a real estate company.

Kate left the parking lot and headed in the direction of a dirt trail that used to lead to a wildflower field and then up a grassy hill to the hidden cave where she and Paul had often met.

The sky was a deep blue, the air crisp and clean, the autumn leaves sparkling, and for a time, she had a startled sense of health and youth. But then her knee and her back began to ache. She had to pause frequently to catch her breath as she made her way across the golden, morning grass and up the slope, toward a grove of trees that covered the entrance to the cave.

She recalled a day in the late autumn of 1968, when she and Paul had climbed the same hill, hand in hand. Clouds were heavy with rain, and before they had crested the hill into the cover of trees, thunder boomed, and the sky opened up and rained buckets. The wind encircled them; the rain slanted into them, and Paul tugged her higher toward the trees, her hair flat, stringy, and dripping.

With wild laughter, they had crested the hill, dropping under the cover of an oak tree, the horizontal limbs dark-wet, fall leaves being ripped from branches and flung away, sailing. Paul's kisses were wet, her clothes clung. Later, when rain-washed sunshine lighted them up, their lovemaking was playful and rapturous.

Kate's memories vanished as she gasped with effort, finally reaching the level tree line and dropping down onto the grass with an exhalation of breath. After a moment, she sat up, her heart drumming, and pulled her knees to her chest, hugging them, casting her gaze out over the gentle hills that were once covered with trees and rolling, green fields.

Below, the town had spread like weeds. Clusters of modern homes and look-a-like condos had invaded the hills, with more under construction. Hammers echoed, electric saws zinged, and a bulldozer crawled about like a toy. And there were two new, multi-story dormitories on either side of the old college chapel. Its spire was lit by the sun, but its majesty was diminished by the size of the other buildings.

Kate released a resigned breath, practicing her philosophy of acceptance. "Of course, it has changed," she said aloud. "It had to change, didn't it? That's life." After another sigh, she said, "But it was so peaceful, and it was so beautiful."

Ten minutes later, Kate pushed to her feet and wandered into the shadowy trees, unsure at first where the hidden cave had been—their cave, hers and Paul's.

Paul would laugh when she called it a cave. He said, "You can hardly call it a real cave. It's just an opening in some rocks."

"But it has an arch, and when you duck and enter, it's quiet, dark and private," she'd said.

Kate made her way through the trees, following a trail on the left through some low brush, and then straight ahead across a narrow ravine and onto another trail, which led to a sandstone cliff. She stopped and caught her breath, proud of her intact memory.

As she approached the cliff where the cave lay hidden by overhanging tree branches and thick brush, it saddened her to see empty beer cans, cigarette butts, crumpled paper bags and paper cups tossed around the charred wood remains of a fire. It seemed a desecration. In 1969, the area had been pristine. If others visited the cave, they didn't leave trash.

Kate crept forward, snaking a hand into her jacket pocket to find her powerful mini flashlight. She kicked the beer cans from the cave entrance and hesitated, glancing about. She heard birdsong and the caw of a crow. She heard a distant siren coming from town, and the wind was chilly, though the sun was still bright.

Inhaling a breath for courage, she parted the branches that obscured the cave entrance, a five-foot high arch. There it was, just as it had been all those years ago. So much had happened in her life; it seemed appalling and yet comforting that all of this remained the same.

Her pulse quickened. First things first. She

switched on the flashlight, allowing the beam to tunnel into the darkness, searching for any animal or snake. Swinging the beam left to right, she saw two more crushed beer cans and a discarded pack of cigarettes.

Because of the trash and the obvious violation of the place, Kate almost left—but curiosity overcame her hesitation. Paul had used his pocket knife to carve their initials into the cave wall. Were they still there? She knew it was silly and sentimental, but she wanted to see that memento of their love. So she crouched below the tree limbs, despite the little pinch in her back, and gingerly crept inside, keeping the flashlight beam active, her eyes sharp.

The tree's hanging branches enclosed her in the cave's space, which measured about 10' x 15', with a ceiling a little over five feet. The air was damp, the smells musty and earthy. And then, in an instant, her nose remembered, and memories flooded her body and mind.

When teaching creative writing, she had often told her students how important it was to include olfactory images in their writing, since the olfactory processing system is very close to the memory hub in the brain. As she stood there, she understood again how powerful a smell can be, how quickly it can trigger memories.

Kate saw Paul clearly in her mind; she heard his voice; she felt his touch. For seconds, she indulged her fantasy that he was with her again in the cave, and all was good and right with the world.

In a slow turn, with her head lowered under the sloped ceiling, Kate shined the beam along the cave wall, noticing discolored yellow and brown water streaks. But there was also something else. When she saw Paul's carving, her eyes expanded. She felt a catch in her chest, and a flutter of love and emotion that stung her eyes with tears. The initials were still there, albeit eroded by time and moisture.

PG
LOVES
KC
10-28-68

The cave was soundless, the moment startling and haunting. Kate stood motionless, remembering those erratic, restless and reckless days. As a twenty-year-old girl, she'd wanted to take big bites out of life. She'd wanted Paul and his baby, and she'd wanted to be a great novelist and write stories that inspired and shocked. She'd wanted to experience currents of raw emotion and moods that soared high and low and crashed. And, in the end, that's exactly what had happened. She had crashed and lost everything.

The dizziness came swiftly. Was it the stale air? She couldn't breathe. Kate heaved in breath after breath, but nothing helped. Her head seemed to spin; her body shook, and her throat went dry.

Panic rose and Kate dropped the flashlight. Her pulse quickened. Her heart stopped. She fell to her knees, mouth breathing, chest heaving. Cries for help were whispers.

CHAPTER 7

Fluttering eyes. Sticky mouth. Cold, damp body. Kate jerked awake with a cry that echoed. Black tomb. Death?

She sat up, searching the dark, her heart high in her throat. She tasted sour, metallic fear. Her head whipped about. Where was she? What happened? The cave! She must have passed out. Yes, she was in the cave! She patted the ground, searching for the flashlight, terrified of touching a snake. Nothing.

Her eyes adjusted, then spotted a faint light a few feet ahead, to her left. Like a panicked animal seeking escape, she scrambled toward the light on all fours, bursting through a leafy door into the shock of sunlight, stopping, a hand covering her squinty eyes.

Her breath came fast, her nostrils flaring, sucking in sweet, cool air. On her knees, she swung her head left and right. A dog barked some distance away; the rowdy cry of a blue jay was close, and the fading moan of a train whistle hung in the air like an old memory.

Kate sat on her heels, light-headed, as she struggled to acclimatize herself to a vague strangeness of body and mind. She listened to her breathing and felt a vibrancy pumping in her veins. Overhead, the sky was a bright morning blue and the eastern sun a rich glow of yellow. The air rustling the autumn leaves was as refreshing as a dip into a clear mountain stream.

Kate unfolded her legs and sat, noticing her jeans were muddy at the knees. Her sneakers were soiled, her flannel shirt and leather jacket were damp, and they didn't fit. They were loose. Too big. The wrong size. A tickle of alarm made her swallow away a dry, tight throat.

Perplexed, she raked a hand through her hair, then stilled. It was long and luscious. Long, thick hair? She didn't have long hair, or thick hair. Her hair had thinned at the top. She lifted her hands and examined them, her eyes widening. Smooth hands. Young, feminine, lovely hands. No wrinkles. No age spots. No blue veins.

In an athletic thrust of hands, feet and legs, she sprang to her feet, agitated, bewildered. With trembling hands raised, she touched her cheeks— smooth, cool cheeks.

Her big eyes blinked into sunlight, searching for the reality of the moment. There was no pain in her back, no stiffness in her knee. In a whirling motion, she faced the entrance of the cave, her eyes moving, seeking to understand. There were no beer cans, no plastic cups, no cigarette butts. The low brush was thick, the trees above flashing autumn gold in the snappy wind.

She swallowed hard, then swallowed again as her mind turned over events. Her clear eyes focused on the lovely autumn day around her, and she saw it all with a clarity of sight she hadn't seen in years. Twenty years? Thirty years? Ever?

A rich, gleaming light fell on everything, like a blessing. Lovely birdsong echoed, and the wind across her face was silky soft. It tousled her hair, her long black hair. The hair of her youth.

For a long moment she didn't move, her heart beating strong, her breath coming soft and easy. As tension rose, she slowly examined her slim, youthful body, her long legs, her slender hips and flat tummy. Who was she? How could this body be hers? This young, lithe body? If it was a dream, then she had to hold on to it. Don't wake up. Don't return to reality! Stay in this incredible and wonderful dream forever!

An idea flashed and Kate reached into her back pocket for her cellphone. It wasn't there. She searched for her wallet. It wasn't there. She'd taken her wallet out of her purse and left the purse locked in the glove compartment of the car. Dream? Reality? A stabbing fear. Unknown. What had happened?

Her mouth opened, and she tried to cry out,

but she couldn't make a sound. She swayed, almost fainting, grabbing the hanging limb of a sapling for support. With her mind reeling, she shambled toward the thick trunk of an oak tree, leaned against it, and caught her breath.

Her eyes tightly shut, she counted to ten, took deep breaths and then opened her eyes, sure the vision or the dream or whatever it was had vanished. It hadn't vanished. She was a young woman again! Strong again, and vital again, and supple, and everything around her gleamed and looked brand new! A brand-new world!

Her thoughts raced, straining to process the impossible moment. Past and present collided; pieces of images, faces, and jagged memories tumbled through her head.

Had she died in that cave? Had she passed through a tunnel of light, and was she on the other side? Was she having a near-death experience, like those she'd read about or watched on *YouTube*?

Recovering her wits, she raced to the tree line, stopped, shaded her eyes, and gazed out over the vast hills and the town of Paxton below. They looked as they had in the 1960s! There were no condos or modern homes. No dormitory towers. The faraway hills lay soft and pristine in the glorious morning sun; the rambling forests were thick with trees and, in the distance, was gentle, rolling farmland.

The weight of the moment froze her for a time, but then she staggered and wilted, bracing her fall on the grass with both hands. She sought answers.

Any answers.

She sat with care. She waited. She stared, and the morning deepened and lengthened. When creamy clouds formed and cast shadows across the land, Kate followed them, allowing her mind and volatile emotions to settle, feeling drunk, and high, and sick to her stomach.

In the cave, she must have had a stroke or a heart attack and died. That was the only thing that made sense. So, she would be patient and wait. Maybe she'd soon pass through a dark tunnel, and then, surely, someone would come for her, or she'd see a white light. Isn't that what happened at death, as many dying people had said? Fine, she would wait. She would just sit and wait.

The sun rose large in the shocking blue sky, the wind whispered, and Kate grew hot. Did dead people get hot and have to shade their eyes from the glare of the sun? Inside her heart, she felt the building of a quiet fire, and she uttered a silent prayer, an urgent plea for clarity and understanding. No one had come for her, and perhaps no one would. What then? What now?

That youthful fire spread through her body and energized her, and so she rose to her feet and set out on a careful descent of the hill toward town. What would she find? Would her rental car be waiting? Would the vision, the hallucination, or whatever it was, melt from her eyes as she approached Paxton, and would dead relatives appear and take her onto new vistas and strange new worlds?

Down an incline, across the tall grass, past yellow and lavender wildflowers and zooming bees, Kate came down from the hill, her legs springy, her breath easy, her mind floating upward through thoughts and memory. The past seemed present, and the present past.

With a start, she realized that her mind and memories were those of a seventy-four-year-old, but in a young body. She stopped, looking around her. Which reality was she in? Past or present? Although her feet were strong and sure, and her pulse throbbed with life, her old woman's mind was stumbling through mental weeds of disorientation and fear. She had shed the skin of an elderly woman and become reborn, but would she shed the skin of an aging mind?

The air smelled of fall, and the world—this familiar old world—seemed to be welcoming her back from a long absence! And so she advanced, leaping a gurgling stream, moving through a thicket, disturbing scattering birds, her anticipation diminishing her fear.

After she crossed the railroad tracks and approached the train station terminal, she stopped, utterly astounded. It was the same structure, the same as it was in the 1960s: a rustic stone base, a long wooden platform, and a broad, shingled, overhanging roof.

Kate advanced, propelled by wide-eyed wonder, like an explorer discovering a new world. Climbing the four wooden stairs to the platform, she stopped, remembering the two ticket windows on her left, the retro looking *Coca-Cola* machine, and the two wooden doors that led inside to the terminal lobby. Billboard signs displayed on the terminal walls advertised *Winston Cigarettes*, the movie *Rosemary's Baby*, and *Jell-O*, with a shimmering red mold above the phrase, *"There's Always Room for Jell-O!"*

Standing on the platform were men wearing suits and ties, and women in lovely dresses, with suitcases beside them, waiting for the passenger train.

Kate twisted her hands. This train station was gone in 2022. It had been torn down, replaced by a professional office building and parking lot, with offices for doctors, lawyers and a real estate company. She'd parked her car there. Of course she had.

Kate stared, turned in place, scratching her head, her mind circling as she struggled to organize time, place, and memory. When a current of wind played over her, and a shadow crossed, she had the peculiar feeling that she was about to meet herself.

Also waiting on the platform was a gnarly, older couple, probably farm people, with one tattered suitcase between them. Their clothes were clean but showed signs of wear. The woman was short and sturdy, with patient eyes turned toward the tracks, anticipating the whistling train and its stabbing white beam. Beside her was a bowlegged man with a weathered-face, wearing brown corduroy trousers, a long sleeve, railroad-striped shirt, black suspenders, and a faded brown felt hat, tugged low over his brow.

The man looked at Kate in a curious way, his mouth a tight line. Kate glanced down self-consciously at her soiled jeans and sneakers, thinking she must look a mess. But his focused attention on her served to anchor her in the moment. She wasn't a ghost. If he was staring at her, then she was real.

Kate had the radical impulse to rush to the man to ask if she was dead—if they were all dead and they were waiting for the train to take them to another world. But midstep, she stopped short when a matronly woman approached, wearing a stylish straw hat and a floral dress. The five-year-old blonde-haired girl in tow was fussy and pouting.

"Oh, miss," the woman said to Kate, in a musical voice, waving a hand. "Could you please take our picture? We're going to see my mother out West, and I promised her a travel picture."

Before Kate could respond, the woman thrust a camera at her and said, "Thank you so much."

Reluctantly, Kate took the camera, feeling the weight of it in her hand, a Kodak Automatic 35, or so read the lettering on the side. She recognized the camera. Her father had one in the 1960s. He'd often said, "Yep, it's the nicest camera we've ever had."

"It has an 'electric eye' feature," the woman said proudly. "It automatically adjusts in the sun or shade."

The woman yanked the girl to her side, told her to be quiet, and then flashed a broad, dazzling smile.

To the girl she snapped, "Smile, Grace! Smile at the camera. It's for Grandma."

Kate raised the camera and pointed it at them.

"Smile, Grace, for crying out loud! Smile for the camera. Say cheese!"

"I don't want to! I don't like Grandma!" the little girl whined.

"Oh, shut up and do as I say, or I'll give you something to whine about."

Kate put an eye to the finder, aimed, and clicked the shutter.

"Oh, take another, will you, please?" the woman asked. "I think my eyes were closed."

Kate nodded, waiting while the woman thrust a shoulder forward in a girlish pose, waiting for the little girl to smile, but when she continued to scowl, Kate snapped the photo anyway.

After Kate handed back the camera, the woman and her daughter walked away to the edge of the platform. The sassy girl was twisting, yanking to break free from her mother's firm grasp, as the woman scolded, and businessmen, ignoring the scene, snapped out newspapers.

Kate was about to leave the platform when she noticed that the weathered, bowlegged man had left his wife still leaning, searching for the train. He was strolling toward Kate, his expression somber, his hat pushed back from his forehead. He drew up within five feet of her and lifted a warning eyebrow.

"Young lady, the past is past. Can't go back. Can't never go back and change nothing. What's done is done."

The hint of a sardonic smile passed over his face as he touched the brim of his hat, turned, and sauntered back to his wife.

Kate's chest tightened. Her shoulders tightened. She felt a pinch in her heart. What was happening to her?

CHAPTER 8

Kate descended the train platform stairs, strode up the steep sidewalk past Chamber's Drug Store, and arrived onto Main Street. The route was familiar. When she was in college, she'd passed this way countless times, to and from the train station. But what was that? More than fifty years ago?

Her spooked eyes took in Main Street and the scenes before her. A blue and cream-colored Chevy Impala drove by, and a 1965 red and white Mustang, a black Ford Fairlane 500, and a blue and cream-colored 1967 Buick Skylark, the same car her father had driven all those years ago. Kate recognized the models—nearly everyone knew them; they had distinctive, one-of-a-kind styles, and they were all considered classics in the twenty-first century.

The street was bustling with students and townsfolk. Kate saw three long-haired hippies, wearing tie dye T-shirts, bellbottom pants and headbands, slouch toward Regal's Record Shop. A girl in a purple and black miniskirt and black go-go boots lingered in a phone booth, and a young black man with an afro guided a hand truck, stacked with boxes, toward The Towne Grocery.

Questions were bursting inside her as two women with beehive hairstyles hurried by, shoulder-close, smoking cigarettes, sharing secret laughter and hard copy photos.

Kate's eyes filled with nervous alertness as she took it all in. Regal's Record shop was there, The Towne Grocery, Kip's Bar, and the bowling alley. All there. And there was McAllen's Department Store, a red brick building with show windows that presented mannequins with attitude, adorned in the latest 1960s fashion.

And down the street to her left was the library. A black banner was unfurled over its double oak door entrance with the bold white words, "**WELCOME BACK, STUDENTS**!

Displayed in the window of the Busy Bee Restaurant was a sign that read **10% Student Discount**. Kate had forgotten that, just as she'd forgotten about the three-story, Federalist style, red brick building next door, where a doctor, a dentist, and a lawyer occupied offices.

Feeling light-headed, Kate saw a wooden bench outside the Paxton Sweet Shop, and she blundered toward it, afraid she would faint. She sat down hard, lowered her head, and inhaled deep breaths.

Music spilled out from the open door of the shop, a radio playing the Mamas and the Papas singing *California Dreamin'.* When Kate lifted her head, she saw two young boys and their mother emerge, each gripping an ice cream cone, their tongues exploring, licking, eyes bright.

"I should have got the strawberry," the redheaded seven-year-old said.

"Yeah, well, I told you vanilla and chocolate was boring. You're not getting any of mine," the other, heavier, and older boy shot back, turning away.

The mother said, "Come on, we've got to meet your father at the smoke shop. Hurry now. He'll blow his top if we're late."

As the trio wandered away, none of the three had noticed Kate sitting there, frozen to the spot, her brain a whirling mass of confusion. There was a madness to the moment that terrified her, and, at the same time, a stark reality that fascinated her.

As she looked at her smooth, pretty hands, the sting of tears misted her eyes. The pulsing vitality that pumped through her veins was exhilarating, and the sharpness of her eyes and ears, and the thrilling possibility that something extraordinary had occurred, lifted her to her feet.

Kate approached the Sweet Shop plate-glass window, staring at the reflection of herself with a blank, entranced expression. As her heart kicked, she stared, moving closer, oblivious to the interior candy cane columns and the counter holding globes of multicolored lollipops, chocolate balls and red and white jelly beans. She didn't notice the soda fountain or the curious teenage clerk who scooped ice cream while studying Kate warily.

"I'm young again," Kate said, in a dreamy wonder, her anxious attention looking herself up and down. "I'm young… so young," and then the words froze to her lips.

She backed away, dropping onto the bench as her brain slowly cleared and caught up to the moment, to the time and to the place. Then two urgent words rang in her head. *How? Why?*

People passed, but Kate didn't see them. The train whistle blew, but she didn't hear it. A curly-haired, adolescent girl on white roller skates raced by, and that awakened Kate from her daydream, as she watched the girl bob and weave through pedestrian traffic.

When she thought of him—Paul—her mind stalled, and she couldn't push through the wall of the impossible. Her mind tiptoed toward the future, to her kids, Ellen and Greg, to her life there, but it all seemed misty and strange, and it brought on a headache.

"How long will this last?" Kate said aloud, glancing about, as a stocky, middle-aged man, dressed in a gray suit and blue tie, hesitated.

"I beg your pardon?" he said, looking at her. "Did you say something to me, young lady?"

Young lady? Had he actually called her "young lady?" Her head had still not caught up to the young lady she'd gazed at in the Paxton Sweet Shop window.

She shifted her eyes to him. "What year is this?" Kate asked in a weak voice.

He screwed up his lips in stern dismay. "What's the matter with you? Look at your jeans and sneakers. Why don't you change your clothes? Are you doped up on something?"

"No... No, not at all. I'm just... I'm just a little lost. Please, what month and year is it?"

He shook his head in disgust. "Your generation are all draft dodgers, hippies, and druggies. God help this country." And then he walked away, muttering.

Kate sat with her hands folded, staring into the air, directionless. All around her was motion and energy, traffic sounds, and passing voices. The song *Hey Jude,* by the Beatles, drifted out from the Sweet Shop, and then *Honey,* by Bobby Goldsboro, a song she'd loathed. By the time *McArthur Park,* sung in the feathery-thin voice by Richard Harris, faded away, Kate's mind had calmed, and she'd formed a plan.

She rose and started off, walking fast. Moments later, she turned left, spotting the Greek column library. Her attention slowly drifted to the right, as she searched for Mackay's Books New & Old. There it was, the very opposite of the chain store bookstores of the twenty-first century. It was a two-story, sooty, brick building, with a green awning storefront and twelve-pane vintage farmhouse windows. Outside were wooden carts filled with stacks of discounted books, neatly arranged.

It wasn't a dream. The bookstore was there,

exactly as it had been over fifty years ago!

Impatient, nervous, and excited, she advanced, crossed Main Street, and started for the bookshop, pushing away apprehension as she drew up to the closed front door.

The afternoon sun lit up the awning and it glowed a forest green. Her nose sniffed at the air, remembering the old book smells. She'd spent so much time working in this little bookstore and roaming its aisles. Would Art remember her?

Kate reached for the tarnished brass doorknob, turned it, and gave the stubborn door a little nudge. It squeaked open with the familiar, tinny, ringing bell, the sound of coming home. For the first time since Kate had left that cave, her shoulders relaxed, and she managed a smile.

It was the same bookstore she'd loved. Just the same. It was old, dark, dusty, and cluttered, with mounds of books to her left, nearly touching the low ceiling, with others neatly arranged on the floor and in wooden shelves near the front door.

She dared to look right to search for Art Mackay. And there he was, seated on his wooden stool, his wire-rimmed glasses perched on the end of his nose, a hardback book in a hand, his eyes moving across the page, completely absorbed.

Kate swallowed, hovering between fantasy and reality, between belief and disbelief. A minute passed before she cleared her throat and spoke in a small, girlish voice. "Hello, Art."

Art grudgingly lifted his eyes from the page and

took her in with a mild curiosity.

Kate was fragile, and she thought she might shatter into a thousand pieces.

CHAPTER 9

A rt removed his spectacles and focused his eyes on her. "This author, Günter Grass, is a bloody sorcerer of literature, and it's a damn good translation. Have you read this, Kate?" he asked, lifting the book, presenting the front cover for her to see. "*The Tin Drum.* It's a helluva book that breaks your insides, makes you laugh like a drunken man, and bloodies your nose. The damn thing is narrated from inside an asylum for the insane, of all places. It's about the human condition, Kate. The human condition in the modern world."

Kate stood stiffly, her eyes moving rapidly. Art had called her by name. He knew her!

Art laid the book aside on the wooden counter beside him, where his heavy, antique cash register sat like a relic from an antique store. He massaged his eyes and kinked his neck and replaced his spectacles. He squinted a look at her, taking her in fully. "What are you doing here so early? You're not working until four o'clock today. Is it bad news? Do you have rotten news to tell me?"

Kate didn't speak. She stared at Art, fascinated. He was very much alive, and just the same.

"Did you take a fall, Kate? Your jeans are soiled. Your eyes look sleepy. Medicated. What's the matter with you?"

Kate stood as stiff as a post. "You know me?"

"What?"

"I mean, you recognize me, right?"

Art inhaled a little breath, sat up straight and gave her a deep, probing analysis. "Pray, not you, Kate. Pray that the gods of madness have not dragged you off into their opium dens of doom."

Kate said, "What?"

Art removed his spectacles again, all business. "You're not on the stuff, are you? LSD? Mushrooms? Come on, you're too smart for that, kid."

"No, I'm not on anything."

"Well, what's the matter with you, then? You look sauced up. Have you been to Kip's and had some of that near beer, two percent crap? Well, no, it's too early for that, isn't it? He's not even open yet. Have you been out all night, tossing back the moonshine?"

"No…"

"So, what then?" he said, spreading his hands, growing impatient. "What are you doing standing there talking to me? Why aren't you walking the aisles, looking for more of that drivel of a book you bought a couple of days ago? *The Millstone,* wasn't it?"

"A couple of days?" Kate repeated.

"Okay, so maybe it was three days ago. I don't know. So, for the last time, what the hell's the matter with you?"

Gathering courage, Kate stepped to the front door, threw the latch to lock it, and turned back to Art, who leapt off the stool, standing with his hands on his hips, studying her anew. Art was just as Kate remembered him, over sixty years old, thin and narrow shouldered, with a gray ponytail, dressed in overalls and a green and black flannel shirt.

"Okay, kid, if you've got love problems, I ain't the guy, okay? I've been married twice and divorced twice, with scars in my heart and bitterness in my mouth. And my exes and me ain't friends, and we never will be, if you know what I mean. Oh, and pardon the verb 'ain't.' I ain't used it in a while, and I like to use it now and then to show that I'm just another dumbass person in this dumbass world. Now, what's on your mind, Kate? Out with it. I'm expecting a bus tour from Cincinnati any minute now, and they'll all want a paperback of Taylor Caldwell's *Testimony of Two Men,*" he concluded sarcastically, with a wink.

Kate lifted and settled her shoulders. "Art... I don't know anyone else I can say this to, and I don't know how to say it."

"A shot rang out," Art said, pointing a finger at her.

"What?"

"All good stories should begin with 'A shot rang out.' You'll grab the readers every time."

Kate was growing frustrated with his smartassed comments. "Art, I think I've time traveled."

Art was still. A flash of confusion crossed his face, and then it was gone.

Kate's words came tumbling out. "I know it sounds crazy... I know it sounds impossible. I know I sound like a nutcase, but... I've been thinking about it, and I don't know what else it can be. I thought I was dead, but I'm not dead. I'm very much alive. And... here's the real crazy part of it, Art. I haven't just time traveled... I'm young again, with beautiful hands and skin, and I see everything so clearly and I hear so well, like my ears are brand new. And listen to my voice. It's mellow and sweet, like it was before I developed vocal nodules because of acid reflux when I was in my fifties."

There was a deep, bloated silence as Art's worried eyes came to hers, and he ran a hand across his mouth. "Well, do you know what, Kate? All kinds of crazy things are happening these days." He shrugged. "UFO encounters and alien abductions. Do I believe it? I don't know. Maybe. Then again, maybe I'm a skeptic. In 1895, Baron William Thomson, a mathematical physicist and engineer, said heavier than air flying machines were impossible. What a knucklehead he turned out to be."

Kate took a step toward him. "Art, what is the

date? What month and year is it?"

Art reached into his overall's pocket, removed a pipe, looked at it and placed it between his teeth. "Blast! I'm out of tobacco. I always forget to buy tobacco. That must mean something, don't you think? I'm sure some damned shrink would have some damned thing to say about it."

Kate's eyes were pleading. "Art, please, what's the date?"

Art scratched the side of his neck, and with his bright, worried eyes, he looked directly at her.

"Okay, kid, I'll play along. It's Wednesday, September 24, 1968."

The confirmation that she had returned to 1968 as a 20-year-old girl, only two days before she had first met Paul Ganic, brought the heat of near panic. Kate lowered her gaze to the threadbare, red and gray throw rug, trembling.

"Haven't you read the papers? Seen the headlines? They'll tell you what day it is."

Kate shook her head.

"All right, then, I've got some coffee made over there, and it's only an hour or so old. It's an A&P brand, but listen to this: it's advertised as being 'vigorous and winey,' and that's the only reason I bought it. I figure that the Madison Avenue ad agency that came up with those adjectives deserves a shot, don't you think? Anyway, I think we should have a cup."

Kate didn't object. She knew where the coffee station was, to the left of the counter on a wooden stand, near a dingy, yellow-curtained window. The window was always open about two inches, and it looked out on the next-door brick building, Paco's Shoe Repair.

Kate sat in the heavy, oak chair while Art poured coffee into two Styrofoam cups, handing one to Kate. Her hand trembled as she took the cup, and Art sensed in her an inner turmoil, an inner demon trying to break free.

He pointed toward the door. "You sip that while I go open the front door. My bills are due soon and I need all the readers I can rope, hogtie and fleece."

Kate took a drink of the lukewarm coffee and was surprised by its bold flavor. It didn't taste 'winey,' but it was almost 'vigorous.'

Art returned with coffee in hand, his expression fixed into fatherly concern. "Somebody slipped you something, Kate. Mushrooms or something..."

She shook her head. "No... That's not it."

"Yes, they did," he said confidently. "I've taken lysergic acid diethylamide, better known as LSD, a couple of times, Kate. In case you didn't know, it's a semi-synthetic hallucinogen. Lysergide belongs to a family of indole alkylamines that includes many substituted tryptamines, such as psilocin, which is found in what is known today as 'magic' mushrooms. I've read all about it, and I've sold a lot of books on the subject to young and old alike, being the true derelict I am. An old lady in her 70s came in about a month ago and bought the book *LSD Dreams and Journeys*."

Kate shook her head, staring into her coffee. "No... I didn't take anything."

Art sighed. "Kate, I've taken LSD a couple of times, and I've had some strange trips. On one, about a year ago, I thought I was living back in ancient Rome. I wore this long, red toga, a crown of thorns and, get this, I was singing *As Time Goes By*, from the movie *Casablanca*. And I met Julius Caesar, and he told me to stay away from knives. Crazy as hell was that trip."

"I didn't take LSD, Art," Kate said firmly. "I didn't. It's not like that."

Art sipped his coffee. "Okay, no LSD. Fine. So, what are we talking about here?"

Kate held up her Styrofoam cup. "See this Styrofoam cup? In 2022, New York City, which is where I live, has a ban on all Styrofoam containers. The law bans any disposable containers, including bowls, cartons, cups, lids, plates, and whatever."

Art looked down at his black Keds sneakers. "That was 2022? You did say 2022?"

"Yes. That's where I came from—I don't know, just a few hours ago. And, in 2022, I'm seventy-four years old."

CHAPTER 10

T he bell over the front door jangled and a young couple entered, their eyes squinting in the dimly lit space. Art turned toward them.

"Do you need any help?"

The young man, in his twenties, with long, reddish-brown hair and beard, started over. His tall girlfriend, with a single braid down her back and her head covered in a red bandana, wandered toward a stack of books.

"Yeah, hi there. I'm looking for *A Clockwork Orange* by Anthony Burgess."

Art pointed to his right. "Down the second aisle, about halfway, on the right top shelf. I've got two left, one hardback, one paper."

Art turned back to Kate, who had her head down. He started to speak, then stopped.

She lifted her head. "Do you still check every book cover and make sure it's placed in agreement with your aesthetic taste?"

He drew his head back. "Do I do that?"

"Yes. I've watched you, ever since I was a freshman. I've worked here for two years."

Art's eyes softened on her. "Kate, is there anything you want to tell me?"

"I've told you, and I'm scared to death, and I'm buzzing with energy, thinking about all the things I have to do, and I don't know what the hell is going on."

Art took nervous sips of coffee as he looked at her, trying to understand. When the guy approached, ready to pay for his book, Art slipped behind the counter and punched out the numbers on the cash register, the bell ringing, the cash door thudding open.

When they were gone, Art ambled back to Kate. "Have you called your parents, Kate?"

Kate blinked. "Isn't that strange? I hadn't thought of them... I mean, about them being alive. Damn, I feel so weird."

Kate dropped her empty cup into the waste basket and leaned forward, placing her head in her hands.

Concerned, Art stepped forward. "Kate, why don't you go into the storage room and take a nap on that old army cot?"

A moment later, she lifted her head, her eyes damp with tears. She nodded. "Yeah, I could use some sleep. Maybe I'll wake up and this will all be gone."

"Okay, Kate. You go back to the storage room and

sleep as long as you like. I'm here until nine tonight. Is there anybody you want me to call?"

Kate shivered a little. "No. Not now. I'm thinking that the world isn't what I thought it was. It's... something else... or many things else... and I know that isn't grammatical. I wish I could explain it. It's so..."

"Lousy sometimes?" Art said, his eyes downcast. "Lousy, and out of its mind, with the flag burning and the race riots and the killing over in Vietnam?"

Kate didn't hear him. "Art, what do you know about time travel? You've read about everything else. What have you read about time travel?"

Art tapped the end of his nose with a finger. "Okay... let's see. Time travel. Well, as I recall, Aristotle seems to have been the first to discuss time critically and informally. He allowed for various notions of time, including the possibility of multiple pasts."

Kate perked up. "Multiple pasts?"

"Yeah, so if the future exists, then we are already 'gone' in the future's past, are we not?"

Kate shook her head. "I have no idea. I already have a headache."

Art continued, while he scratched the back of his head. "And I remember reading in some book about a theory that time is an illusion; that rather than time passing us, humans pass through what we perceive as time, which is actually stationary."

Kate stared at Art in weary confusion. "Well, there's a scientist out in the future, whose name is

Neil deGrasse Tyson, and he said, 'The universe is under no obligation to make sense to you,' and right now, nothing is making much sense."

Art chuckled. "I believe it was Johann Wolfgang von Goethe who said, 'Ignorant men raise questions that wise men answered a thousand years ago. Not that I think you're ignorant, Kate. Just sleepy, a little loopy and maybe hopped up on something."

Kate looked at him earnestly. "You have a daughter, don't you, Art?"

"Yeah, a daughter and a son."

"How old is your daughter?"

"Oh... well, let me see. She'd be about... yes, she just turned thirty-five in May."

"What's her name?"

"Lana, her mother's choice, not mine. I wanted Emily, and being the old bastard I am, I still want Emily. Better to be named for a poet than a movie star."

"What would you tell her to do if she told you she'd time traveled?"

Art removed his spectacles and pinched the bridge of his nose. "Lana and I don't talk much, Kate, I'm embarrassed to say. I never was worth a damn as a father. I didn't know what to do with kids. I was a drunk then. Did I ever tell you that?"

Kate shook her head. "No, you didn't."

"In my younger days, I was a lawyer, copyright law, and I hated it. I walked out one day. Couldn't breathe. Thought I was having a heart attack. Well, that was my first marriage. The second only lasted a year. Brought a boy into the world. Byron is his name. We talk now and then. He's married to a pleasant wife who cooks like a champ, and has a little girl, and, sorry to say, I haven't seen them in a while. My son's a numbers guy, a bean counter, and he makes good money. Well, he doesn't call me much, either. What does that say about the old man?"

Kate stared at him with a grappling, restless mind. "Don't beat yourself up. I know more about kids and marriage than you think."

Art opened his eyes fully on Kate. "In case you haven't surmised by now, Kate, I'm stalling, because I don't have any idea what to say to you. The only thing that comes to mind is a quote my father used now and then. He hailed from Kentucky, and he always had a good story or a quote for every occasion. Daniel Boone was reported to have said, 'I have never been lost, but I will admit to being confused for several weeks.'"

Kate rose, with a grateful nod. "I can't think anymore. I *will* take that nap."

"You do that, Kate. I'll be around if you need anything. And let's see how you feel when you wake up. Maybe you should go back to your apartment later on and not worry about working today."

Kate tilted her head. "My apartment? Yes... that's right. I have an apartment with Vicki Allen."

"And how is your short story progressing? Almost finished?" Art asked.

Kate stared at him, not recalling any short story.

She'd have to lie. "Yeah… Yeah, okay."

Art flicked a hand. "Okay. Go! Go lie down and stop thinking!"

And Kate did.

The green, canvas army cot was on the left side of the square room, flush against the wall, with stacks of boxes at the head and foot.

She lifted the single window above the cot, feeling the welcomed breath of a breeze, then she turned off the overhead light and sat on the edge of the cot. She took off her sneakers and socks. A moment later, she teetered over and fell fast asleep.

Her last thought was of the wizened man who had approached her at the train station. "The past is past. Can't go back. Can't never go back and change nothing. What's done is done."

Who was he, and how did he know she had time traveled?

CHAPTER 11

Kate awoke to gray light and the sound of gentle rain tapping the window. Consciousness came back quick and frightening. Her eyes were heavy with sleep, her back stiff, her mouth sour. The cot. The army cot. She was lying on it and a woolen blanket covered her.

Rising hysteria awoke her fully. Still in her muddy jeans, she kicked off the blanket, swung her legs to the floor and shot up.

She stuttered out, "Time... Time... Travel."

Time to run. Time to scream.

Stay calm!

What maze of time was she in? A glance brought a new recognition of time and place. Art Mackay's storage room, stacked with boxes. The day? Unknown. How long had she slept? It was day, for sure. Why didn't Art awaken her? The year? Was it still September 1968?

A quick look at her hands confirmed it. Young hands. Twenty years old? Her head felt stuffed with rags, and too many thoughts. Too many emotions came crashing in. Too many questions. Time travel? Paul Ganic? The future? Her kids?

Her stomach growled from hunger. When was the last time she'd eaten? Couldn't remember. Did she have any money? No.

She leaned over the cot, parted the pitiful, dingy white curtains, and gazed out. Stringy fog shrouded the distant trees and made a ghost of the library, but the gentle rainfall was comforting, and it relaxed her. Bringing a hand to a yawn, Kate faced the closed door. What time was it? She hadn't worn a watch the day she'd climbed to the cave. How long ago was that? Time and her memory were disjointed.

Sitting on the edge of the cot, she put on her socks and sneakers, rose, and hesitated before opening the door. Standing in the doorway, Kate viewed the five aisles of books, seeing shafts of gray light streaming in from the windows, making shadows.

"Hello? Art?"

Kate walked across the creaking, uneven wooden floor to the front of the shop. Hanging on the front door from a rope, the reversible double-side OPEN/CLOSED sign was turned to closed.

Kate ran a hand through her tangled hair and moved to the counter. She glanced up and saw the IBM wall clock, the one Art had bought at a flea market in 1967. Yes, she recalled that. He loved the thing, the domed glass lens, the hour hand thicker than the minute hand, and the red, continuous sweep of the second hand that always seemed to move in slow motion.

She'd never thought much about time in those days. She'd never considered that a clock didn't really measure anything, except itself. It now occurred to her that time could not truly be measured. It had its own play, and it was never impatient, and yet it was always on the march. Though the same age, one person appeared younger than the other. An hour could be long or short, depending on the activity or the focus, or if one was asleep.

Kate stared blindly, seeing the faces of her children in her inner mind. How odd that she could recall the future, even though she was currently only twenty years old. Her vision had expanded; her mind could recall past, present, *and* future events.

She thought of her kids, Greg and Ellen. Their births had changed her in myriad ways, each an irresistible wonder. She'd been humbled and blessed and scared for their safety, for their minds and for their souls. She'd been awed by them, angered and matured by them, and daily aged by them, as they stumbled out into the world, crying in pain and dancing in triumph.

Ellen and Greg had seemed to grow to adulthood slowly, at least that's what it had seemed at the time, like the slow movement of the hour hand on a clock. But as Kate reflected back now, they'd grown in minutes and seconds, first babies tucked in their cribs, then toddlers reaching to be held, and then school kids running, screaming gleefully through sprinkler spray across glittering spring grass. In a flash, they were sassy teenagers, and in their twenties, imposters of wisdom. A blink of an eye had Ellen off to France, and Greg living in L.A.

Kate's mind shifted to her husband, David. She recalled his last moments. As he lay silently dying, time seemed precious and fragile. She sat by his bed and watched as his breaths strained, as he clung to life, until his ticking heart ceased, and the clock of his measured years stopped.

And then David was gone, and she was alone, an old woman, staring at the red, continuous sweep of the second hand on the clock as it mocked her, measuring silence, memories, and old age.

Time existed, of course, but it was illusive, clever, and puzzling. Now, having blundered through some syncopated tick-tock of time, she was a young woman again. A young woman who felt the fresh bloom of youth again, and a surge for the passion of life again. If she could release the past, now her future, and the negative emotions and memories, and let go, she would soar with those girlish wishes and desires and be newly born.

But could she let go? Those wishes, those delicious desires, were also tangled in the memories, experiences, regrets, and rational mind of a 74-year-old woman.

Kate stared at the clock. It was 5:42 a.m. She had slept more than eighteen hours! Were things the same? Was it still September 1968?

She found a note from Art, written in black ink and taped to the counter, along with a five-dollar bill.

Kate: When I checked on you at 9 p.m. you were sleeping like Kate Van Winkle, so I didn't wake you. Whatever it was you swallowed today, Kate Clarke, it knocked you on your ass. I won't say "bad girl." I'm too bad myself. And didn't somebody back in my Bible days in Kentucky say, "Don't judge?"

You know that I'm upstairs if you need me. I'll be down in the morning, about nine. You know where the bathroom is. Sorry, the shower's kaput, but the sink has hot and cold water. I gave the thing a lick and a promise last night (even scrubbed the toilet) so you wouldn't call me ugly names. I know you like the bathroom clean. I even gave it "a woman's touch," as you would say, by putting out a nice and clean little yellow hand towel that somebody gave me last Christmas. Ain't I a nice guy, after all?

My rooms aren't so tidy, so I'm not inviting you up for breakfast. Here's five bucks. If you wake up early, get something to eat at The Busy Bee before you head back to your apartment. After your classes, come back and let's talk. I need to know you're all right.

Okay, kid, signing off. This wasn't supposed to be a novella.

-Art

Kate found a pen and scribbled a response.

Thanks for putting me up, Art. I can't believe I slept so long—but feeling much better this morning. Thanks for the money. I'll pay you back when I see you again, after class. Off I go.
-Kate

Kate turned and leaned back against the counter, pondering. After class? Yes, she was a student, a twenty-year-old student, majoring in English Literature, and she lived with a roommate, Vicki Allen, who was working on a B.A. in social sciences.

Kate considered the strange moment. Did she really want an education do-over? She had already completed a master's degree in education and had taught for years. On the other hand, it might be fun to experience it again, knowing all that she knew about the future.

But first things first. Kate was young, rested, and ravenous. And tomorrow, if history was about to repeat itself, she'd meet Paul Ganic.

Kate said his name softly, as if she were under a spell. It would be a terrifying encounter, like meeting a ghost, like meeting an incarnate dream she'd conjured up from the depths of her soul. Although she was seeing and experiencing the world of 1968, she wasn't ready to admit that it was real. How could it be?

Part of her was waiting for the vision to come crashing down—an old woman's shattered fantasies

—and then she'd awaken from a dream with a start to find herself in her New York living room, sitting in her recliner, watching the awful twenty-first century news cycle on her wide screen TV.

After Kate washed up, finger-combed her hair into place and wiped the grime from her jeans and sneakers, she left the quiet shop in a misty rain, the five-dollar bill stuffed in her pocket. Her apartment on Telford Street, and her encounter with Vicki Allen, would have to wait, even though Kate longed for a change of underwear and clothes. But she was hungry, and she wanted to see more of 1968, just in case it vanished in the next hour or so.

Kate's pulse jumped, and she quickened her step, ready for her adventure. Sleep had revived her, and she allowed herself a tentative happiness, like dipping a toe into the water to check the temperature of a lake.

For minutes or hours, or for however long her time travel experience lasted, she was going to reach out and grab a big handful of this past life in 1968.

And she would soon see Paul Ganic. Dream or reality, she would see Paul again. He was here, in this time, and she would find him, and they *would* meet. But then what? Could she change the past?

Kate strolled the quiet sidewalk in the early light of morning, in a cool wet wind, stepping across damp leaves, approaching The Busy Bee restaurant. She looked to her right to see moving fog crawling across the campus buildings, and she wondered if she had already changed the past. Each step she was taking was not a step she'd taken all those years ago. And what about her conversation with Art the day before? That certainly had never occurred in the past.

Over a breakfast of scrambled eggs, ham, toast, orange juice and coffee, Kate thought about the cave. She could return and climb inside, couldn't she? If she did, would she return to 2022?

She raised the coffee cup to her lips and swallowed the last of it, noticing the swirl of cigarette smoke from a table nearby. A man was smoking in a restaurant, a detail about 1968 she'd forgotten.

Kate stood by the cash register, staring at her check in astonishment. The entire breakfast cost $1.77. The eggs, ham, white toast and coffee were $1.45, with .25 cents for the orange juice, and seven cents for sales tax.

With a little smile, Kate handed the five-dollar bill to the cashier, a pleasant woman in her forties, with a beauty-shop sculpted beehive and a red and white, polka dot dress. She said, "It's so nice to have you students back. It's so darn quiet in the summer. Would you like your ten percent discount?"

"Oh, well, I don't have my student ID with me."

The cashier's smile was generous. "Well, we won't worry about that, honey. I can clearly see that you're a student. And I've seen you in here with Art Mackay."

Outside, the fog had lifted, and a weak sun peeked through broken, murky clouds. Kate would not return to the cave, at least not until she saw Paul again. A fever of delight and a stab of fear sent her walking briskly toward her apartment to see Vicki again, and to attend class at Paxton College again.

Kate recalled a quote she'd recently read, by the writer Sherrilyn Kenyon. "I don't suffer from my insanity—I enjoy every minute of it."

CHAPTER 12

T he footsteps came close, slowed, then advanced again. The metallic click of the lock was loud, and Kate inhaled a sharp breath.

The apartment door swung open and 20-year-old Vicki Allen stood slumped in a ratty blue terry robe, her face pale, mouth slack, her sleepy eyes dull with irritation.

"Stop forgetting your keys, Kate," she said, in a scratchy voice, her thick helmet of blonde hair in tangles. "You're really ticking me off. I didn't get to sleep until three."

Vicki backed away, not bothering to cover her cavernous yawn. Kate stood transfixed, staring at her old roommate with rigid curiosity, an old memory alive in the flesh.

Vicki narrowed an eye on her. "What's the matter with you? Are you coming in or what?"

Kate stepped into the room and closed the door,

struggling to accept the moment.

Vicki examined her. "What's with those jeans? Loose, aren't they? Top's too big. Groovy jacket and sneaks though. Never seen them. Futuristic looking or something. Where the hell have you been? You were out all night? Shackin' with who?"

Vicki always had talked a lot—was all motor-mouth in the morning, when Kate wanted her to shut up.

Vicki slouched, tilting her head, her eyes holding questions. "Out with it, Kate. Who is he?"

It was a shock when Kate realized that over time, she had conjured up an alternative physical look and memory of her roommate. Vicki wasn't as tall or as pretty as Kate had recalled, although she was certainly attractive. Her blue eyes were lovely, and she had a dancer's chiseled neck, but she was a bit overweight, her nose sharp, her lips thin. But her voice was just the same, a chocolatey, sultry alto that enhanced any song she sang. It was a late-night radio voice that lured men, young and old; a resonate, secretive voice that some girls on campus, who'd witnessed Vicki's vocal power over men, tried to imitate.

"Are you still high?" Vicki asked, growing progressively irritated by Kate's lack of response.

"No, no... I was just... I was studying and writing, and, well, you know?

"No, I don't know," Vicki said with a challenge. "Pray tell and enlighten this sleepy, sixty percent hungover chick."

Kate blurted something out just to get Vicki off her back. "I was with Art."

"Bookstore man, Art? Cranky, old man, who I don't know how he sells any books because he'll tell you to go to hell anytime, day or night, Art Mackay?"

"Yeah, and he's not so old," Kate said defensively, a chunk of her mind still aware that she had been seventy-four years old yesterday morning.

"Really? He must be like sixty or something." And then Vicki's face scrunched up in disgust. "Don't tell me you and him are..."

Kate cut in. "... No! We were just talking."

"All night?"

And there it was! Vicki's irritating manner had jerked Kate back fifty-four years, and it was as if they'd never grown up and moved on.

"Yes, all night. Okay? So big deal. Yeah, we talked all night."

Vicki leaned her head back. "Okay, groovy. Hope you had a blast talking about boring authors and their books, that I'll have to read next semester."

Kate ignored that. "Then I had breakfast at The Busy Bee."

Vicki looked at her skeptically, lifting a hand, still not entirely convinced. "Hey, whatever blows up your dress." And because Vicki's mind was as changeable as a sparrow in midflight, she asked. "So, where did you get those clothes and those sneaks? I've never seen them. They're far out, but just too big, Kate."

Kate glanced about the living room, and as her

eyes settled on the wicker couch with its burgundy cushions, on the red beanbag chair and the hanging lamp with its bamboo shade, her memories of them returned in a rush.

And there was the Motorola console radio and record player, the two guitars propped in the corner, and a small, square TV with rabbit ears, the ends of the antenna wrapped in aluminum foil to improve reception.

"What are you smiling at?" Vicki asked, following Kate's eyes as she took in the room.

"I'd forgotten about the aluminum on the antenna."

"What? What are you talking about? Luke did that for us."

Kate snapped Vicki a look. "Luke!"

"Yeah… You know, Luke. Hello? Luke, my boyfriend. You're all whacked out today. You must have taken some bad shit or something."

"No! I don't do drugs. You know that."

"Fine, but you're like dizzy, on a head-trip merry-go-round or something."

Kate pointed toward the bathroom and started toward it. "I need to take a shower and change clothes."

"We have Psych at ten o'clock, you know," Vicki said. "Human Growth and Development. Our second class with Mr. Horstman, the guy who notices every girl and ignores the guys."

Kate glanced back. "Oh… Yeah. Right. Psych."

"And guess what? My Dad's coming tomorrow

night to see me at the Candlelight Coffee House, and he's bringing my brother. You said you'd come."

Kate smiled. "Of course, I'll come. I wouldn't miss it."

The Candlelight Coffee House had been lodged in Kate's mind for over fifty years. It's where she'd first met Paul Ganic. While Vicki sings and strums her guitar, Kate's and Paul's eyes will meet, and it will be magic.

"You'll meet my brother," Vicki said. "He's twenty-four and has a '61 jet-smooth Ford Galaxie Starliner."

Kate didn't remember much about Vicki's brother except that she didn't like him or his conceited manner.

Kate retreated to her bedroom and reintroduced herself to the single bed, narrow closet and small mahogany desk and chair, where she'd written several short stories and stored them in the top drawer. Although she was anxious to read them, it would have to wait until later.

Moving to her chest of drawers, she slid open the top drawer and saw them: her wallet, her apartment keys, her car keys and the black savings account passbook from the Union National Bank of Ohio.

Kate hadn't forgotten about her car, purchased from a neighbor the previous year. Kate's father had bought it for her, a light blue and white 1963 Ford Falcon Sprint. It was her first car and she'd loved it. She recalled what Paul had said when he first saw it. He'd stepped back, hands on his hips, looking it over with boyish delight. "Well, look at that. I haven't worked on one of those for a while. Since before I left for Vietnam. If memory serves, the engine is a 144-cc 90-hp inline-6, it's got a coil-spring suspension in the front and leaf spring in the rear. Brakes? Four drums. And if that wasn't enough, you've got the two-speed Ford-O-Matic. Who can't like a car that has a Ford-O-Matic?" he said, with a little laugh.

"I don't know what any of that is," Kate had said. "I just love the car. Is all that good?"

Paul had circled the Falcon, nodding his head. "Yeah… One downside, though. When you turn the key, the little engine kicks on and shakes the casing to the point where you feel like you're sitting on an over-full dryer in the spin cycle."

Kate had grown defensive. "It doesn't bother me."

"Well… everything calms down as the engine warms up a bit, so there's nothing to worry about."

Kate considered that time traveling was a peculiar and paradoxical matter of place and mind. She hadn't thought of that conversation in years, and yet, here and now, holding her car keys in her hand, she recalled her talk with Paul nearly verbatim, even the engine size and suspension—information that normally would have dropped from her mind in seconds.

And she could almost smell the Ice Blue Aqua Velva Paul wore, a cologne many men splashed on in those days. How did the commercial go in the 1960s? "*There's something about an Aqua Velva man.*"

When Kate had been in the hospital in 2022,

recovering from her encounter with the SUV, she'd read an interesting magazine article. It stated that *A poll of 2,000 adults revealed that freshly cut grass, crayons and certain meals, such as baloney, mac and cheese, and roast dinner, are among the top scents that take a person back to childhood.*

Kate's conversation with Paul had occurred in the past. It *had* happened. But since Kate left that cave, returning to 1968, she'd taken actions she'd not taken in the past. Her encounters with the people on the train platform, and her conversations with Art and Vicki, and her breakfast at The Busy Bee, were novel events, never taken before, not in her first past of 1968.

She was leaving fresh footsteps, and she was a 74-year-old woman in a 20-year-old body. As a result, she had a broader picture of the world, of people, and of herself, than she'd had when she'd been alive for only twenty years.

What did that mean? What would the result be? Would history repeat itself, or had her seemingly insignificant actions already formed new patterns that would shift the course of history and produce alternative outcomes?

The old man on the train platform was wrong when he told her, "Can't go back. Can't never go back and change nothing. What's done is done." No, she'd already changed the past.

Kate stared at her car keys, then tossed them up and caught them. So, would it matter if she drove to Paul's trailer near Cove Lake?

She was desperate to see him again—breathless and eager to see if he would be there.

CHAPTER 13

No, she would wait. She would not drive to his trailer near Cove Lake. What if she messed everything up—the natural course of events? She was supposed to see him tomorrow night, so she would wait and be patient.

Kate held her passbook in her hand. What was her bank balance? She opened it, leafing through the pages, running a finger down the lined itemized page. There it was, $238.28, and the bank was paying an interest rate of 7.5 percent! She did some quick calculations, estimating that her bank balance, adjusting for inflation, would be worth about $1,500 in 2022.

After a hot shower, which did her a world of good, Kate fluffed and blow-dried her hair. She applied makeup, pausing often to nose toward the mirror, mesmerized anew by her taut skin and flawless complexion. She felt silly, happy, and desirable.

When was the last time she'd felt desirable? She moved her head close to the mirror and then back, enthralled by how attractive she was. Maybe she was even pretty—very pretty?

In her bedroom, she searched her closet, picking through slacks, tops, and dresses she'd long forgotten about. She chose a pair of tan pants with a high waistline and a side zipper, and a cotton/polyester, long sleeve sweater with paisley swirls and neon flower daisies. It was definitely 1960s style, and she loved it.

Ten minutes later, she found a purse, stuffed her wallet and apartment keys inside and met Vicki in the living room. Vicki was smoking a cigarette and sipping a mug of coffee, dressed in faded bellbottom jeans, a loose-fitting top, and a denim jacket. She wore no makeup, and her hairdo was just a classic knot and bangs.

Kate stopped short. "Oh, I'd forgotten you smoked."

Vicki glanced up with bored interest. "Forgotten? What does that mean? I've been smoking since I was seventeen. Did somebody hit you on the head or something? You smoked, too. You quit last summer because your father said it made you appear unattractive. I loved the 'appear unattractive.' So articulate. Anyway, Earth to Kate? Whatever you're doing for kicks, I could use some of it. Let's get to class before we're late."

Paxton College was just as Kate remembered it: quaint and serene, with lovely red brick buildings, leafy walkways and quiet areas with gardens and marble benches. The oldest building on the campus was the Pickney log cabin, built in 1816. Kate remembered that Paxton had produced eight Union generals and two Confederate generals in the Civil War.

Kate and Vicki entered the Psychology Building with a group of scurrying students, climbed the stairs to the second floor and moved across the gray-and-white, polished tile hallway floor to Room 210.

The two girls found seats near the windows and slid into their oak tablet arm desks, across the narrow aisle from each other. That's when Kate realized she hadn't any books, notebooks or even a pen. She rummaged through her purse but found no writing instrument.

With a shake of her head, Vicki handed Kate some paper and a pen, and Kate shifted in her seat, glancing about nervously at the other sixteen students, most of their faces familiar, but long forgotten.

Mr. Horstman entered, closing the door behind him. He paused to glance up at the wall clock to insure he was on time. He was always punctual, demanding his students be on time and seated when he arrived. Once his leather briefcase was on his desk and open, he shouldered out of his dark brown suit jacket, arranging it on the back of his chair, and then adjusted his tie.

With cool, appraising eyes, he looked at his students. "Good morning, class," he said, in a clear, tenor voice.

They weakly returned his greeting. Mr. Horstman was a tall man in his forties, wearing a crisp, white shirt, forest green and gold tie, fashioned into a perfect Windsor knot, and dark brown trousers with a razor-sharp crease. His short, chestnut hair gleamed, his manner was subdued, and his deep brown eyes were penetrating.

Mr. Horstman was younger than Kate had recalled, but then again, she was seeing him as a woman of seventy-four, not a girl of twenty, and she swiftly made the adjustment. Her mind also flashed back to a raw, half-buried memory, not one she'd entirely forgotten, but one she'd kept in some humiliated corner of her mind.

Mr. Horstman had flirted with her, had cornered her in his room one November day, and kissed her. She was so stunned and intimidated by the man that she'd let him kiss her, not fighting him or twisting away.

And then he'd threatened her. "This is our little secret, Miss Clarke. Let's keep this between us, so you can pass my course and stay in the good graces of the school."

Seeing the man again, after fifty-four years, still made her nauseated, and the older, wiser woman wanted to stand up, march up to him, and slap him hard across the face.

And just like that, Mr. Horstman's piercing eyes landed on Kate, and he seemed to see right through her, as if he'd read her thoughts.

"Miss Clarke," Mr. Horstman said, still standing. "I see you are testing your mental abilities this morning. And perhaps you're testing my patience?"

Kate squirmed, feeling all eyes stuck to her. She did not feel seventy-four, nor did she feel twenty, nor any age at all, but under water, struggling to rise to the surface so she could breathe.

"I'm sorry, Mr. Horstman... I'm..." and she didn't finish the sentence.

"You haven't any notebook, and only a pen and two scraps of paper. You have no books. During our first class last week, you carried your textbook and took copious notes during my lecture. Has your passion for this course so swiftly waned to such an extent that you are now blatantly apathetic?"

Kate saw the insidious attraction for her in the depth of his eyes, and when he strolled toward her desk, that attraction turned to an insolent resolve to intimidate her.

"Something has changed in you, Miss Clarke. You seem preoccupied and a bit nervous. Are you nervous?"

Kate stayed quiet, feeling anxious and unprepared.

"I hope and trust it is not I who am making you nervous, Miss Clarke. I'm sure the rest of the class does not feel that way."

And then he turned to face the class. "Am I right, class, in my assumption?"

There were vague murmurs and some nods.

His gaze returned to Kate. "That is not my wish, I

assure you."

Kate thought, *Bullshit!* The first time around in 1968, the 20-year-old Kate had been intimidated by the man. But suddenly, the mature Kate took over, shoving the 20-year-old meek and insecure Kate to the side. Mature Kate had acquired a lifetime of experience by being a wife, a mother and a teacher, engaging with students, parents, faculty, and the politics of bureaucratic management. She easily recognized Mr. Horstman's devious little sexual power game, and she was ready for him.

Yes, he'd singled her out to nudge her off-balance, to make her feel insecure, while he performed in his private theater to show he was the "big man" in charge, and she was just a silly college girl he could toy with. Not this time around.

Most students were well aware that Mr. Horstman flirted with, and often dated, some of the more attractive female students, taking them to shadowy places off campus. It was even rumored that Mr. Horstman got a girl pregnant the year before, and that the administration had kept it quiet.

He stared at Kate, waiting. "Don't you have anything to say, Miss Clarke? All right, well, let me ask you a question about today's lesson. It is a subject we are all interested in, and it concerns the psychology of relationships. In our society today, the women's movement is having a transformative effect. To wit, Bob Dylan's song, '*The Times They are A Changin.*' For all of us, and especially for the men in the class, in your view, perhaps, however limited, Miss Clarke, what is the key to having a good relationship? And what are the qualities that make for a good relationship between the sexes? And, finally, if it isn't too much to ask, perhaps you can enlighten us as to your views on marriage in this time of 'free love,'" he concluded with a self-satisfied smile.

Mr. Horstman leveled his condescending eyes on Kate. "Please, Miss Clarke, you have our full attention."

Kate sat up, not the least bit shy. To her surprise, she felt the words gush out of her, merging the emotions of a 20-year-old with the intellect of a 74-year-old.

"Relationships, good relationships, like love, are first and foremost built on respect. Respect is the foundation, and it must be strong, just as the foundation of a building must be strong. Good relationships have a structure and, if one truly loves, one must maintain that structure to keep the thing standing, through honesty, tolerance and patience, practiced daily. Love takes time… perhaps a lifetime.

"Love is not some silly emotion in a fairytale, or some grabby thing, a sexual object that you must have, like a selfish child's new toy. Love stands tall, and it is lovely, and it is formidable, and it is a pretty, infinite thing."

Vicki angled her body toward Kate, her mouth open, hanging on every word.

Mr. Horstman took a step back with a worried little frown. "Well… isn't that edifying, Miss Clarke, but it sounds as if you read it in a book."

Kate continued, ignoring him. "But let's talk about marriage. Marriage is not just a love affair. It changes over the years, and, in many ways, it becomes an ordeal. Ideally, marriage becomes a method to help the couple grow up spiritually and emotionally. It's sharing the good and the bad and learning from each other, and forgiving each other for all the many mistakes they both make and will continue to make.

Mr. Horstman's snide face fell a little.

Kate wasn't finished, and she could see that he wished she were. "And when the children are grown and gone, if the marriage has not truly bonded, morally, economically and spiritually, then, most likely, the marriage will fall apart. All this is only my opinion, of course. Oh, and one more thing. Older men, who are married and who have the power to pass or fail a student, should not be dating... how do I say it? Young and vulnerable female students. That is, for obvious reasons, a really bad thing, a selfish thing, and a very immature thing. It's very bad for any true, lasting and loving relationship."

Mr. Horstman stood rigid, although his tight mouth twitched. His expression held first surprise, then unease, and finally anger. As the second hand on the wall clock advanced, slowly, relentlessly, an icy silence filled the room, and Mr. Horstman's face grew tight with the glare of an insult, and his hands moved in his pockets.

Kate cast her gaze over the class, and most were

staring down at their desks. She then looked boldly into Mr. Horstman's stormy eyes. It was a sweet revenge.

She said, innocently, "Have I said too much?"

CHAPTER 14

Kate and Vicki walked swiftly through the Arts Quad, heading to their next class, and Vicki was still buzzing about Mr. Horstman's class and what Kate had said.

"What were you thinking, Kate?" Vicki said. "I mean, what in the hell was going through your head? It was wild what you said. I couldn't believe it. The whole class was like stunned. I mean, it was like you were in Horstman's face about him dating students. It was crazy."

Kate laughed.

"Yeah, it was, and I loved it, and he deserved it."

"He was so ticked off that steam was coming out of his ears, and he didn't look at you for the rest of the class."

"I noticed, and I was thrilled. The jerk—and I'm being nice."

Vicki said, "Well, it was tense... the whole class

was really tense, and I just wanted to get out of there. He'll flunk you, you know, like he flunked a couple of other girls who rejected him. Remember Jill Chase last year? He flunked her, and she had to change majors, and she didn't come back this year."

Kate snapped her a glance, fire in her eyes. "If he flunks me, I'll go straight to the dean and scream my head off, and if the dean doesn't listen, I'll keep screaming to anyone and everyone until they call him in and confront him. And he's married, you know. I'll even scream to his wife if I have to. I'm not putting up with his shit! Not like the last time. No way."

Startled, Vicki slowed her pace, looking Kate straight in the eyes. "Last time? What does that mean?"

Kate waved a dismissive hand. "Never mind."

"You're like... I don't know, you're not yourself or something."

Kate grinned. "No, I'm not, and I like it."

Vicki trudged off, shaking her head.

Professor Conning's Creative Writing class had always been an oasis for Kate. It had been easy to get lost in words and plots and characters, just as the professor was often lost in his own world, with his messy cloud of white hair, like Robert Frost's, and his pale face drawn tight against sharp bones.

Connie Poe sat next to Kate, her wide-open, dreamy eyes taking in every word Professor Conning said.

"This is 1968," the professor said, standing

before his desk, both hands stuffed into his brown corduroy jacket that had patches on the elbows. His eyes lifted toward the ceiling as if he were calling down inspiration from the gods. "There is so much to say about world events, about world leaders, about social unrest. You truly do live in interesting times, and you should be grateful for it."

Professor Conning rounded his desk and sat, deep in thought, his hands folded on the desk.

"Now, as to your assignment. During our first class, I asked you to write some small fiction, just a three-page story, using character, atmosphere and plot so that we might have a measurement of where we are technically and creatively. During our second class, when you turned them in, most of you lent the impression of confidence, and even enthusiasm."

Professor Conning rose and pursed his lips. "Now, I have read them."

Kate couldn't remember what she'd turned in, and no amount of straining her brain would bring it back into her consciousness. It was too long ago.

Professor Conning continued, turning to stare at the stack of corrected stories on his desk. "Class, you must remember the words of Marcel Proust. 'The real voyage of discovery consists not in seeking new landscapes, but in having new eyes.'"

Kate considered that. Is that what she had been given by time traveling? New eyes?

Professor Conning faced the class and narrowed his watery eyes. "The work of Rosenthal and Jacobsen, pioneers in education, have written that the teacher's expectations influence student performance. Positive expectations influence performance positively, and negative expectations influence performance negatively. All right, then. I want you to rewrite your assignments, knowing full well that I have high and positive expectations that not only will you succeed in improving your work, but you will also exceed your own and my expectations."

He held up a hand. "Now, having said that, and at the risk of appearing blatantly partial, I do want to read a portion of Kate Clarke's story, because it is an example of energy, imagination and, shall I dare say it? Fun."

When all twenty students swung their gazes at Kate, she blushed, staring down at her desk.

Professor Conning lifted a page from the stack, cleared his voice, and began to read.

In Marietta, Ohio, river stories and tall tales were interwoven into the cultural fabric: the floods, the fishing, the drownings and the ghost sightings. Some old timers wrote their stories down in their Bibles or diaries; some recounted them in saloons, or on riverbanks while they whittled, or at church funerals after a drowning.

Some sang songs to the dead and about the dead— and they were mournful, wailing ballads—about how the bad ole' river had done them in, and how their ghosts roamed the river banks and the unplowed fields, and how those ghosts made melting tracks in the newly fallen snow.

Many Ohio folk fled after a flood, unable to accept or forgive the river for their loss. They mounted buggies, raising fists at the river and at the sky, cursing God and their own sorry fate.

Annie Atkins grew up by the river, and she loved the river. She loved the changing expressions of the seasons that surrounded it and were reflected in it. She loved the constant, heavy weight of the water, as it moved in a tragic and relentless, hypnotic poetry. She loved the style and textures of currents and eddies and the pitch of the water.

Often, while Annie sat staring at that river, she had the wish she could time travel, go back in time, and take a paddlewheel riverboat downriver to New Orleans. She would meet a handsome, card-sharking gambler, who would kiss her, rude and sweet, and they would sail off into the sunset and live happily ever after.

After the professor concluded the reading, Kate's eyes were turned down.

Professor Conning quietly replaced the page on the stack and then folded his hands. He cleared his throat.

"I don't know about you class, but I would like to take that riverboat trip with Kate and her no-good, card-shark friend. What grand adventures we might have."

Professor Conning put his warm eyes on Kate. "This is the work of a talented and hard-working student, who could, if she chose, have a career as a writer. I hope you do write a novel someday, Kate. I, for one, would like to read it."

After class, when she thanked the professor, she didn't meet his gaze. The compliment made her sad. In the future, she had never finished her novel. She'd started it so many times but hadn't completed it. Why? As she had grown older, her responsibilities had piled up, and her marriage had declined, and something indefinable had gone out of her writing, some aspect of joy and freedom.

Kate left Professor Conning's class feeling ashamed, and she felt baffled, and she felt the urge to write as she'd never felt before.

CHAPTER 15

In July 1968, Paul Ganic was finally going home to Ohio. Although he'd been discharged from the Marines late in 1967, he'd rented an apartment in Jacksonville, North Carolina, and hadn't returned to his parents and old friends because he wasn't ready to face them. He'd called his parents, struggling to explain how he felt and what he'd planned to do. They were quietly supportive, but he'd heard the disappointment in their voices, and in the long pauses before their words.

His emotions and memories often flared into night sweats and nightmares, and he found himself back with the 2d Battalion, 9th Marines, and their move into the safety of the 4th Marines perimeter. In July 1967, after their foray into the Demilitarized Zone (DMZ) led to a running battle with North Vietnamese forces, three of his buddies had been killed and others injured, but he had miraculously survived. And that wasn't the only time. He'd been in many firefights, with men dying all around him, and he'd survived without a scratch. Not a scratch to his body, but wounds to his mind, or so his assigned shrink had written.

Paul got tired of sitting around the plastic laminate conference table with other worn and weary vets discussing their feelings, or lack of, and so he'd stopped going. With his savings, he bought a 1957 black and white Pontiac Star Chief, rebuilt the transmission, replaced the brakes, points and plugs, sprang for good tires, and hit the road to see the USA.

The miles fled by in hazy visions of splattered raindrops, slapping windshield wipers, sunbaked days, lowering clouds and distant flashes of lightning. Every mile that separated Paul from the war was a healing mile. Paul felt pushed by the wind, as if the hand of some benevolent god were shoving him along, helping him flee a world of violence, loss and despair.

He slept in cheap motels and ate in cheap diners, where pretty waitresses flirted and hovered. When his car broke down, he found friendly garages, and the owners were generous, letting him use their tools and their lifts for repairs.

In Patterson, Missouri, they hired him as a mechanic, and he stayed about a month. When he needed money again, he spent a few weeks working as a mechanic at car repair shops in Kearney, Nebraska and San Bernardino, California.

He lost track of the days. He grew a beard and let

his thick, reddish-blonde hair grow. In the West, if they learned he was a veteran, they bought him beer and dinner and offered him a place to stay for as long as he wanted. In the South, they didn't like his hair and they called him a hippie. He didn't care, and he wouldn't fight when they taunted him.

On July 20, Paul was on his way home to Wilmont, Ohio, a little town just outside the college town of Paxton. Sunlight broke through the clouds, streamed through the windshield, and warmed him. He thought it was a good omen. How long had he been on the road? He didn't know and didn't care, but he felt better. The nightmares were gone, and he was ready to return to school and restart his life.

Myron Ganic, Paul's father, was a thick-chested, tall, muscled man. He was serious, restrained and intelligent, and he was good with his hands, a good carpenter and mechanic. Known throughout the area for his moonshine, he'd been making corn whiskey since he was fifteen years old.

Myron had cash stashed in many nooks and crannies of the house, and it was said that if any neighbor needed help, money or otherwise, "Big Myron" would be there. "He may not say much," neighbors said, "but he don't need to. He says all he's got to say with his hands."

Paul's mother, Edna, was a quick, talkative and careful woman, who loved to read, liked to argue and liked to cook. If Myron wasn't so fond of "her tongue" he was fond of her wisdom, her steady nature and her fine cooking.

Edna and Myron were on the front porch, waiting with anxious patience, when Paul turned the Pontiac into the gravel drive, came to a stop and switched off the engine.

He climbed out and stretched, wearing faded jeans, a blue cotton shirt and brown cowboy boots he'd bought in New Mexico. Clean shaven, and with a short, brush haircut, just for his parents, Paul smiled and waved.

Lifting his face to the sky, he inhaled, feeling the blowing rush of warm summer air across his face. He saw circling crows and blue jays darting after them with their sharp cries. He heard all the pleasant and familiar sounds of nature, and he was happy to be home.

Paul advanced toward the two-bedroom house, painted blue and white with new mahogany shutters and a porch swing. He stopped at the base of the porch stairs, smiling warmly at his parents.

He shoved his hands into his back pockets and shrugged. "Hello, folks. I guess I'm home."

His mother wore a cream-colored dress and blue print apron, her brown hair piled on top of her head, her eyes glistening with tears. "Is the war out of you, Paul?" she asked.

During the Second World War, Myron had been a left waist gunner in a B-24 bomber and flew thirty-five missions in Europe. He said, "It don't go away easy, does it, son?"

Paul glanced toward a grove of majestic trees moving in the wind. "My days are better, and I want to move on. I want to go back to school."

Edna looked at her son, and she was filled with love and pride. Paul was tall like his father, his jaw like granite, his eyes very blue, his blonde hair military short, his features well-made and handsome. His broad shoulders had carried fighting things, the weight of battle and wounded men. Edna knew this from letters. Paul wrote good letters, in fine cursive handwriting. His sharp descriptions revealed Vietnam's fertile rice fields, America's industrial Midwest, the wide prairies of the golden West, and the South's lush, green farmland and misty swamps.

Edna had thankful prayers on her lips and grateful tears in her eyes when Paul climbed the stairs and embraced her, whispering that he had missed her. Myron stood by, his face held under tight control.

Paul shook his father's hand and said, "The house looks good, Dad. The shutters are expert and fine. I see Mom finally got her porch swing."

Myron nodded, his throat tight with emotion, and it took moments before he responded.

"Thank you, son. It's good to have you home again."

Within days, Paul found a job as a car mechanic at Pete's Texaco Service Station and Auto Repair, just outside Paxton. Paul was going to explore the GI Bill to help pay for his college tuition when he spoke to Al Haynes, a recently discharged vet who worked the full-service gas pumps and sold products in the automotive store. Al had been a helicopter doorgunner in Vietnam.

"The Veterans Administration place was cold, man," Al said. "I was just there last week, and I went in a suit and tie and cut my hair, because I wanted to show them I wasn't a junkie on the hustle. So, I told the guy I wanted to go to college, and he looked at me like I was out of my mind. He slapped the papers down. I could see he wanted me out of there. Cold reception, Paul. Still, I stood in this long line, and then another long line, and filled out all these papers. I'll get my GED and then we'll see what they do."

Paul decided to pay his own way. The idea of standing in any line after the endless lines he'd been in during the service didn't inspire him. He wanted freedom—his own kind of freedom.

Two weeks later, Paul was enrolled in Paxton College as a sophomore, not a junior, because the college would not accept the credits he'd earned at a community college before he entered the Marines.

Some days later, over dinner, Paul told his parents that he'd found an old trailer near Cove Lake, and he was going to buy it, fix it up and live there.

He saw the disappointment in their eyes. "It's close. Only five miles away. I guess it's time I had my own digs."

"Digs?" his father asked, not understanding.

"It's a word the Brits use for my own place. I learned it from a guy I made friends with over there."

"You do as you need to do, son," Myron said softly. "You've given your time to your country and now it's time for you to live your life."

Edna took a sip of her iced tea, keeping her eyes down. "Paul... do you have a girl? Have you given any thought to settling down... well, I mean, after your schooling is over?"

Myron shot her a glance. "Edna, let the man have alone time. He don't need to be thinking about family responsibilities after what he's been through."

"You and me got married before you went off to fight," Edna said. "Even with a war going on and when Paul was born, we got on with it, didn't we? I don't mean nothing by it, Paul, but I'd be a lying woman if I didn't speak my mind and say some grandchildren would be welcome."

Paul scooped up some mashed potatoes and smiled at his mother. The smile reached up to his warm eyes. "Mom, your mashed potatoes are better than they used to be."

Edna blushed a little. "They're just the same, Paul. I haven't done nothing different."

"I dreamed about these mashed potatoes," Paul continued. "And your fried chicken. I used to spend hours thinking about your dinners."

That pleased Edna, and her pleasure softened the mood.

"No, Mom, I don't have a girl. I dated a girl out in Tucson, Arizona, a few times. She was nice, and came from a good family, but I only stayed around for a couple of weeks, and I told her that when we met. I told her I wasn't ready for anything too serious. I got a letter from her just the other day, and she said she might come for a visit. I guess... well, I guess that's okay."

His parents stopped eating, hanging on his words. Myron cleared his throat as he reached for his frosted glass of iced tea. "Well, like I said, you don't need to rush into anything, son. Plenty of time for all that later. Now, about that trailer, I can help you fix it up if you want."

"Yeah, sure, Dad. Thanks. It doesn't look so good on the outside, so some paint might help, but the inside's okay, except I'll have to replace the old carpeting. I didn't see much mold. The plumbing's okay, the bedroom's small, and the kitchen will do. Nothing fancy."

A minute later, Myron added, "I guess you heard that Will Glover died over there in Vietnam some months ago?"

Paul didn't look up. "Yeah, I heard."

"Your mother and I went to the funeral," Myron added. "She brought a casserole and a pie, and I gave Willard one of my drills. He's been working on his house... and who can't use a good drill? Anyway, we said the decent thing and stayed for prayers."

Paul felt the darkness trying to pull him back into memories of war, death, and loss.

Edna said. "You take all the time you need, Paul, and if the trailer suits you, then so be it. If you get lonely, your bed's here... and so are we. I know you'll find the right girl when it's time."

Myron nodded. "We'll fix the trailer up nice, Paul. You'll have a good place for your studies come September."

CHAPTER 16

I t was a daring choice—given the unpredictable nature of time travel and the past. But she didn't care. Kate made a left turn onto Pike's Lane, a narrow, asphalt road that led to Cove Lake—to where Paul Ganic's tan and white trailer was parked. The September wind was rising through changing maples, oaks and elms, and the shadows of creamy clouds swept across autumn hills to the edge of the eastern sky.

Kate Clarke rolled down the window of her Ford Falcon and inhaled the Friday afternoon breeze. Geese honked overhead, winging south over the shining lake, banking left over the far hills, flying in a V formation. Coming to a small hill, Kate turned onto a part-gravel, part-asphalt, single-lane road, as the afternoon sky widened, as the broad, shining lake dominated her attention, and Paul's trailer came into view.

Kate's car went sneaking ahead, and her pulse quickened. She braked to a stop, and sat in a paralyzing silence, stiff-shouldered and anxious. There it was, the newly painted tan and white trailer resting on cinder blocks, looking fat, with bulbous rounded corners, and an aluminum ladder that led to the roof. It was just as she'd remembered it from all those years ago. Paul's car was parked beside it under a steel carport, the black and white Pontiac. Yes, he was there! He was inside the trailer!

Her jaw clenched as memories flooded in, and the sorrow of remembering that awful rainy night robbed her of giddy anticipation, seizing her with pain. The small, wooden bridge was only about a mile away. She was driving too fast, and the back end of the car came around, and there was a shriek of rubber, and the car slammed into the bridge guardrails, broke through, and plunged into the lake, killing Paul and their baby, and nearly killing her.

But time, by some strange twist of fate, had been reset. Paul, her soon-to-be husband, was inside that trailer, and, incredibly, she would meet him that night at the coffeehouse.

She strained now to remember what had happened to her after that accident. She knew she had gone to college, but she couldn't recall where. In fact, ever since Wednesday, the day Kate had returned to 1968, she'd begun to notice small memory slips about her life in 2022. With everything else that was unfolding, it was alarming.

She was having difficulty remembering where she lived in New York, where she had taught, and even her children's names. For the life of her, she couldn't recall her husband's name, his face, or what his profession had been. At first this startled her, but as she relaxed into 1968, she grew less concerned, allowing herself to live fully in each unraveling moment.

Staring at Paul's trailer now, Kate realized she didn't feel like a woman in her seventies. She felt the incendiary thrill of a 20-year-old's playful recklessness and desire. Otherwise, why would she have piled into her car and driven to Paul's trailer, risking the chance of messing up time? What if she and Paul met now, instead of at the Candlelight later that day?

Every cell was alert, her body ripe for love, for Paul's kisses, his touch, his body. In only a few hours, their eyes would meet, strong and quiet.

Kate nudged the car ahead, approaching Paul's trailer, ducking her head, raking a strand of hair from her eyes, swinging a hopeful glance toward it. The sharp glare, glancing off the trailer's picture window, made her squint, but she saw no one inside. Afraid of being discovered "before the right time," she burned rubber and shot away down the road, dust spinning from the back wheels.

In her rearview mirror, through the swirling dust, she saw a tall figure emerge from the trailer, his hands on his hips as he stared curiously at the retreating car.

An extraordinary expression passed over Kate's face: shock, excitement, wonder. It was Paul! Whatever was true or not true, whatever was fiction, fantasy or reality, there he was, the love of her life, Paul Ganic, alive again!

***

After seeing Paul and his trailer, Kate drove into town, parked and breezed into Art Mackay's bookstore at four o'clock, on time for her shift. That morning, she recalled she worked part time at Mackay's Books New & Old four times a week: Wednesday, Friday, Saturday and Sunday.

Art glanced at her from the center aisle, where he was helping two female students search for copies of used novels that were required reading for their English Literature class.

He hadn't seen her since Wednesday, when she'd come crashing into his store with her wild tale of time travel. She waved, and he waved, and when she stepped behind the cash register and stored her purse, the front door "dinged" open, and Kate glanced up to see an older man enter. He had a work-tanned, weathered face. She immediately recognized him. He was the same man she'd seen on the train platform on Wednesday morning, and he was dressed the same, in brown corduroy trousers, a railway-striped, long sleeve shirt, black suspenders, and a faded, brown felt hat, tugged low over his brow. Stepping inside, he closed the door and shifted his gaze to her. As he approached Kate, she unconsciously took a step back.

He stopped within a few feet of her and touched the brim of his hat. "Afternoon, ma'am."

Kate noticed his hands were rough and veined, his black boots scuffed and in need of polish. She spoke just above a whisper. "Can I help you?"

He pulled a toothpick from his top shirt pocket and stuck it between his yellow, tobacco-stained teeth. He cast his eyes around the place while he worked the toothpick back and forth with his tongue. When his eyes returned to hers, the skin around his eyes crinkled. "You didn't heed my warnin'."

Kate retreated another step. "I don't know what you mean."

"Time is what I mean. You didn't heed my warning about time, and about changing time, and about all the things that turn and twist when time is played with. Well, all right, young woman, now time will have to adjust itself, just like a stream when a tree topples down, blocking its normal flow. Then that stream must alter its course and flow in a new direction, into an uncharted and mysterious direction."

Kate shivered, her eyes narrowing. "Who are you?"

"Don't matter none, ma'am, who I am. Just a messenger, that's all, and the message has been delivered."

Kate stared into his dark, hollow eyes, and then

he touched the brim of his hat with two fingers and gave her a little, gentlemanly bow. "Good day, ma'am."

The man had crossed the room and closed the door before Kate released a trapped breath. She stepped aside when Art moved behind the cash register and rang up the four books the students had chosen.

When they were gone, Art looked at Kate, who'd remained next to him, her eyes staring.

"There's that look again, Kate. When you walked in here a few minutes ago, you looked fine. Just like your old self. Now... I don't know. What's going on with you? You're as white as a ghost."

She shook her head, struggling to recover. "I'm okay. I'm fine. I just need to get busy."

"Well, at least tell this rusty old man that you've gotten over all this time travel crap from two thousand and something."

Kate looked into his eyes and saw it was a lost cause. Art would never believe she'd time traveled. Of course he wouldn't. Would she believe it if someone had approached her when she was living in the twenty-first century and said they were from fifty years into the future?

But it was unsettling, and frightening, that memories of the future were melting away, hour by hour, it seemed. What did that mean? She had to hold fast to her memories. Without them, she'd forget about that horrible night when Paul and her baby were killed.

And who was that scary man who'd just left the shop? Whatever had happened, she had to remember so she could ensure that she and Paul would not be in that 1962 Chevy Bel Air on March 23, 1969, crossing that wooden bridge in a rainstorm.

Kate was shaken from her thoughts when Art said, "We got a delivery this morning. Three boxes of books from the Hunter mansion in Columbus. If you want to stay busy, go check them, catalogue them, price them, and put them on the shelves."

Kate brightened a little, shaking off her angst. "Okay, good. It will keep me busy, and it'll be fun."

Art shook his head. "Do you know something, Kate? It's when I see your eyes light up like that over books that, if I wasn't sixty-three years old, I would fall head-over-heels in love with you."

Her eyes lit up to his smile, and she thought, *Art, part of me is ten years older than you, and if you had lived in 2022, I'd have asked you out on a date, you younger man.*

Kate said, "I bet you were a heart breaker, weren't you, Art?"

"Nah... Like I told you before, I was never very good with issues of the heart in the real world. Grown-up love? It was not for me... Only the kind of love written about in novels is the love for me. The fantasy. The unattainable. Only when I read do I dream and play the foolish lover, and perform the noble act, or do the red-roses, romantic thing. But do you know what, Kate?" he asked with a little wink.

"When I read books, I'm a regular Casanova, Don Juan and Rhett Butler all rolled up into one, and I live in an extravagant palace with golden balconies, opulent fountains and scented gardens."

He lifted his hands. "In that most romantic of lands, no woman can resist me."

Kate's laughter burst out. "Art, you're a quintessential romantic, and I never knew."

Art pointed at her. "And you, Kate Clarke, should be in love."

"Oh, I am in love... and I'm going to see him tonight."

CHAPTER 17

T he Candlelight Coffeehouse was located near the Village Green, only a block from the Aurora Movie Theater and Schmitt's Bakery. It was a square room, with a black-and-white tile floor, open brick walls and soft lighting, which lent an intimate look and feel.

A small stage, with an overhead spotlight, faced the wooden tables with their flickering tea candles encased in small, red globes. To the left of the stage was the generous, dark mahogany bar that served up wine, beer, burgers, snacks, and coffee, especially Irish coffee, with lots of Irish whiskey and lots of whipped cream.

Whenever the live performer finished a set and took a break, the yellow and green neon jukebox was put into action, thumping out 1950s and 1960s rock.

On the walls were hung framed concert posters

featuring The Doors, Judy Collins, Pink Floyd, Bob Dylan, the Grateful Dead, and Janice Joplin & the Holding Company, all lit by dim spotlights, the psychedelic art eye-catching.

Kate entered at 9:20 p.m., facing a room that was bustling. Cigarette smoke hung in stringy clouds and ceiling fans whirled lazily. Two waitresses, wearing bellbottom jeans and sunburst T-shirts, one with a headband, the other sporting a long braid, worked the room, trays held aloft as they dipped, swerved, delivered, and bussed tables.

On the stage, Vicki strummed her guitar and sang the Bob Dylan song, *Don't Think Twice It's All Right,* in a lusty tone. Her boyfriend, Luke, standing beside her, juiced up the tune with his harmonica, finding off-centered rhythms and working the instrument from side to side to produce the melancholy moan of a train-whistle.

Kate took it all in, high on anticipation. Her hair was shoulder length, slightly teased up on the top and lightly sprayed. She wore slim, flared, dark slacks, an orange and yellow V-neck sweater, and low heels with pointed toes that she'd bought that morning at McAllen's Department Store.

Before she left the apartment, she'd examined herself in her bedroom's full-length mirror and was startled by her appearance: she looked like Mary Tylor Moore as the character Laura Petrie, on the old *Dick Van Dyke Show*.

For hours, Kate had agonized over what to wear, sampling countless outfits until there were piles of discarded clothes on her bed, shoes scattered on the floor and the lingering smell of hairspray. She had no memory of what she'd worn the first time she'd met Paul, and she prayed it wouldn't make a difference.

Kate merged into the coffeehouse crowd, her nerves like broken glass as she scanned the room, looking for Paul. The music and the applause were loud; the sing-a-longs spirited; and a glass, sliding off a tray and shattering onto the tile floor, distracted her as she searched for Paul.

If memory served, Paul should have been sitting at a back table with another guy. The previous time Kate had entered the coffeehouse, all the tables had been taken. She'd glanced to her right and there he was. Their eyes met, and it was, as they say, love at first sight, or at least an attraction so powerful that neither looked away.

But Paul wasn't sitting there. Three girls were, and they were singing along with Vicki, the folk song *If I Had a Hammer*.

Kate recalled what that dusty old man had said to her in Art's bookstore. "Time will have to adjust itself and flow in a new direction, into an uncharted and mysterious direction."

Kate picked her way through the crowd to the front door, where she had a good view of the room. She waited ten, fifteen, twenty minutes, glancing around, glancing outside, but Paul didn't come. She fought a sinking despair. If Paul didn't appear, then how would she meet him?

Vicki finished her set and rose from the stool, bowing to applause and whistles. Preoccupied, Kate applauded while she continued searching for Paul. A growling stomach reminded her that she hadn't eaten since lunch.

The three girls sitting at the table where Paul should have been stood up, ready to leave. Kate surged ahead and sat down in a chair that faced the front door, and she prayed, with all her heart, that Paul would enter at any moment.

She massaged her forehead, struggling to climb over her anxiety and come up with a plan. Fear pulsed. What if she didn't meet Paul? What if he was with someone else? What would that do to her destiny? Would she want that destiny? She was positive that she'd been hurled back in time to save Paul and their unborn child.

A waitress hustled over in a hectic flush. With nimble fingers, she forked the three empty glasses, setting them on her tray, and then reached for the empty basket of French fries.

"Can I get you something?" she asked. "Need a menu?"

Kate struggled to clear the fog from her mind. She had to eat. "No... Just a Coke and a burger."

"Deluxe?"

"Yeah, sure. Medium."

As the waitress hurried away, Vicki and Luke came over, he flipping his shoulder-length blonde hair from his face. Vicki's mane of long hair was tied into a loose topknot. She wore platform shoes, bellbottom jeans and a black turtleneck.

"Hi, Kate!" Vicki said brightly, still high from her performance.

She and Luke sat.

"Look at you," Luke said with a grin, his speech slow and lazy. "You are lookin' so fine, and you smell good, too."

"What's with you and the smells, Luke? Are you some kind of hound dog?" Vicki said, with a chuckle.

"No... I'm just noticing that Kate looks different and she's wearing something I've never smelled, some perfume or something. Okay? That's all," Luke responded, a little defensively.

"How different?" Kate said, leaning forward, seizing on his comment, as if it might hold a clue as to why Paul hadn't shown up.

Luke shrugged. "I don't know. I've never seen your hair styled like that, and I've never seen you dress like that."

"How do I normally dress?"

"With... I don't know, bellbottoms and neon pink and yellow T-shirts. And you also..."

Vicki rolled her eyes, cutting him off. "Let's drop it with the smells and the hair and the clothes, already."

Luke gave her a look, spreading his hands. "Hey, I'm just talking, that's all."

Vicki swung her hopeful attention to Kate. "So, how did you like my set, Kate?"

Kate was lost in her whirling thoughts and didn't respond for so long that Vicki thought she hadn't heard her. "Kate?"

Kate snapped out of her anxiety. "Oh, I'm sorry, Vicki... No, I liked it. I loved it! I really liked the *Blowin' in the Wind*."

"Thanks!" Kate said, with a lift of her proud chin. "I'm in good voice tonight and it's a great crowd."

"I didn't remember that you played the harmonica, Luke," Kate said, making conversation.

Luke and Vicki exchanged a glance.

"What do you mean, you don't remember? You know I play," Luke said. "I practiced with Vicki in the apartment just a few days ago. Don't you remember? You said I sounded real good."

Kate's eyes slid away. "Oh, yeah. Sure... I just... I... Yeah, of course, I remember."

"Did you come alone?" Luke asked, looking around.

Kate nodded. "Yeah... I mean, I thought I was supposed to meet somebody, but..."

"... Stood you up?" Vicki said.

Kate folded her hands, then unfolded them. "I don't know," Kate said, glancing toward the front door. "I just thought he'd be here, that's all."

"Your parents called again," Vicki said. "Did you get my note?"

"Yeah, I called them back, but they weren't home. I'll try again tomorrow."

Vicki scratched the left side of her lip. "Are you okay, Kate? You don't... I don't know. You seem different, like something's bothering you."

Kate sat up, forcing a smile. "I'm fine. Just fine. I'm

starving. I always get weird when I'm hungry."

"Yeah, I know you do," Vicki said.

"I ordered a hamburger deluxe."

"Good... Are you going to hang around for my next set?"

Kate wanted to eat and run. Literally. She wanted to rush to her car and drive back to Cove Lake to Paul's trailer, but, for now, she'd have to stay for Vicki. "Yeah, sure..."

Luke glanced over his shoulder. "So, Kate, why don't you sit with Vicki's father and brother? Vic Jr. keeps giving you the eye, if you haven't noticed."

Kate hadn't noticed. "No... I think I'll just hang out here and, you know, wait. The guy might show up, and I don't want him to think I'm with someone else."

Vicki's eyes narrowed. "And who is this mystery guy, Kate? The guy you're so secretive about? It's not like you to be so secretive."

"You don't know him."

"But he does have a name, right?"

"Yeah... It's Paul."

"Paul what?"

"It doesn't matter!" Kate said, much too sharply.

Vicki leaned back. "Okay... Okay. Touchy you are tonight, Kate."

"No, I don't mean to be. It's just that..." And then Kate's mouth froze when the front door opened, and Paul Ganic entered, tall and handsome.

But he wasn't alone. A tall, thin, pretty girl, wearing jeans, a brown leather jacket, a cowgirl hat and cowgirl boots, was hanging on his arm, all smiles.

Vicki and Luke followed Kate's astonished and wounded eyes to the couple.

Vicki cleared her throat. "Okay, so, from your expression, Kate, I'm guessing that must be Paul."

Kate mouthed the words, "It can't be."

CHAPTER 18

On Saturday morning, Kate spoke with her parents on the phone. Hearing their voices again brought a full range of emotions: love, bewilderment, compassion, a haunting sense of loss. The sharp pictures of her parents in her head were mostly of their last days, her father dying of pancreatic cancer, her mother dying in her sleep from a heart attack.

Kate's childhood memories of her father were of his patient bicycle-riding instructions as she wobbled and spilled to the ground; of his drilling multiplication tables at the kitchen table until she rattled them off with militaristic precision; and of their common love of reading and books.

Kate's mother was a quiet, private woman who taught elementary school and attended the Methodist church regularly. She was also somewhat of an enigma. She hid gin bottles in all sorts of places in the house: in her back closet in a pair of boots; in a box filled with World War II photographs; and in the kitchen cupboard, behind the five-pound bag of Gold Metal flour.

Several times as a teenager, Kate had smelled the gin on her mother's breath and, being the mischievous girl she'd been, she'd embarked on numerous "gin hunts." Once, she found a half-drunk bottle in the umbrella stand, another in the linen closet, with but a single swallow remaining, and yet another in the laundry basket, not touched.

Kate did not get to know her mother well; they'd never had a real mother and daughter heart-to-heart talk, and Kate always blamed herself for that. After Kate was married with kids of her own, her father told her that her mother had had "a drinking problem" ever since the war, after she'd lost her brother and the boy next door, who had been the love of her life—or so she'd told her husband several times when she was drunk.

On the phone, Kate told them she loved them, and that she promised to visit soon, although she wasn't sure when she'd honor the promise. Her mother was quiet, and her father asked about her reading, as he typically did. "Have you read *Confessions of Nat Turner,* by William Styron?"

"No, Dad, but I'll check it out."

"You might find it interesting. See if you have it at your bookstore."

"I will." She waited for her mother to say something, but she didn't. "Mom?"

"Yes, Kate."

"How's school?"

"It's just fine. Every year I'm surprised by how cute the kids are. I wish they didn't have to grow up and go out into this miserable swamp of a world."

Kate ignored her comment, and said brightly, "Hey, you two... I miss you. I love you, and I'll see you soon."

"Can't be soon enough, Kate," her father said.

***

For a time on Saturday afternoon, Kate moved restlessly through the bookstore, as if searching for something, strolling up one aisle and down the next, her head down, a thoughtful expression on her face, a fingernail to her lips. Art watched her, concerned, but he said nothing, because whenever a customer came in and needed help, Kate hustled over to help them. And then her eyes lit up as she led them to the book they were looking for, offering opinions and answering any questions.

As the afternoon lengthened, Kate kept busy, ringing up sales and rearranging table displays to feature best sellers, popular romances, and required reading for students. During a slow period, she dusted the shop and cleaned the paned glass windows with Windex.

"Are you going for a merit badge or are you hinting at a raise?" Art finally asked, smoking his pipe and glancing over the display tables, impressed.

"What do you mean?" Kate said, standing by the cash register, the windows behind her shiny clean.

"First you pace around the shop like Hamlet's ghost, quiet and sulky, and then you're busier than a rabbit with four dates, talking to customers, rearranging the displays, and cleaning, and then, if that weren't enough, you grab a copy of *Listen to the Warm* by Rod McKuen, and you are actually reading it. Okay, Kate Clarke, look at my blank expression."

"Okay. So?"

Art puffed his pipe and blew a cloud of smoke toward the ceiling. "Kate, you're just not yourself. You don't read Rod McKuen. You wouldn't. You couldn't. I've never, not ever, seen you read Rod McKuen."

Kate turned defensive. "I was curious, okay? I haven't read him in a while." She wanted to add, *not in over fifty years*, but she didn't.

"Fine, fine, whatever, but you haven't been yourself since you showed up here last Wednesday. You're smoke one minute and fire the next. You're brooding and insular, and I even saw you talking to yourself, lips moving, head shaking, nibbling your thumb."

Kate crossed her arms. "Okay, well, *you're* brooding sometimes—maybe dour is a better word. And you're insular, too, or maybe I should use the word detached. And you definitely talk to yourself, or I should say, curse to yourself. And you can be very grouchy."

"Yeah, well, I'm over sixty. That's what people

do when they jump over sixty. They're grouchy and they talk to themselves. But 20-year-old girls shouldn't be so wadded up with life. All that will come later. What's going on, Kate? Something's bothering you. You can tell your old Grandpa Art. I'll keep it locked up in the vault of my head. Promise."

Kate couldn't have agreed more. As she'd aged, she'd started talking to herself, especially after her kids were grown and gone.

Art pointed at her with the stem of his pipe. "Now tell me true, Kate Clarke, you're not doing a *Valley of the Dolls* on me, are you, getting addicted to barbiturates, a.k.a. 'dolls?' I read the book and saw the movie, as awful as it was, although I liked Susan Hayward."

Kate lowered her arms to her side. "No. I've told you. For the last time, I'm not taking any drugs."

"Yeah, and maybe I believe you, and maybe I don't. You were out of your head on Wednesday, talking about time traveling, and I don't know what the hell else. You didn't even know what day and year it was."

Kate turned away. "I was just... I was exhausted. I hadn't slept well. And I was a little sick, but I'm better now."

Art puffed on his pipe. "Okay, kid, it's just that... I don't know. I'm just a little more than uneasy about this world right now, and especially your generation. Your music stinks, your clothes are shabby and ugly, and while I can't say I'm wild about us being caught up in the Vietnam War, me thinks you all protest too much. Anyway, things just don't seem so stable to me. So, maybe I worry about things... about you."

"I'm okay, Art, really, I am. Thanks for worrying about me, but you don't have to."

Art kept his eyes on her, smoking pensively.

Kate inclined her head forward and lifted her hands. "Okay? What else?"

Art pulled the pipe from his teeth and looked at it. "So, what happened to the guy you met last night? The one you said you were in love with? Is that what's bothering you?"

A shadow crossed her face.

"Aha! There it is!" Art exclaimed. "That's what it is. Something happened last night."

Kate shook her head. "I don't want to talk about it."

Art nodded. "Fair enough. None of my business."

He pointed to the door. "All right, kid, then get out of here. It's Saturday night. Go find some friends and have some fun. Go to a movie or a drive-in or something."

"I can stay and close up," Kate said.

"No, you've done enough today, and so maybe I *will* give you a raise, say twenty cents more an hour."

Kate grinned, batting her eyes. "I'm rich," she said, with a playful toss of her hair.

"Don't be a smartass, or I'll change my mind. Now, get your purse and jacket and go. And grab an umbrella from the rack. It's clouded up; it might rain and spoil your pretty, clean windows. I'll see you tomorrow."

Kate shrugged, went to the cash register and reached under the counter for her purse. At that moment, the door "dinged", and Paul Ganic and his girlfriend entered, their hands joined, she again wearing cowgirl boots and hat. She playfully tugged him inside, her worshipping eyes fixed on him.

Kate froze and squeezed her black leather purse until her left hand turned white. Art noticed. He also noticed that Kate didn't make a move to ask if they needed help, and they were staring at her, obviously wanting to be helped.

Art spoke up. "Hi, there. Can I help you?"

The girl smiled, showing perfect white teeth on a lovely, tanned face. "I'm looking for a book about the West and horses, and my boyfriend wants a book about natural things or…"

Paul spoke up. "… Something about the Earth's ecosystems… the environment. Non-fiction."

Art's gaze flicked to Kate. "Kate's our environment expert. She collects fallen leaves and twigs, and she grows plants and things."

Paul grinned at the joke, but his girlfriend didn't.

Kate's hesitant eyes lifted onto Paul's warrior-handsome face, his chiseled good looks, the broad shoulders and deep blue eyes; his mouth she had kissed all those years ago. She knew his naturally muscled body, vital and strong from hard work since he was a child, working with his father. She knew he had a two-inch scar on his right hip, from when he'd been in a car accident at sixteen, and that when he was eight years old, he had named his dog Jackson, after President Andrew Jackson, whose biography Paul had read.

Kate knew all that, and more. Paul also had an impressive collection of jazz and classical records, his favorite jazz singer being Billy Holiday. His favorite classical composer was Brahms. Rock and roll and blues favorites included *The Who, Motown* and *The Paul Butterfield Blues Band.* She and Paul had made love to some of those records and, after the accident, whenever she'd heard them playing in a club or restaurant, she'd grabbed her purse and left.

The night before, when Kate saw Paul and his cowgirl enter the Candlelight Coffeehouse, everything in her began to shake and bust loose. After canceling her order with the waitress, Kate had made an abrupt exit, wandering the town aimlessly until she found a White Castle Restaurant, ordered, and ate alone, lost in memories.

Now, in the bookshop, Kate had a good look at Paul, and it was wonderful, and it was terrible. She loved his quiet dignity and the power of his gaze, which had always drawn her ever closer to him. And she loved his clever, exploring fingers as they caressed her. Standing there in a kind of trance, she could almost feel his fingers touch her lips, her neck, her breasts.

Kate saw Paul's eyes examining her, and the awkwardness of the moment caused Art to clear his throat and clasp his hands. "All right, then, Kate, go find them their books."

"Oh, yes," Kate finally said, pointing toward the third aisle. "Over here."

Paul's eyes lingered on Kate, and he realized she was familiar, and she was magnetic. The cowgirl gave Kate a frosty, jealous stare as she witnessed the spark in Paul's eyes.

"We don't need any help," Cowgirl said flatly. "We can just browse the aisles. Come on, Paul."

Kate backed away, feeling the impulse to bolt out of the door and run from the nightmare; run as fast as she could back to the cave and vanish.

But she gained control of herself, and the rise of a challenge galvanized her. Her lips formed a business smile as Paul drifted away with his girlfriend.

She called out, "Have you read *Silent Spring* by Rachel Carson and Linda Lear?"

Paul stopped, turning to face her. "Yes, I have. It's a great book and ahead of its time, I think."

"How about *Ring of Bright Water*?"

Paul thought about it and shook his head. "No, I don't know it."

"We have one hardback copy from a recent estate sale. It was published in 1960, I think, maybe earlier, but the reviews were excellent."

Cowgirl's face tightened as she looked Kate up and down.

"What can you tell me about it?" Paul asked.

Kate took two steps toward him. "It doesn't sound as good as it is, and I didn't read it all, but what I read, I really liked. It's about the experiences of the author with otters at his remote house in Scotland."

Cowgirl rolled her eyes. "Otters? You've got to be kidding me."

Kate ignored her. "It's also about wildlife and understanding nature. Well, now that I think about it, it's really about nature and animals."

Paul nodded. "All right. May I see it?"

Kate pointed to an aisle. "It's over here," she said, walking toward the far aisle. Paul followed and Cowgirl was right behind him, not happy.

Kate found the book on the upper shelf, pulled it down, and handed it to Paul. He took it, studied the dust jacket, and opened the book, leafing through it. "Thanks. Looks interesting."

Cowgirl's hard stare directed at Kate had the desired impact, and so Kate excused herself and returned to the front counter, trembling, her hands flat at her sides.

Art was at the coffee station, pouring himself a paper cup of coffee. He reached for the glass sugar dispenser and let the sugar flow for a good five count. After he stirred the coffee several times with a plastic straw, he lifted his eyes to Kate and spoke in a near whisper.

"That book you recommended only came in three days ago. Did you really read it?"

Kate shrugged a shoulder. "I read the description on the back when I placed it on the shelf yesterday."

He shook his head. "I'm glad I'm not young anymore."

Kate had a thought. She left the counter and angled right, leisurely strolling the aisle parallel to

Paul and his girlfriend. Hidden by book shelves, Kate cozied up to one, pretending to tidy up a section of leaning poetry books, while she strained to hear their conversation.

CHAPTER 19

"HAVE YOU THOUGHT ANY MORE about what I said this morning?" Cowgirl asked.

Kate's head was canted, her ear close to the bookshelf as she rearranged books.

Paul said, "Yeah, I've thought about it."

"You said you liked Arizona," Cowgirl said, caressing the words.

"Yeah, I do. I love the sky and the desert, and especially the northern rim of the Grand Canyon."

"Daddy will get you a job, and he knows everybody, including the President of the University of Arizona. They'll transfer all of your credits, and you can finish in a year or so."

Paul was quiet.

"We could finish school together," Cowgirl continued. "I only have fifteen more credits to complete."

Paul sighed. "I don't know, Myra. I need more time

to think about it, and I don't want to be so far away from my parents."

"That won't be a big deal. We can fly back often. As often as you'd like."

After a brief silence, Myra said, "They like me, don't they? Your parents?"

"Yeah. Dad thinks you're pretty. Mom likes your boots and hat."

After another brief silence, Myra said, "Do you mind if I stay another couple of days?"

"No... Stay."

Kate's shoulders sank.

"You won't have to work as a mechanic," Myra added. "Daddy likes you."

"I only met him twice."

"Yes, and he said he liked you. He said he could tell you were a 'steady and upright young man.' His words. Before he put me on the plane to come here, he said he could put you to work in one of his real estate offices or in insurance, whichever you want."

"I like working with my hands," Paul said. "And, as I said, I want to do something in conservation, or work with the environment."

"Well, okay, you can do that on the side, can't you?"

"I don't know... I have to think things out."

When things got quiet, and Kate heard creaking floorboards, she was sure they were kissing. Kate's chin fell to her chest as she stared at the floor in thoughtful astonishment. How could this be happening?

Kate heard boots moving across the floor and she skedaddled toward the rear of the shop, staring up at an upper bookshelf, looking engrossed and preoccupied but feeling utterly deflated. At the sound of the ringing cash register, she walked to the front in time to see Art slide Paul's book into a paper bag.

Paul turned to Kate with a smile, pulled the book from the bag and held it up. "I bought it. Thanks."

Kate placed her hands behind her back, managing a thin smile. "I hope you like it."

Myra's expression turned sour. "I didn't find anything. I didn't find the kind of books that appeal to me." Then she glanced about, searching for something polite to say. "But the shop is well… I mean, it's old and quaint. Nice."

Kate gave her a cool glance, but Art was amused by the statement, and he chortled. "Well, young lady, you know what Mark Twain said, 'Books are for people who wish they were somewhere else.' Perhaps you're happy being just where you are."

Myra's face turned sunny, her adoring eyes lighting up on Paul. "Yes, I think you're right about that, sir."

When they were gone, Kate wilted.

"What a face you have, Kate… a Greek, tragic-mask sort of face. The face of a mourner."

Kate lowered her head, her voice barely audible. "It's not the same… Not at all the same."

"What's not the same?"

Kate looked at Art with vacant appraisal, not

really seeing him, but seeing her thoughts play out in her mind. She visualized the dusty old man who told her she couldn't change the past. When she'd left him and walked into town, she had already changed the past, hadn't she? So, the old man was right. Her old past was not being repeated, while a new, unknown past was coalescing and taking shape. How would the "new" past unfold? Would she and Paul get married as before, and would she get pregnant as before?

Kate didn't want to face it, but the pageant of time had changed, and the players were acting in variation. The clock had been reset when she arrived, but the events, disturbingly unique, forced brand-new actions and brand-new choices.

"Kate?" Art asked. "There you go again, tuning out on me. Talk to me."

Art stared into the depths of Kate's eyes, and what he saw troubled him. He saw storms and confusion, and as her eyes widened and cleared, he saw a cold, entranced comprehension.

"Kate? What's the matter with you?" Art said, in a cracking, worried voice. Had the girl completely lost her beautiful mind?

Kate turned away, grabbed her jacket and purse and gave him a final, uneasy glance as she left the shop. "I've got to go."

Outside, she walked as if in a dream, oblivious to place or time, her mind a restless autumn wind. A light rain fell, glistening the streets, and the rain and wind ripped leaves from the trees and blew them in circling gusts. Some leaves crabbed across the sidewalk; some flew past her face; some landed on passing cars.

Without an umbrella, Kate was wet and chilled, but she kept walking, finally ducking in for cover under the awning of a jewelry store. When the rain stopped, she moved on, her bold, stunned eyes staring ahead, tunneling through the dim daylight as it slowly emptied into twilight, and then into darkness.

Kate sat under the protective roof of the gazebo on the village green, her breath puffing white vapor. Wet as she was, the cold and dampness did not reach her inner skin, the skin of a stranger she didn't know.

Kate created a movie in her mind. She drives to Paul's trailer and finds him with Myra. Kate tells him she loves him, and she will always love him. She tells him she came from far away to love him again, and to save them both from an unthinkable tragedy.

He stares at her. He pities her. Tells her she should go home. Myra shouts at her to leave, and Kate, humiliated and lost, turns and slinks away.

Sitting on a wooden bench in the gazebo, Kate wiped wet strands from her face, staring, thinking, planning. She sat up, shivering and hungry, slowly recovering from the shock of her discovery, a discovery she should have made right at the beginning, but her head had been too blunted and confused.

All right. The game was brand new now, which meant there was the real possibility she could make a play for Paul. If he'd fallen in love with her the first time, then he could do it again, couldn't he? She doubted whether that had changed. She'd seen that something, that spark of attraction, that "Hey, haven't I seen you somewhere before?" in his eyes. Yes, she was sure of that.

She knew where he lived and where he worked. Those things hadn't changed. She also knew where he attended classes.

A mind made up had power—the power of decision-making and focus. No more waiting for fate to repeat itself. She would act and bend fate to her will—and to her desire.

Kate did not intend to lose Paul, her only love, to Myra, the cowgirl from Arizona. Kate was determined to have the life she and Paul should have had the first time around.

It was time to think anew and act anew.

CHAPTER 20

P aul sat on a flat rock behind his trailer, staring out at the morning fog that curled across Cove Lake. He wore a navy-blue sweatshirt, jeans and comfy old brown shoes that should have been tossed months ago.

His arms were folded tightly against his chest, bracing himself against a chilly autumn wind that circled him, subsided, then returned, repeating the pattern. He hitched his knees up to his chest for warmth and gazed out in a drowsy peace. Paul loved the early morning, the timeless moments, the view of the flat lake, the smell of scented damp leaves and the music of echoing birdsong.

Myra had left the night before. She had to get back in time for her Wednesday classes at UA, and Paul had driven the sixty-two miles to the Columbus airport, with her cozied up next to him, the scent of her tantalizing, the memories of loving her, fresh.

At the airport, after a warm, deep kiss at the entry gate, Myra had stared at him longingly, stroking his cheek. "I'll miss you, you sexy man, who drives me crazy in all the indecent ways a girl wants to go crazy," she'd said in a breathy voice.

"It's good to be missed," Paul answered.

"Will you miss me?"

He lowered his voice. "I thought we covered all that this morning in my squeaky, lumpy bed."

She leaned the warmth of her full breasts against his chest. "I want more."

"Here?"

Her grin was sexy, her gray/blue eyes sultry. "Yeah, why not? I can find us a corner and make it look like we're just talking."

He kissed her again. "I won't be talking."

"Then you'll miss me?"

"Yeah, I'll miss you, Myra. I'll think of you every time I work on a crankshaft."

Her face fell. "What? I don't even know what a crankshaft is."

"It rotates inside the engine, and it rotates hundreds or even thousands of times per minute."

Myra leaned her head back, taking him in with a lusty amusement. "Ooooh, you make car repair sound so erotic."

He spoke in a southern drawl. "Yes, ma'am. The pleasure is all mine, ma'am."

She touched his lips with a finger. "I love you, Paul. I know we haven't known each other long enough for me to say that, but I don't care. I do love you, and that's just the way it is."

When he opened his mouth to answer, she covered it with her elegant hand and glossy red nails. "You don't have to say anything. I just want you to know how I feel, okay? That's the kind of girl I am. I don't hold back. When I feel it, I say I feel it. When I want it... Well, you know I'm not shy about that, ex-marine. But just promise me that you'll think about moving to Tucson."

He removed her hand and held it. "I told you this morning that I'm half-way there. Just give me a few more days."

She took his hand and kissed it. "We could have so much fun together, Paul. We can have it all, you know. Love, family, travel. And I won't get in your way. You can be who you want to be and do whatever you want to do, a car mechanic, a forest ranger, whatever you want."

"How about agricultural engineering? They offer courses at UA."

Myra lit up. "Then you *have* been thinking about it? You read the course book?"

"Yes..."

"Well, I don't exactly know what agricultural engineering is, but I'm all for it."

They heard the last call for Flight 309 to Tucson.

"You'd better go," Paul said, staring at the corners of her lovely mouth and the elegance of her neck.

"I'll go, but I don't want to."

After a goodbye kiss, Paul watched her sashay away, the body of a goddess, the cowgirl hat cocked confidently to the right, the jeans, a perfect hug-the-hips-and-buttocks-fit, her scent lingering in the air.

Outside on the observation deck, he watched the 707 roar down the runway, lift sharply into the night sky, landing lights blinking, and aim itself West.

The morning wind was shredding the fog. Paul's sitting bones ached, and the damp rock chilled him into a shiver. He stood, stretched his arms high into the low, gray sky and yawned dramatically, allowing his sleepy howl to disturb the delicate silence.

He was more or less awake, and his mind cranked up like a car that needed a tune-up. The night before, sleep hadn't come easily. His dreams had been flickering scenes of frantic battle, of his greased-up hands tangled in Myra's hair, and of standing stark naked in a car dealership, staring at a 1960 Chevy Impala's outward-pointed tail fins and bat-wing rear end. What the hell did that dream mean? He didn't really want to think about it.

Inside the trailer, Paul wandered into the kitchen, with its gray Formica table and two matching chairs. He scratched his head, contemplating breakfast. His first class wasn't until ten o'clock, and he wasn't due at the garage until four.

On the counter, the flip numbers of the yellow and white clock radio said it was 7:32 a.m. While he boiled water for coffee in a black tea kettle on the two-burner range stove, he dropped a slice of white bread into the toaster that burned the toast no matter what the setting was. From the turquoise Frigidaire, he retrieved a quart of milk and a stick of butter.

While he sat at the table munching buttered, burned toast and a banana, and sipping coffee, his mind unexpectedly flashed back on the attractive girl he'd seen on Saturday at the bookstore in town. The girl who'd recommended the book—and he liked the book. What was it about her that had seemed familiar? He couldn't put a finger on it. He thought, *Have I seen her before?*

No, he didn't think so. Maybe their paths had crossed on the Paxton College campus, or maybe he'd seen her in town. Paul pursed his lips in thought, pondering.

Myra had taken an instant dislike to the girl. That was easy to see. As they left the bookstore and started down the street, Myra glanced back and said, with distaste, "I don't like that girl. She had her eyes all over you."

Paul closed his eyes and reviewed the scene in his mind. What was the look the bookseller girl had given him? Seductive? Maybe, but maybe he'd also seen troubled unease. Maybe that's why her face had stamped itself on his mind.

Whatever the look was, he'd felt a little jolt of surprise, and he'd seen her, unexpectedly, in a kind of soft focus. For infinite seconds, he'd become aware of inexpressible emotions rolling through him, like tides of the sea. When their eyes first met, before he noticed her unease, he saw a magical loveliness and vulnerability that had captured him and frozen him to the spot.

Paul leaned back and looked up at the ceiling. Why was his head so thick? Why did it take him so long to understand his feelings? Was it the war? Had it beat the feeling out of him? Did he love Myra? Could he love her?

After breakfast and a shower, Paul drove his Pontiac along the old asphalt road that curved around Cove Lake. When he approached the wooden bridge and heard his tires rattle across the old beams, a memory was triggered. He recalled when he was sixteen, driving an old rattletrap of a 1954 Ford Fairlane. The radio was blasting *I Walk the Line* by Johnny Cash, the car fishtailing around curves, spitting gravel, and shooting across the bridge, bouncing, his laughter high and loud.

That had been before he'd gone to war, and he'd been a little crazier then. Maybe a little too wild, and a little too reckless with cars, and a little too irresponsible with his money, and maybe he'd tossed back a little too much moonshine.

He was twenty-five now, and the years behind him seemed like echoes. Whenever he thought about the war, he thought of shadows and boredom and fear and loneliness.

Paul attended his classes at Paxton College, returned home, ate lunch, and read more of the book he'd purchased at the bookstore, *Ring of Bright Water*. It fascinated him. The bookstore girl had been right. It wasn't just about otters. The author lived, off and on, in a remote house in Sandaig bay, Scotland, where he interacted with stags, wildcats, seals, porpoises, killer whales, and many wildfowl.

It was as if an entirely new world had opened up to him. The thought of living quietly in nature, away from the madness of the world, appealed to him on many levels. He got so immersed in the book that he was nearly late for work at Pete's garage.

At five minutes to four, Paul swerved into the service station, tossed a wave to Al Haynes and parked his car near the chain-link fence. He got out, closed his door, and as he started for the garage, he saw a light blue and white 1963 Ford Falcon Sprint parked near the air pump meter. He'd seen that car. Some people never forgot a face. Paul never forgot a car.

A moment's thought lit up his memory. Some days ago, from his trailer picture window, he'd seen the car creeping along the road, then stopping. He left the trailer to see who it was, when, for no reason that he could see, it shot off, with a jet of exhaust smoke and burning rubber.

Paul started over to the pretty little Falcon, and just as he arrived, he saw the bookseller girl exit the auto store, an unwrapped Snickers candy bar in her hand, her purse in the other.

He stopped and stared. She stopped mid-step and stared.

"Hi there, again," he said, with a friendly smile.

Kate released a little sigh. She'd planned the meeting. She knew Paul began work at 4 p.m., so she had parked her car by the air pump meter and waited. When she saw his car pull into the service station, she hurried inside, bought the candy bar and exited.

"Oh... Hi," she said, pretending surprise, but not pretending a fluttering heart. Her eyes expanded on him with pleasure. "Nice to see you again," she said, with a little smile.

"Yeah... You, too. I was reading the book earlier, the one you recommended."

"Then you like it?"

"Yeah, I do. I'm surprised at how much I like it. By the way, my name is Paul Ganic."

The golden afternoon sun lit up Kate's face, her raven black hair glazed by it, and Paul's eyes lingered on her, the sensation of *the familiar* rising again, pressing in on him. *Bookseller girl's face is pretty*, he thought. More than pretty. *Lovely*, not a word he used much. Ever? There was mystery in her eyes —imploring, beautiful eyes that reminded him of spring flowers. Bright, like spring, too. She was taller than he'd recalled, and her creamy white skin was flawless.

She stared back at him, waiting, appraising him. "I'm Kate Clarke."

Paul snapped out of it, turning to her car. "Well, it's good to meet you officially, Kate. And, by the way, you have a great car here. Nice 260, 4-speed, with a wood-like steering wheel."

Kate narrowed her eyes. "Wood-like?"

"Yes... Not real wood. 'Wood... like.'"

"Oh, I thought it was wood. Real wood."

"No, but I could put a real wood steering wheel in, if you want."

"No, I'm... Well, I mean, I probably *wouldn't* know the difference, pardon the pun."

"Pun?" Paul asked, lifting an eyebrow.

Kate moved her head right to left and left to right. "Silly... *'Wouldn't'*... you know, like wood-n't. Wood-like steering wheel."

Paul nodded, scratching his nose, grinning. "Oh, yeah. Got it. Not bad. You sneaked that one in on me."

"I love puns," Kate said, feeling the rise of a natural happiness she hadn't felt in years.

Paul moved toward the hood of the car and placed his hand on it. "Did you know that all those guys out there driving those groovy Mustangs are really driving a Falcon? This was the prototype."

"Really?"

"Yeah, really. I love the body on this thing. And did you also know that both Ford and Chrysler wanted to use the name 'Falcon,' but Ford registered the name twenty minutes before Chrysler? How's that for a bit of useless information?"

Kate shaded her eyes from the sun. "I like useless information. You never know when you might use it. Who would have known?"

"And, to bore you further, before 1963, the Falcon was just an economy car with two six-cylinder engines. I think one was the 140 or the 144, and the other was the 172, but don't quote me on that."

Kate pointed her Snickers candy bar at him, her forehead wrinkling into a mock stern warning. "Oh, you bet I'll quote you on that, pal. I'm holding you to it. If it's wrong, I'll pull out the handcuffs."

Paul laughed, and it was an easy laugh, a deep-in-his throat laugh. "And did you come all the way down here from town just to buy a Snickers?"

Kate had her answer ready. "I came for gas, and one of my tires was low."

"Mission accomplished?" Paul asked.

Kate had to be bold. Time was running out. She took in a sharp breath and went for broke. Everything happening had not happened before. None of it. She was improvising.

"Now that I'm here..." she said, shifting her weight from her right foot to her left, "... On Saturday morning, I'm going to drive to an old house about forty miles from here. The grandfather who owned the place just passed away, and his granddaughter wants to get rid of his rather extensive library. I want to get there before the big guys pick everything over. Would you like to come?"

Paul glanced away, considering her offer. Two cars were parked by the gas pumps and Al Haynes had pumps going in them both, while he reached to squeegee a windshield, the glass squeaking under his work, and the gas pumps clanging away, ringing on the dollar.

Paul observed Kate's elegant awkwardness. "I'd like to say yes, but..." He lifted a hand.

Kate rushed out her words. "Oh, it's okay. It was

just a spur-of-the-moment thing. No big deal. I mean, I know you have a girlfriend and…"

"But you know what?" Paul said, with a nod and a shrug. "I'd love to go. Why not?"

Kate wanted to leap up, stretch her arms to the sky and shout, YES!

Instead, she smiled demurely. "Okay… Good. How about we meet at ten o'clock at the bookstore on Saturday?"

CHAPTER 21

W hy did it have to rain? Kate thought it was a bad omen, and it was the reason she'd asked Paul to drive. As the windshield wipers slapped away rain, Paul was enjoying himself behind the wheel of the Falcon, shifting through the gears with ease, a boyish smile on his lips.

"You like driving, don't you?" Kate asked.

"What's not to like? And I love this car."

"Even on a rainy day, you like to drive?"

"Rain doesn't bother me. I got used to it in Vietnam. When it rained there, it poured buckets."

"Then I'd think you would hate it," Kate said, looking up at the gray, wind-swept clouds.

"Rain brings life. Anything that keeps life going is okay with me."

"I never thought of it that way. How long were you in Vietnam?"

"Thirteen months."

"In the Marines?"

"Yes."

"And you were in combat?"

"Yes. As a platoon sergeant." He glanced over, and Kate saw he didn't want to talk about it. "It was hell —rain flooding down, mud, swamps, rice paddies, disease and brutal death. War is hell, Kate. That's all anybody needs to know about it."

They were silent for a time.

"Do you like being a car mechanic?"

"Yes, I do. I also work part time for a couple of insurance companies."

"Doing what?"

"After a car accident, I appraise the damage so that claims can be fairly adjusted. Insurance adjustors and lawyers handle the liability and all that, and I just make sure the claimant doesn't get a complete body job just from a banged-up fender, if you know what I mean."

"How do you have time to study?"

"I don't sleep much. Never did. And there's something about surviving a war that makes you glad to be alive, and glad to be awake. Okay, enough about me. Why do you like books so much?"

"I have, for as long as I can remember. My father always read a lot. Maybe I got it from him."

"Do you remember the first book you read?" Paul asked, over the sound of a thunder roll.

"Oh, yeah. *Anne of Green Gables*. I read it five times. What was your first book?"

"I don't remember the first one, but I read a lot of

Louis L'Amour westerns. My dad had a stack of them in his workroom, and I found them there."

"What's your major?" Kate asked.

"I'm on a science track right now, but I'm looking for a degree in environmental studies, climate trends, and agriculture. I just learned that the University of Arizona offers a degree in agricultural engineering. I might end up there."

Kate's worried gaze darted across his face. "Doesn't Paxton have a degree in environmental studies?"

"A few courses, but no degree program. They might offer one in the future, but that would be too late for me."

They left the main road and found Route 9, which went rising, falling and twisting through wisps of fog and sailing autumn leaves. They soon arrived at the small town of Monroe. On the other side of town, the impressive Victorian house, with its turrets and towers, appeared out of the half-gloom of fog and veiled sunlight. It was a striking house, dark, secluded by massive hedgerows.

"Impressive," Paul said, as they passed through an open, wrought-iron gate, drove up the driveway and parked beside two late-model cars near the front entrance. "It reminds me of the house in that Hitchcock movie, *Psycho*."

"It's prettier than that, don't you think?" Kate said. "I'd say it's historical, and I love old things."

Paul nodded. "It's the gray clouds and the mist that make it look foreboding, along with all the wrought iron. And there's a cemetery over there to the right. Now, that gives the place a kind of gothic touch, doesn't it?"

They left the car, mounting the stairs to the broad porch and oak front door. The doorbell brought a matronly woman in her 50s, who stood before the couple with an air of polite dignity. She wore an expensive gray suit and low heels, and her medium length, gray and black hair was brushed back from her solemn face.

After introductions, Mrs. Larson led them up a wide staircase, with a broad, polished, mahogany railing, to the second floor. Across the lush, burgundy hall carpeting, they turned left, passed through a set of French doors and entered a lofty, dark wood library that smelled of pipe smoke, lemon wax and wealth.

Walking across oriental rugs and parquet floors, they frequently stopped to admire the room. The floor-to-ceiling, cherry wood bookshelves were impressive, with two winding, wrought-iron staircases that led to the balcony level, where one could roam and browse. Two rolling ladders allowed access to rare, leather-bound volumes, displayed on the upper shelves of both sides of the vast, impressive room. Kate felt a rush of excitement, as if she were a kid at Christmas.

Mrs. Larson folded her hands, and, with a gentle melancholy, she said, "My grandfather was a reclusive man who loved his books, and I promised him that I'd give them a good home. Many are already spoken for, and you'll notice they are clearly marked. Feel free to browse and make your selections from the others. Art Mackay and I have known each other for over ten years, and I know he will find a good home for these."

Kate smiled. "Art said you used to come to his bookshop."

"Yes, before I moved to Chicago, a little over a year ago. It's a lovely shop, and Art has such eclectic tastes. I'll try to drop in before I return home."

Mrs. Larson turned to business. "As you know, there's one price for leather-bound books, another for hardcover books, and still another for paperback books. I'm afraid the bulk boxes have all been taken."

Kate nodded and thanked her, anxious to begin.

Mrs. Larson left them, walking swiftly and quietly across the floor, closing the French doors, enclosing Kate and Paul in a cocoon of library silence.

Paul followed Kate up the winding, wrought-iron staircase to the balcony and Kate went to work, the tip of her tongue poking out from the side of her mouth. He watched her closely, taken by her passion and concentration. She was absorbed as she searched the shelves, and when she pulled a book down and examined it, her eyes lit up.

Kate sifted through the books and set aside the ones she found visually appealing, thus minimizing the amount of time she'd have to spend examining each book on a shelf.

Paul said, "So, what am I looking for?"

Kate glanced over, her focused eyes clearing. "Oh,

yes… Sorry. I get so…"

"Hypnotized?" Paul asked.

"You're not bored, are you?"

"Not at all, but let me help. Tell me what to do."

"Okay," Kate said, pointing. "Check the novels over there. Simple. Who wrote it? What is the edition? What condition is it in? Check for missing pages, ripped pages, mold, whatever. Is it signed by the author? Does it have the original dust jacket?"

He snapped her a salute. "Yes, ma'am."

Their eyes met, and it was electric. They were both surprised by its strength. Paul felt an intense, unknown emotion, and he stared at her eyelashes, which were black, dense, and very long.

Kate was surprised by the moment's powerful desire, as fresh and alive as it had been over fifty years ago.

And then Paul tilted his head a little to the right, pocketed his hands and said softly. "Hello, Kate Clarke."

She examined him, unsure of what was behind his words.

"I guess I'm saying I'm having fun…"

Kate felt the hair lift at the nape of her neck. It was as though no time had passed—and there had been no tragic deaths and no agony of guilt. She'd not had a life way out in the future, where she'd been a teacher, a wife and a mother, and was now a seventy-four-year-old widow. Those memories were like old movies, and they were receding a little more every day.

This series of events was novel, but the emotions and desires were the same. The sound of Paul's name when she said it, or even thought it, warmed her to her soul. The look of him, masculine and magnetic, brought quick desire, and the ease of his step, the cut of his jaw, the hot memory of his touch she could never forget.

For Paul, the moment froze him to the spot. In that instant, this girl, Kate Clarke, had become a part of his future—not that it made any logical sense. It was as though some mystical hand had appeared and opened, revealing a snow globe world, where he and Kate were living happily together as man and wife. Paul felt the power of it, and the startling reality of it.

But he couldn't hold on to the images or the emotions. The smoky vision faded, and then it vanished like an airy, morning dream, and Paul stood staring and mystified.

They went to work, concealing their feelings and thoughts. Instead, they focused on the task at hand. The books were removed from the shelves, examined, considered, and then set aside or boxed. A little over two hours later, while Kate wrote Mrs. Larson a check, Paul loaded the trunk with their treasure.

As they were driving back to Paxton, the sun peeked out from behind a bank of clouds, sprinkling sunlight on wet leaves and grass. Kate's mind was active, pitching about, searching for an excuse to arrange another meeting or date.

Paul gave her a side glance. "I have an idea.".

Kate's eyes jumped to his.

"There's a little grocery store just outside Paxton, called Vans, and on summer and autumn weekends they make up little picnic baskets. Ham and cheese sandwiches, chips, soda pop and apple pie. Why don't we swing by, get one and head up into the hills for a picnic? I think the rain is finished for the day."

Kate sat up, delighted. "I love apple pie. Let's do it."

The local grocery store was busy, but Paul edged his way past a bickering, retired couple, two sun-streaked, giggling college coeds, and a big-mouthed woman protesting the price of sirloin. He snatched a lunch basket, waved five dollars at the alert cashier, slapped it on the counter, and darted away.

With the wicker picnic basket in hand, Kate and Paul left the Falcon parked in the lot at the train station. Paul led the way as they climbed a hill, descended the other side and roamed across a gentle, sloping meadow that led into a valley of damp grass and trees. In a sheltered grove they found some boulders, perfect stand-ins for a picnic table.

Kate spread the red and white paper tablecloth over a mostly flat rock surface and emptied the wicker basket. She arranged the items strategically to keep little puffs of wind from sweeping away the tablecloth.

"This is pretty impressive," Kate said. "Did they charge for the basket?"

"You're supposed to return it. I know the couple

who own the place. They don't give a wicker basket to just anyone."

"So, you're a VIP wicker basket person," Kate said with a laugh.

"Yeah, and they know where I live, and their son's a town cop."

The grass was still damp from rain, so they leaned against the rocks and ate, feeling the warm sun on their faces.

"This is perfect," Kate said, feeling intensely alive, her voice on the wind.

Paul looked further up the hill. "There's a cave up there, you know. Right over there," he pointed.

Kate lowered her eyes, swallowing a bite of her sandwich. Yes, she knew, and she wanted no part of it. Her voice dropped. "Really?"

"Yeah. After we finish, I'll take you up. I used to go there when I was a boy to escape from everything... mostly from school."

Kate shrugged. "I don't know. Maybe we should drop the books off. Art's probably waiting."

Paul said, "It won't take long. You'll love it. Promise."

CHAPTER 22

A s they polished off their pieces of apple pie, Paul described the entrance to the cave and how startlingly quiet it was inside. One part of Kate longed to go there with him, as they had in her life before, but she was too afraid to enter the cave so soon after time traveling. Who knew what might happen if she stooped back into that place?

"I'm sorry, but I get spooked out in caves," she said, glancing at her watch. "And it's getting late. Art will wonder where we are."

"Okay, maybe next time," Paul said. His words gave Kate hope that there *would* be a next time.

When they arrived at Art's bookstore, they were surprised to find the place lively, with Art hustling and not dressed in his usual denim overalls. He was wearing jeans and a black T-shirt from Kip's Bar, with bold white letters across the front proclaiming:

Kip's Bar - We Have Beers as
Cold as Your Ex's Heart

They quickly unpacked the car, Paul hauling the boxes into the storage room near the cot Kate had slept in. When they returned to the store, Art gave Kate a pleading look and a wave, mouthing, "I need help!"

There was little time for her to invent a reason for a next date with Paul. She turned to him, and, for just a moment, she allowed the vulnerability to show in her eyes. She prayed that he'd ask her out, but he didn't. He thanked her for the day and backed out of the shop, his very handsome face catching the light as he waved and shut the door behind him.

Kate hid her disappointment and turned to the waiting customers. She forced smiles, searched for books, and talked about books. She and Art bumped shoulders and thighs as they arched, skidded and slid behind the counter, taking turns punching the cash register keys and ringing up sales. The cranky old cash drawer thudded open, and dollars and cents swiftly exchanged hands. No credit cards. No swiping. No tapping. No cellphones with electronic wallets.

At seven o'clock, Art locked the door and turned the door sign from OPEN to CLOSED. When he faced her, his eyes were weary, shoulders slumped.

"You made some money today," Kate said.

Art inhaled a breath and blew it out. "This was the busiest day in months. I'm glad you came back when you did. What took you so long?" And then, he thudded his forehead with his palm. "Art Mackay, what a dumbass you are."

Art lifted the back of his hand dramatically to his forehead and, in a stage voice, said, "'My bounty is as boundless as the sea, my love as deep; the more I give to thee, the more I have, for both are infinite.'"

Kate emerged from the counter and went to the coffee station, glancing back over her shoulder. "Come on, Art, *Romeo and Juliet*? Really?"

With another heavy sigh, Art sagged into a wooden chair next to the door. "He's the guy, isn't he? I mean, the man you don't want to get away? Paul is his name, isn't it?"

Kate poured old coffee into a Styrofoam cup, keeping her back to him. "Yeah, he's the guy, all right."

"So, what's the story with the cowgirl he came in with the other day?"

Kate turned. "Don't know. Don't want to know."

Art leaned back, pulled a handkerchief from his jeans pocket and mopped his brow. "Well, I'll tell you this. She was composed, observant, and smart. I could see it in her eyes. She was also extraordinarily attractive and jealous of you. Oh, and I loved her cowgirl hat and boots."

"Yeah, so maybe I don't give a damn what you think," Kate said, more harshly than she'd meant to. It was a youthful reaction. A rash, emotional reaction. A-girl-in-her-twenties reaction, not a 74-year-old woman's response. But then, she *was* twenty, wasn't she? And the future was, ironically, a kind of past, and half-forgotten, right? And good riddance to it, and good riddance to being old. She was young again, and she was going to stay young, and she was going to find a way to marry Paul and get pregnant again.

"Feisty today, you are, Kate."

Kate leaned back against the counter. "Sorry, Art. I'm... I wish I could explain everything."

"You can. We're closed. We have time. I can take you to dinner at the Busy Bee and you can tell me all about it."

"And you won't believe me."

"Try me."

"I did."

Art shook his head. "Oh, for crying-out-loud, Kate, you're not going to tell me you've time traveled again, are you?"

Kate lowered her head, realizing it was pointless to go on. "No..."

The phone rang.

"Don't answer it," Art said. "We're closed."

"Maybe somebody left something."

Kate reached a hand and lifted the receiver. "Mackay's Books New & Old."

It was Vicki. "Kate, glad I caught you. Your father just called. Your mother's sick. He took her to the hospital."

Kate straightened up. "What's the matter with her?"

"He didn't say. He gave me the number at the

hospital."

Kate wrote it down and hung up.

Art waited, observing her worried expression.

Kate strained her memory. Her mother had never been admitted to any hospital when Kate was in college. It was only after Kate was married that her mother had a hysterectomy.

"What's the matter, Kate?"

"Mom... She's in the hospital."

Art rose. "Then you should go see her."

Kate glanced around, distracted by all the changes. Too many events were happening that hadn't occurred before, and it was nerve-racking. How would it end? Could she bend current events to mirror the events in the past?

"Yeah, I'll go. I'll drive or take the train or something."

But Kate didn't stir. Her thoughts circled around Paul. She knew they were inevitably, completely, and glowingly perfect for each other, and she'd seen and felt his attraction for her. They'd lost it once fifty-odd years ago, but an ineffable magic had brought them back together. If she left for home, would that small quantity of time destroy the possibility of their surviving and living the life they should have lived?

It was an agony to have to make a choice.

In the end, she went back to her apartment, packed an overnight bag and decided she was too tired to drive the hundred and ten miles home. She'd take the 10:15 p.m. train. She called her father and left a message with an answering service he had for emergency customers, asking him to pick her up.

That gave her some time to kill, so she drove to Cove Lake and parked in the deep shadows, a few yards from Paul's trailer.

Gathering courage, she exited the car, stretched, and nervously appraised the area. Ten yards away was a flickering street light, the only one on the narrow, desolate road, which was flanked on both sides by quiet trees. Near the trailer stood a leaning, yellow road sign that read **ROUGH ROAD**.

Kate said aloud, "Really? Like I need a reminder."

She heard the low hum of insects and ringing crickets. She heard the lake lapping at the shore and the sound brought memories of loving nights with Paul, their quiet confidences and laughter, their future plans.

Looking skyward, she saw the pale glow from a three-quarter moon, which seemed to travel as the blue clouds slid around it, and when her gaze found Paul's trailer, resting alone, nestled in trees and haunting shadows, she felt a catch in her throat. It was dark inside, and his car was gone.

Kate breathed in apprehension and disappointment. All the emotion of the day rose, peaked and drained out of her. Who knew when he'd return, and she had a train to catch.

The first time they'd made love, it was in Paul's trailer, and it had been urgent and bold. They had collapsed on Paul's double bed, fatigued and sweaty, she quivering and he breathless. Her eyes had filled with tears, the impact of new and fragile emotions engulfing her.

Paul lay beside her, staring into her candle-lit eyes, gently stroking her cheek. He wiped her tears, and his voice was low and seductive.

"What is it about us, Kate? Everything fits, doesn't it? You make the world look brand new to me, and I didn't think that was possible after what I'd seen and gone through in Vietnam."

But after that night, Kate had spent the days in dreams and worry. Most of the novels she'd read about lovers did not end well. There was *Women in Love* by D. H. Lawrence, *Anna Karenina* by Leo Tolstoy, and *Tess of the D'Urbervilles* by Thomas Hardy. And the first time, their love *had* ended tragically.

"Not this time," Kate said aloud. She vowed that they would marry, have a family and live as happily ever after as they possibly could.

Kate's tentative plan to knock on Paul's trailer door to ask for a beer or a glass of wine, to ask if he wanted to take a walk, to ask if she could see him again, was not meant to be. He wasn't there.

She wandered the road aimlessly, praying that Paul's car headlights would come swinging into view and she'd wave him down, and she'd spend the night in his arms and catch a morning train. But he didn't come.

Kate ambled back to her car, subdued and dispirited, feeling a loss of strength and dignity. As she drove away, her eyes glimpsing Paul's trailer in her rearview mirror, another memory intruded, and the sound of Paul's voice was a whisper in her ear.

"What should we name the boy?" Paul had asked.

They were standing on a hill above town, under the wide dome of blue sky, on a cold, January day. Snow lay in patches around them, and they heard the moan of the train whistle approaching Paxton.

"What if it's a girl?" Kate asked, linking her arm in his, their breath smoking in the chill air.

He had stared at her for a long time. "Whatever we name her, I'm going to have to fight a lot."

"Fight? What? Because?"

"Because she'll like guys, and I won't."

"And what if it's a boy?"

"Easy, we name him Ethan, after my favorite grandfather. How does that sound?"

Kate turned the name over in her mind, pursing her lips in thought. "I think I like it. How about Ethan Paul Ganic?"

"Do you think so?" Paul asked, obviously pleased.

"Strong name. Yep. That's it."

Kate bought her train ticket, bounded out of the Paxton train station and darted across the platform, hustling toward the open train doors. From the corner of her eye, she saw him—the dusty, suspendered, bowlegged man—standing twenty feet away. He touched the brim of his hat with two fingers and grinned.

Kate quick-stepped into the train just as the ringing doors were closing. Carrying her overnight bag, she entered the half-filled coach, found two empty seats together and dropped, placing her bag to her left on the seat beside her. As the train lurched ahead and picked up speed, Kate refused to look out the window at the platform, where the man surely stood, staring at her.

Within minutes, Kate settled into her seat, crossed her arms across her chest, and sighed. Her heavy eyelids fluttered, then closed, her head rolled left, and she dropped into black waves of bottomless sleep.

CHAPTER 23

K ate exited the train and entered the small round terminal, where the big white clock on the wall said it was 1:13 in the morning

Her father had a smile for her, and he was patiently waiting, his full head of salt and pepper hair and blue pin-striped suit giving him a senatorial look. She felt an immediate gush of love for her father, who came toward her, alive again, his eyes lit up with love, his smile warm. He was an attractive, solid, and intelligent man, who was trusted and liked by his customers and his neighbors.

Kate drew up to him, lowered her bag, and they embraced.

"Glad you got my message."

When she leaned back, he cupped his hand on her chin and kissed her nose.

"Hello, Katy Girl."

"Hello, Dad of mine," she said, tenderly, and then the tears came, as images of him flooded in. Images of him lying in a hospital bed, his face wan, body thin and eyes drawn, as he lay dying of pancreatic cancer.

As Kate had aged, she'd realized her father had been a quiet man, a romantic man, bewildered by the changing world and by his wife's remote demons, which she never talked about.

"Hey... why the tears?" Oliver Clarke asked.

Kate pulled a tissue from her purse and blotted her eyes. "I'm happy to see you again. And I guess I'm tired and worried about Mom. How is she?"

Oliver's mouth turned down. "She passed out, so I called an ambulance. Turns out she has an ulcer, for one thing. For another, she developed a urinary tract infection and she let it go for too long. A little longer and we'd have lost her. They're keeping her in the hospital overnight for observation, but she'll probably be released sometime tomorrow."

Oliver lifted Kate's overnight bag, and they left the terminal for the parking lot, where a snappy, autumn wind smelled of leaves and damp earth.

"Sorry it's so late, Dad. Way past your bedtime."

"Don't give it a care. I haven't been sleeping all that well, anyway. And who cares about sleep when my Katy Girl is home? And I bought plenty of chocolate chip ice cream and Cheerios."

Kate applauded. "Yay for Cheerios!"

As her father walked to the driver's side of the car, Kate stopped, staring.

"This isn't your car, is it, Dad?"

He turned to her. "Of course it is, Kate."

"But this is a Chevy Impala."

"Yes, a 1967 Chevy Impala."

"But you drive a 1967 Buick Skylark."

Oliver studied her. "No, Kate, I've never owned a Buick. I've been driving Chevys since 1954."

Oliver saw the unspoken worry and confusion in Kate's eyes. "Kate, what's the matter?"

Kate glanced away. Granted, it wasn't a 1962 Impala, like the one she'd driven into Cove Lake, but it was the same color, and it was an Impala. Did that mean anything?

"Nothing, Dad, I'm just tired."

They drove the quiet streets of the town with the radio turned low, playing sappy old songs with lots of lush violins.

"What have you been reading?" Kate asked, making conversation, shaking off her unease. She didn't like being in the car. It looked the same, and it smelled the same as Paul's 1962 Chevy Impala, and she was positive that her father—at least in that other world of 1968—had driven a blue and cream-colored Buick Skylark.

Oliver said, "The last book I read was *Where is Janice Gantry*, by John D. MacDonald."

"What did you think of it?"

"Brief, taut, violent and suspenseful. Not for you, Kate. What about you? What have you read lately?"

"I haven't had much time to read what I want. For class, I had to read *The Mill on the Floss* by Edith

Wharton. It's a tragedy, but it has a cozy, cheery ending for a tragedy, if that makes any sense."

"I'll take your word for it. How's your writing coming?"

"Too busy to write much. I've started two short stories but haven't finished them."

"Oh, by the way, I ran into Jerry Baxter at the store a few hours ago," Oliver said, "and I told him you were coming for a visit. He's finishing up college this year, and he's going to law school. He said he might call."

Hearing the name Jerry made Kate a little nauseous. *High-school-prom-Jerry*, Kate thought. *Pinned-her-in-the-backseat-of-his-father's-Dodge-Polara-Jerry.* She'd scratched his face, and he'd slapped her, bringing the taste of blood.

Being too embarrassed and humiliated by the awful night, she hadn't told her parents. She hadn't told anyone, and Jerry had threatened her if she did.

"I'll tell them you made it all up," Jerry had said, sneering. "I'll tell them you were drunk, and you were asking for it, and you slapped me when I didn't give it to you. If you didn't want it, then why did you get in the back seat with me, you little bitch tease?"

She remembered that night vividly, and she remembered Jerry's mocking and defensive expression when he'd slapped her again before pushing off, climbing over the seat and sliding behind the steering wheel.

Yes, they had been drinking, and, yes, she had used bad judgement climbing into that backseat, but it hadn't occurred to her that he'd become aggressive and violent. Romantic kisses and some "playing around" she'd wanted, like in the novels she'd read, but she didn't want abuse.

Maybe it had been the booze that had turned Jerry into a creep, or maybe it was an authentic part of his true character, and he'd been clever at masking it. His All-American, boyish charm and good looks had made him one of the most popular boys in school.

Now, she didn't give a damn who knew.

"If he calls again, tell him he's a bastard and he can go straight to hell," Kate said acidly.

Her father snapped her a look. Her parents didn't swear, and neither did she.

"What did you say?"

Kate faced her father boldly. "He tried to rape me, Dad. Senior prom. I never told you. He threatened me not to tell anyone, and I didn't. Now I don't give a damn... Sorry, I mean, I don't care who knows about it. I never want to see or talk to him again."

Oliver stared ahead, eyes blinking. He lifted and resettled his shoulders. "Yes... well, I wish you would have told me. I would have spoken to his parents. I would have ignored him today, or something."

There they were again. Her 20-year-old girlish emotions flared raw and hot, and the fresh burn of rage demanded action and revenge. Or had those emotions been buried for all those years and locked up inside? Or perhaps, this time around, it hadn't happened at all, or maybe it had been someone else, just as her father's car had been a different model from the one in the past.

In Kate's bedroom were scents of soap and perfume. Fabergé had been her high school choice. The primrose wallpaper she'd forgotten, but not the cream lace curtains, or the Édouard Manet print of the painting *A Bar at the Folies-Bergère*, which hung on the wall above her writing desk.

A rose quilt with a white floral pattern covered her double bed, along with matching pillows. Propped against the pillows was the teddy bear her father had given her when she was nine, and the rag doll she'd named Betsy Straw Hair, a gift from her grandmother. They seemed to be staring at her with glassy, accusing eyes, as if to say, "What the heck are you doing back here, Kate?"

There was a sewing machine that her mother used, and a small, pink, portable TV with rabbit ears, placed on a bookshelf next to her many books. In her closet, she found a rack of hanging clothes, a crate packed with paperback books, an old tennis racket, tennis balls and way too many pairs of shoes.

Kate slumped down into a chair, her mind full of noisy memories. It was almost as if she'd returned from the dead, a ghost lost and wandering, with too many thoughts and emotions. Her eyes strayed toward her top dresser door. She'd kept diaries and stored them there, but she was too exhausted to even think about reading them. Kate recalled that when she'd turned twenty-three, she'd burned them, not wanting anyone to find and read them.

Kate showered, slipped into a nightgown she'd found in her closet, flipped off the light and crawled under the quilt. Sleep came swiftly, and Paul's heroic face swam in and out of her dreams. So did the menacing, dusty man, who stood rigid on the train platform, waiting for her return.

In yet another dream, a faceless cowgirl galloped across tall, green, flowing grass, on a magnificent, white horse. She ascended the hill, where the cave lay hidden, and the horse reared back on its hind legs. The cowgirl dramatically yanked off her hat and shouted, "Hey, Kate, get back into that cave, go away, and leave us all alone!"

CHAPTER 24

The curtains whipped and billowed in an early morning wind, and Kate snapped awake. It was cold, and she left the bed, crossing the room in haste, shutting the window and scurrying back to the bed, feeling cozy under the warmth of the quilt. For minutes, she lay on her back, staring up at the ceiling, her mind muddled.

As all her other dreams had faded, one had not. It was a strange and disturbing dream that clung to her eyes. She'd been an elderly woman in her seventies, living in New York City. Her husband was dead, but she had two children. What were their names? A son named Greg. She couldn't recall her daughter's name. The dream had been clear, immediate and tangible, and as real as anything she'd ever experienced.

In her closet, Kate found a light gray top, jeans, and sneakers. As she dressed, the same troubling dream blinked in and out of her mind, a clear picture one minute, but then staticky and out of focus the next, as if wires were crossed.

Kate was in the kitchen early. The yellow wall clock said it was 6:17 a.m. She should have slept more, but the dream had startled her awake. As she made coffee in the percolator, she was shaky, increasingly concerned that she was losing her mind.

When her father entered the kitchen, she was staring into her Cheerios, trying to make sense of her life and dreams.

"Good morning," Oliver said, dressed in a white shirt, tie, and charcoal suit. "You're up early. I thought you'd sleep in."

"Weird dreams," Kate said.

Oliver reached for a cup and poured himself some coffee. "I know what you mean. I didn't sleep so well either. I called the hospital a few minutes ago, and the night nurse said your mother slept well. Dr. Banks will look in on her first thing."

Kate looked at her father peculiarly, and he noticed.

"Yes? What is it, Kate?"

Kate had a sudden flash of the cave—of her bursting out of the cave and of seeing herself young again. Kate stared ahead at the wall as if seeing the cave projected there.

"What is it, Kate? What's happened?"

In that instant, her memory returned. She had time traveled! She hadn't dreamed she was a 74-

year-old woman, she had *been* a 74-year-old woman! But she was losing it, forgetting—and she couldn't forget!

"Kate..." her father pressed, his eyes opening on her, round and wide. "What is wrong?"

Kate didn't meet his eyes as she stuttered out the words. "I'm... I just need... I guess... I need to see Mom, that's all. And then I have to get back to school. I realized something. Something I have to do."

Oliver blew the steam from his coffee. "Kate... you're all right, aren't you? You're not taking... taking any drugs, are you? They're everywhere, these days. Please tell me..."

Kate cut him off, her response quick. "No, Dad. No. Nothing like that. I don't take drugs."

He eased down in the chair opposite her. "You seem, well, a bit erratic and not quite yourself."

"I know... I just haven't been sleeping so well, and school... School is busy, and work at the bookstore is busy, too."

"Then quit the job. I'll give you money. You don't have to put all that pressure on yourself. I have plenty of money to help you. I know you want to be independent, and that's fine and admirable, but it's more important that you stay well and happy, isn't it? That's what I want most for you."

Kate rose. "I'll be fine, Dad. Really. I'll sleep more when I get back to school. Anyway, I'm okay, so don't worry. Now, can I fix you some eggs?" she asked, smiling. "I know you always like to have your eggs and bacon in the morning."

He softened. "Yes, if you don't mind. I always need the fortification of a good breakfast to face the day, and I love the way you scramble the eggs. They always taste better when you make them."

"They're just eggs, Dad."

He nodded. "Yes, yes, I know that, but they really do taste better with you at the helm, Kate."

She stepped to him, leaned, and kissed him on the cheek. "And I love you more than you'll ever know."

He lowered his eyes, his smile shy. "Well, what a nice thing to hear on a day like this. After breakfast, we'll go straight to the hospital and see your mother. She's so excited you're coming. It gave her such a lift when I told her you would be with me."

"What about the store?" Kate asked.

"I called good, old faithful Ronnie a few minutes ago, and he said he'd open and get things going. And Agnes will be there."

"The drill sergeant?" Kate asked, laughing, as she went to the stove. "Isn't that what Mom used to call her?"

Oliver chuckled. "Yes, and she still calls her that. But Agnes doesn't take any guff from anyone, including me, and she runs a tight ship."

Kate went to work, praying her mind wouldn't drop into another partial blackout.

Oliver observed his daughter, and he was worried about her. And he was tired, and his spirits were low, and he was struggling to stay cheerful.

His wife, his dear Carolyn, was an alcoholic, and on days like this, he felt the agony of his failure as a husband most acutely, for Carolyn did not love him and never did. However, he knew she cared for him, at least as a friend, and as a friend, he could never tell Kate about Carolyn's sickness. It was a secret Carolyn wanted kept, and he'd made a vow. Kate would never know.

CHAPTER 25

C arolyn Clarke stared up at her husband and daughter from the fog of medication, from a half dream and groggy regrets.

"Hello, Mom," Kate said, with a soft smile and wonder on her face. This was her mother at forty-seven! She barely remembered what she looked like.

"Good morning, Carolyn," Oliver added, with an encouraging smile. "Hope you're feeling top notch today."

Carolyn lay in the hospital bed covered by a sheet and blanket. A privacy curtain separated her from her roommate, an elderly woman who snored, coughed, and complained.

Carolyn appeared older than her years, her once pretty face now puffy, her eyes lusterless, her skin pale. Oliver gently raked her graying black hair from her forehead, and she gazed at him with searching eyes, as if trying to pull him into focus.

"It's me, Carolyn. Oliver. And Kate's here. Right here. Remember? I told you she was coming to see you."

Carolyn cleared her throat, her gaze sliding from Oliver to Kate. "Well... Kate. Why?"

"Why?" Kate said, leaning over a bit. "Because you're in the hospital, Mom. Have you ever been in the hospital since I was born?"

"The war..." Carolyn said thickly. "After... he... Tom was killed."

"Tom?"

Oliver broke in. "... Have you had your breakfast, Carolyn?"

She blinked several times. "Your father was in the Navy... Tom, the Marines."

Oliver tried again. "Have you eaten anything this morning, Carolyn?"

"I don't know. Don't want it."

"Well, you have to eat something. You have to get your strength back."

"Don't fuss," Carolyn scolded. "You're a fussy man... pushy and fussy about things."

Oliver felt the sting of her words and he stepped back, wordless.

Kate spoke up. "I hope you can come home today, Mom."

Carolyn rolled her head toward the window, covered by a beige curtain, glowing with morning sun. "I want to sleep here. They let me sleep. I need sleep... and they give me, you know, pills to sleep."

Carolyn closed her eyes. "They're all gone. All of

them, gone... So sad."

"Who's gone, Mom?"

"I was dreaming about those days. Back there... I was, yes, back there. Happy. Happy days."

And then Carolyn was asleep, and the woman behind the privacy curtain broke into a ragged snore. Kate looked at her father for answers, but Oliver stared ahead, lost in a defeated, temporary paralysis, his hands pushed into his trouser pockets.

Kate touched his arm. "She's not herself, Dad. It's the drugs, you know that."

He gave her a hasty glance and a twitch of a grin. "Of course, Kate. She'll be her old self again once we get her home."

Kate knew how he felt, stuck in a marriage that wasn't working, neither of them happy nor satisfied, but neither having the strength or courage to move on. That's what had happened to her marriage way out in the future.

Oliver glanced at his watch. "I think she'll sleep for a while. We could catch Reverend Waddell's sermon, if you want."

"Shouldn't we speak with the doctor?"

Oliver nodded, pulling his hands from his pockets. "Yes... yes, of course we should. We'll find him and get the latest."

"Then why don't we go for a drive? Maybe get some coffee and a donut somewhere?"

The sadness left Oliver's face. "You and your coffee and donuts, Kate. I think you could eat them three times a day, and you never gain a pound. Not one pound."

Dr. Banks suggested that Carolyn stay another day and leave on Monday afternoon. Oliver nodded his consent, and then he and Kate left the hospital and went for a Sunday drive in the sparkling, morning sun. Autumn blazed out magnificence, trees shimmering red, yellow and orange, and leaves sailed by, meandering like little kites.

"Why don't you two get a divorce?" Kate blurted out. "You have plenty of money. Mom could keep the house and you could move closer to the store."

Oliver didn't speak.

"Neither one of you is happy, Dad. I see it now. Mom's a complicated woman with emotional problems that she can't handle, and you're just a good man who wants a normal life and home. Mom should get some therapy, but she won't. She's too scared and too private."

Oliver gave Kate a side glance. "You don't sound like yourself. What's going on, Kate? I've never heard you say things like this. It's just not you, and you haven't been yourself since you arrived."

Kate wished she could tell him. How she longed to tell someone and have them believe her, but her father was a practical man, a straight-lined man, a man who would never be able to get his head around time travel.

"I'm just growing up, Dad. That's what kids do, isn't it? They go through this crazy life and they either grow up or they get stuck."

After a moment of silence, Oliver said, "So, you

think your mother and I are stuck?"

"Honest? Yes."

"I wish life was just that easy, Kate. But it isn't. I love your mother. I would never divorce her and leave her alone. She wouldn't make it."

"I think she's stronger than you think, Dad."

"And I think you don't know everything you think you know, Kate. You're a young woman with not much life experience. When you get a little older, you'll understand what I'm trying to say."

Kate turned her body toward him. "Forgive me, Dad, but Mom has never been a kind woman, or a warm woman, or a generous one."

Oliver's eyes jumped to hers, his mouth open and ready to speak.

"Now, wait a minute, Dad, and let me finish. She's my mother, and she was a good mother to me, and I love her with all my heart, but when I left that house for school, I never wanted to go back. It was not a happy home. It worked, I mean it functioned, and everyone was nice, most of the time, and our lives were on automatic pilot, but, let's face it, we had to work to keep it all together. Mom... Well... Mom is not a happy person, and I know you have tried your absolute best to make her happy, but she's lost in herself. Lost in some old sorrow, and she can't break free of it."

Oliver's chin lowered, his hard gaze focused on the road.

"I don't want to hurt you or Mom. I love you both. I love you more now than I did when I was a girl... I mean, when I left for college. My point is, maybe you both need to let go, and try to find some happiness while you still can. Mom will be just fine, maybe even better, if she understands that you can let her go."

Her father's hand trembled as he wiped his mouth. "Maybe we've talked enough, Kate. Yes, I believe we have talked enough now."

Fred's Diner was ahead, and Oliver turned in and found a parking space. Without speaking, they went inside and sat at a yellow booth. They ordered a pot of coffee, Oliver a piece of cherry pie, and Kate, two sugar donuts.

They stared out the window and watched cars come and go. A family of five burst from a Ford wagon, kids pushing and yelling, parents scolding. Oliver smiled, nodding at them.

"I wanted a big family. Three kids. Four even. I made my success so I could have a big family. I wanted plenty of money for them, so we could all live well and be happy. I wanted to buy them things, and spoil them, and slap them, ever so gently, with my leather belt when they sassed me. I wanted to play ball with my boys and teach them how to throw a fast ball."

He looked at her. "Did you know I pitched on my college team?"

"Yes, Dad, but I never get tired of hearing about it."

Oliver wanted to tell it again. He needed the escape. He needed a distracting, remembered glory. "When I was in the navy, I learned how to throw a curve ball from a guy who had pitched for the St. Louis Cardinals. In college, I could throw a curve ball and a fast ball that only a few could hit. The team manager said I could go pro. But I didn't want to go pro. After the war, I wanted to get a good education, and I wanted security. I wanted a family."

When their food came, they ate in silence. Kate was worried about her parents, and she was deeply surprised at her love for them. How could she have forgotten that? Her kind and warm father. Her tortured and heartbroken mother, who'd lost the man she'd truly loved and had settled for Kate's father.

Kate smiled at her father, tenderly, remembering how he'd been as a grandfather. He'd loved tossing a rubber baseball with little Greg, and he'd spoiled Ellen with dolls and doll houses, pretty dresses and candy.

It was a burden to remember. It hurt. It was almost too much to bear the pain of reliving her past life and remembering her life in the future. It was a feeling of becoming oddly fictional, like an actress in a play, moving in and out of the first and second acts while the playwright kept writing new lines, changing the characters' movements, the furniture, and the scenes.

"Will you leave in the morning?" Oliver asked.

"No, I'll stay until Mom comes home."

"You'll miss classes."

"It's all right. I can get notes from my friends. I want to be sure she's okay."

Oliver cut into the last of his pie.

"I know she's an alcoholic, Dad."

His eyes lifted on her. After he'd set aside his plate and fork, he folded his hands and drew in a little breath. Kate couldn't read him, and she'd always been able to read him.

"I'm sorry, but I know," she added.

Oliver's expression held a pleading compassion that nearly broke Kate's heart. "Don't be hard on your mother, Kate. She's a good woman in her heart. She has her demons, all right, but then who hasn't? I'll help her with it, and we'll be all right. She'll beat it. She'll beat the alcoholism."

His hurt wrenched the attempt at a smile, and he teared up. "I love her, Kate," he said, looking away. "I don't care what happens, or how lost she is, or how others may whisper behind her back. I don't care. I love her, and nothing, and no one, will ever come between us and that love. And I will never leave her."

It was a stunning, unpredictable moment, and Kate reacted spontaneously, reaching for her father's folded hands, taking a hand, and kissing it. "I didn't know... Forgive me, Dad. All those years, and I didn't know you. I didn't know how truly special you are. Thank God, I've been given the gift of telling you now, face-to-face."

Oliver stared at her, trying to understand.

CHAPTER 26

T he train whistled, clanged and hissed into the Paxton Station on time, at 3:12 on Tuesday afternoon, October 8, three days after Kate had left for home. From her window, her wary eyes searched for him, the dusty, bowlegged man on the platform, but he wasn't there, and she sighed and shut her eyes in relief.

With urgency, Kate clutched her bag, wishing for a modern overnight suitcase with roller wheels, and crossed the platform. She descended the stairs and hastened to her car, storing the bag in the backseat and getting behind the wheel.

She cranked the engine and rolled out of the lot, turning right, heading out of town toward Cove Lake and Paul's trailer, hoping she'd catch him before he went to work at the garage.

Kate had left her father more contented, and her mother in her upstairs bed, smiling and happy to be home. Their conversations had been less formal, and Kate and her mother had caught up, and held hands, and made small talk. At one point, as Kate left the room, she heard her mother thank her "patient husband" for waiting on her, and that made Kate smile.

On the platform, before Kate had caught the train back to Paxton, she'd hugged her father and told him she hoped her mother would maintain her cheerful mood and not start drinking again, and not spin the cycle of suffering again.

Her father had said, "Don't you worry about us, Kate. We're going to be just fine."

Kate's Falcon descended a small hill and turned onto the single-lane road. She saw a slice of Cove Lake shining through the trees, and she smiled with delight when Paul's trailer came into view. He was home! His car was parked in the carport.

Kate pulled the car onto the shoulder of the road near the trailer and killed the engine. She got out, nerves building in her gut, closed the door softly, walked the length of the trailer, turned right, and climbed the three concrete steps to the closed door. She was about to knock when it opened and Paul stood staring at her, dressed in jeans, a blue and black flannel shirt rolled up at the elbows, and black sneakers.

"Kate!" he said, looking genuinely happy to see her.

Kate's smile was timid. "Hi... I just came by to see if you... well, I don't know if you wanted to go out for some coffee or a beer or something."

Paul shoved his hands into his pockets.

Before he could answer, Kate said, "Maybe you have to work or…"

"No, I'm not working today. Actually, yesterday was my last day."

That puzzled her. "Last day?"

"Yeah, I'm leaving town in a couple of days."

Kate was immobile, and then a gush of panic rose. "Leaving?"

"Yeah, I'm going to move to Tucson. Can you believe it? The University of Arizona is going to transfer all my credits, and they're giving me a scholarship. Myra's father—Myra's my girlfriend. You met her in the bookstore. Anyway, her father is going to fix me up with a job in wildlife and conservation. I talked to a guy on the phone who has his own company and he said they're working at the Grand Canyon. He said there are uranium mining issues, contamination of water sources, and a lot of proposed developments that I can get involved in. He said I can do a work/study program until I graduate, and then I can work full time for his company—after I interview and get the job, of course."

Paul was bubbling with excitement. "Oh, sorry, Kate. I guess I'm pretty wound up, and it's happening so fast."

Kate stood, braced and tense, her body turning cold, her voice flat. "You'll get the job, Paul. I know you will."

Paul glanced about. "I feel like I just moved in, and now I'm leaving. And after I cleaned the place and scrubbed the bathroom for days!"

Paul straightened, winced, and spread his hands. "Look at me and my bad manners. Do you want to come in? The place isn't much, but it was home for a while."

Kate mechanically entered the trailer, noticing the beige, pleated curtains, an egg-white, leather recliner, a rickety-looking coffee table and a chocolate brown rug. It was all as she'd remembered it. Exactly.

"Can I get you something? I have beer, and I can make coffee."

Kate felt the life seeping out of her. She shook her head slowly, incomprehensively. How could he be leaving? What did it mean? What would she do with herself?

She found her weak voice. "No, nothing. I'm fine."

Paul clasped his hands together, his face lighting up. "Do you know what? I was going to get out of here and take a ride across the lake in my skiff. I've got so much to do before I leave and my head's spinning. It always relaxes me to get out on the lake. Would you like to come?"

Kate stared blankly ahead. *Maybe this was it*, she thought. *Maybe they would both die in the lake.*

"Kate?" Paul repeated, breaking into her thoughts. "Want to come?"

"Yes... Of course. Why not?"

From the six-foot wooden dock, Paul helped Kate

step down into the boat. It was an aging, sixteen-foot, white and gold striped aluminum skiff, with a stubby foredeck, an eighteen horse Nissan outboard, two swivel seats and life jackets. Paul cast off the line, put the engine in gear, and the boat went burbling and mumbling out toward the center of the lake as Kate presented her face to the sun, feeling the wind whip her hair.

"I've got a cap if you want it!" Paul called. "Just under the seat there."

She found it, a cap with an embroidered fish on the front panel, and pulled it on. A big, fat cloud swallowed the sun for a time, and they moved in and out of shadows, chugging along, dead slow. Kate heard the gentle slap of the water as Paul steered toward a quiet area beneath the reaching branches of colorful autumn trees. The dreaded wooden bridge came into view only about fifty yards away.

Paul cut the engine, and they glided toward shore, disturbing a family of ducks that went paddling off to find other, more private water.

Paul eased down next to Kate, reached and opened a square red cooler, retrieved two cans of beer and handed her one, nodding. "Like one?"

Smiling, she took it. They popped them, toasted, and drank.

Two minutes can be a long time, and to Kate it seemed timeless as she listened to the birds, the lapping water at the rocky shore, and the hum of a single-engine airplane passing over. Her mind drifted and wandered and couldn't settle. It had nowhere to go, so it kept wandering, homeless.

"I'm going to be silly and honest," Kate finally said. "I'll miss you."

He turned his head, giving her a thoughtful look. "How do you think it all works?" he said.

"What do you mean?" Kate wondered if he'd heard her say she'd miss him.

Paul looked skyward. "I don't know, life, I guess. I met Myra when I was driving around the country, trying to shake the war from my head. I saw something over there, in Vietnam, that I'll never forget... well, maybe I saw lots of things that stick in my brain, but after a firefight one awful day, I went looking for three of my men and the medic. The fight had been quick and fierce and, as much as I was trying to look out for my men, the battle became one of those 'every man for himself' things. When it was over, I circled back and searched the jungle, and I finally found them. Two men died twenty feet from each other. And then I found my buddy and the medic. They were lying in each other's arms, dead."

Kate lowered her head as if in prayer.

Paul continued. "Dead eyes take on a dusty look and reflect no light. But I swear... theirs had light. Do you know what I thought as I stared at them? What an unforgiveable waste. What an absolute waste of men who would have had families, who would have grown old and died old, the way a man is supposed to die, and not in some God-forsaken jungle far from home, away from the people who love them."

They sat for more long moments.

Paul tipped back the can, swallowing most of the beer. "That's why I drove, and drove, and looked at this big country that we fought for. And do you know what? I met good people. Good and kind people, and I went to see my friend's parents, Ed's parents, in San Jose. I told them I'd try to live a good life, to honor their son and my friend, Edward Tyler Jessup. I told them I wouldn't forget him, and what he did for his country."

Kate kept her head down, both hands holding the can of beer.

"I met Myra on the road. She had a flat tire, and I fixed it. We hit it off. She laughed easily, didn't take things too seriously, and she had her own mind. Anyway, I want to do something useful, Kate. I want to help this country the best way I can. I've seen most of it and I love it, and I don't care how that sounds. The sooner I can finish my degree, the sooner I can get out and do some good in the world... Do some good that Ed, and others like him, would have been proud of."

Paul ran a hand through his short hair and stared out at the water, squinting in the late afternoon, glowing sun. "I'm not going to say that I'm not attracted to you, Kate. I think we both feel that attraction, and we felt it right from the beginning when you suggested that book, which I love, by the way."

Kate was still, desperation filling her up. "But do you love her, Paul?"

Paul leaned back, gazing up into the creamy

clouds. "I'm not sure I'm ready for all that, but I am ready to try, and right now, that's what I need."

Kate looked away, tears hanging in her eyelashes.

"I guess we just met at the wrong time, Kate."

Kate wanted to lash out—she wanted to tell him the truth—that she'd time traveled. She wanted to explain to Paul what had happened the first time. She wanted to tell him about their marriage, their happy marriage, and about their baby, and about that stormy night, the bridge, and the water. She wanted to... But she didn't. How could she? She would sound like a lunatic.

Kate felt the energy between them disintegrate, and she looked at Paul, wild and vacant. "I don't understand" was all that came out.

"What?" Paul asked, looking at her. "What do you mean?"

Kate turned from him, shaking her head. "Let's go back. I want to go back now."

Paul returned to the outboard, revved it, swung the stern around, and pointed the boat toward home.

On the dock, Kate handed Paul his fishing cap and said, "Goodbye, Paul. I truly hope you have a great life. You deserve it."

Paul stared into her eyes and Kate sensed he wanted to say something, but he didn't.

She left him there, climbed the short incline to his trailer, walked to her car and drove away, not looking back, and not looking into her rearview mirror.

Kate drove aimlessly, thinking the irrational thought that time would somehow make it right. The turtle, helpless on its back, would finally flip over, go lumbering on its way, and everything would be as it should be, and they'd live happily ever after. Paul wouldn't really leave and move to Arizona and marry Myra. How could he?

In a feverish moment of madness, Kate's mind flashed on the entrance to the cave. The cave she'd entered in 2022 and exited in 1968. Could she enter it now and return to the future? What future? If the past wasn't the same, then how could the future be the same? If she stayed in 1968 and lived out her life, the chances were that the sequence of her life events would be different, based on her choices. She would not marry David Cunningham, because she didn't love him. But if she didn't marry him, she wouldn't give birth to Greg and Ellen, the children she loved more than her own life.

Kate drove the road that circled Cove Lake and, when she came to the bridge, she sped up, smashing the accelerator to the floor, her jaw set, her eyes hard, her arms braced. It was time to choose her own destiny.

CHAPTER 27

The knock on the door brought Kate out of sleep, and brought Paul back into her mind so vividly that she knew he'd been in her dreams the entire windy, rainy night.

"You're going to be late for class," Vicki called, knocking again.

Kate lifted up. "Okay! Okay!"

"Coffee's on. I'm outta here. Bye," Vicki said, her voice already fading.

The front door closed, and Kate flopped back down, listening to the rain strike the windows, sounding like little pebbles. Blurry images swam before her eyes, faces she should have recognized. An older man, leaning over, was ready for a kiss, but Kate mentally slapped him away. Who was that?

Had she been an elderly woman? Why did that dream repeat every night, and dreams about kids, and teaching in some school in Manhattan? Dreams that insisted and harassed her.

Kate sat up and leaned back against the wooden headboard. She blinked, breathed, pondered. In degrees, two realities bubbled up, and she mentally worked to separate them. Here and now was 1968. She was in her bed, a throb of a hangover reminding her that she'd left Paul's trailer, driving much too fast. She'd thought better of plunging her car into the lake and, instead, she'd gone to some dive bar ten miles away. A skinny bartender with a bandito mustache and beady, bird eyes kept pouring her shots of Jack Daniels.

"There you go, little lady. That'll fix you up," he'd said, with a narrow-pinched face and a smirk of a mouth.

"I'm not a little lady, okay?!" she'd snapped.

He'd grinned, delighted by her sassy attitude, leaning in, one arm on the bar. "Well, then, I could call you a little bitch, couldn't I? And then I could toss your sexy underage ass out for drinkin' 'Jackie Dan' whiskey, and not the Near-beer you're legal to drink. Now what do you have to say about that, bitchy girl with the hot ass and sweetie-pie lips?"

He knew that would shut her up, and it did. Kate wanted to slap him, and heave the shot glass at him, but she didn't, because she also wanted the booze, and she wanted to get good and drunk, and forget the past, the present, the future, and Paul Ganic.

Grudgingly, she'd slapped a ten and a five down on the bar, and the smirking bartender took a pull from his cigarette and poured her another two shots, sliding them toward her. He snatched up the bills and moved away, his face shiny in triumph, his bar buddies chuckling.

How many shots did she have? Not a clue, but her head suggested it was more than five. What a stupid 20-year-old thing to do, to get drunk.

And then a thought stiffened her spine. Wait a minute! The dream about the elderly woman. No, it was not a dream! No! She was forgetting again. The future was melting away again. She *had* been seventy-four years old! She had time traveled!

Kate flung the blanket away, swung her feet to the floor and shot up. She and Paul were over. They wouldn't be married, and she wouldn't have his baby. She pushed a trembling hand through her hair, emotion almost taking her again.

One day soon, she'd awaken, and she wouldn't remember the future. The dreams would persist for a time, and then vanish, and she'd be trapped in 1968, to live out her life.

Kate crossed to the window, and gazed out through the beaded-up glass, at the silvery, rainy day and the wind shaking the trees. Last night's thoughts returned, so it was time to make up her mind. If she couldn't have Paul, then there was no reason for her to stay in 1968, and there was no way she was going to live her life again without Paul and his love.

He had loved her the first time. That was real! The child she lost because of the accident was real! It happened. It all happened, so why didn't it happen the same way again? What was the reason? A cruel joke by fate? Did they conspire up there, somewhere in the heavens, and say, "Let's send Kate back to 1968 so she can change the past, and make things right, and good, and happy? But, just for the fun of it, let's mix things up a little. Let's see what she does now."

Kate's mind was the flaming mind of a twenty-year-old kid, and she was fine with that. She was going to go with that; give into that. No caution or careful, methodical, mature thinking. No!

She shimmied out of her night gown, went to her chest of drawers, reached for a bra, then grabbed a pair of jeans and a turtleneck. Tugging on thick socks, Kate slid her feet into lace-up boots, tied them, and shook out her hair.

Rain or no rain, she was going to march back to that cave, duck inside, and plant herself. There she would wait, and she would dare the fates to send her to an alternative version of 1968, or return her to the future to continue her life in 2022. She would not be left dangling in this failed version of 1968.

For her blinding headache, Kate grabbed two Excedrin from the medicine cabinet, downed them, and then snatched her raincoat, cap and umbrella from the hall closet, and left. Rain exploded off the sidewalks and bounced off the roof and hood of her car.

Inside, she cranked the engine, backed out of the driveway, bounced onto the street, straightened out, and pointed the car toward the train station. To climb the hill to the cave would be a slog, and the cave might be damp and muddy, but she didn't care. Her mind was made up.

By the time she parked in the train parking lot, the rain had subsided, but thunder rumbled, and streams of water formed pools in the lot and poured from the station's roof gutters.

Kate shoved the door open and got out, not bothering to open the umbrella. She bounded up the train steps to the platform and took cover under the overhanging roof, where eight people waited for the train, some reading newspapers, some craning their necks toward the tracks. Thankfully, the dusty, bowlegged man was nowhere to be seen.

It was time. Kate took a deep, shuddering breath and squared her shoulders. For days she hadn't been able to predict her next mood, her next thought, her next step. She had been a puppet, her strings jerked, and her mouth made to talk, her mind made to remember, her heart made to hurt. "Get to that cave," she said softly, sharply.

The bright, hot pain of the headache nearly bent her over, and she shut her eyes, massaging her forehead. She'd never had such a brutal hangover. And then, with a single heavy thud of her heart, she staggered, found a bench and slumped down.

Minutes ticked by, and the red second hand on the big terminal clock flicked through the seconds, as time passed, as fog rolled in, as the train approached, and passengers gathered up their suitcases.

Kate lacked the strength to rise and start for the cave, so she sat, staring. She was still sitting when the train rumbled in. Passengers exited and embarked, the conductor shouted, "All aboard!" and a bell clanged, and the train gathered speed and rumbled off.

Kate listened to the drumming rain and the mournful call of a bird, and she inhaled the wet scents of autumn. As time appeared to pause, she had the odd feeling of being unfinished. An unfinished person. An unfinished life. Words fell short to describe the feeling and the swift, strange mood. It was as though one curtain had descended and another rose. The play must go on.

And then her headache was gone, just like that, and the platform was empty. She was alone. The rain had stopped. A spear of sunlight shot down from a broken, gray cloud, pierced the fog, and lit up the wet train tracks.

Kate canted her head. What had just happened? Her mind stilled, and she glanced about, struggling to remember why she was sitting there. Did she have a train ticket home to see her parents? No. Hadn't she just been there and seen them? Her mother was home. They seemed happy.

Kate pushed up, left the platform, and descended the stairs to her car. Behind the steering wheel, she turned the key and boosted the engine, then drove away, splashing through puddles, turning onto Main Street, heading back to the apartment.

Then she realized. Didn't she have some unfinished business at the train station? Isn't that why she was there? She touched the brake at the first cross street, doubled back, and entered the parking lot from the other side. Again, she parked, and the engine idled. She didn't move.

Kate felt an unlikely confusion. Why in the world was she sitting there? She had a psych test to prepare for, and a history paper on John Adams was due. And she was hungry. Maybe she'd stop at the Busy Bee and eat breakfast.

Paul filled her mind, bringing an aching sadness. Then came the selfish wish that his relationship with Myra wouldn't work, and it gave her a pathetic and meager hope.

How could Kate move on without him? He was the love of her life, and she knew that without any doubt. She hungered for him. She was born to be with him, so why hadn't it worked out?

Finally, she backed up, nudged the car into gear and drove away, her heart heavy. Maybe she'd blow off her classes for the day and begin work on her first novel, *Between the Shadows.* Later, she'd swing by the bookstore and tell Art about it. He was always pushing her to write.

As Kate drove through the early Main Street traffic, she got a flash of memory from last night's dream. She'd been a woman in her seventies. How weird was that? And she'd been married with two kids, and her husband had died from some weird pandemic disease.

Maybe she'd tell Art about it. He was good at interpreting dreams and dream symbols. He'd probably say something like, "You're out of your mind, that's what it means. You and your entire spaced-out generation are heading down the road to perdition."

Kate stopped at a red light. To her left, passing through the green light, Paul's black and white Pontiac moved across Main Street to Lake Road, and she watched, sick and haunted, as his car slowly drifted out of sight.

She felt a terrible and inescapable rage. How could she live the rest of her life—a life that could last another sixty or seventy years—without Paul? How could she let their relationship go, leaving them to travel down separate paths? He was her soulmate. She was sure of it.

The red light flicked to green, and Kate drove off into a shroud of morning fog. There was only the present hurting moment, without Paul. No future and no past. She had but one reality and one wish: that she and Paul would somehow find each other again, somewhere, in some other time.

PART 2

CHAPTER 28

May 2022

S eventy-four-year-old Kate Clarke pushed through the glass revolving doors of Macy's Department Store and stepped out onto 34th Street. Her purse hung over her left arm; her right hand clutched the rope handle of a heavy shopping bag containing an aqua enameled steel tea kettle she'd just purchased on sale.

As hectic shoppers flowed around her, she dodged and weaved and struggled ahead, feeling like a salmon swimming upstream.

On Seventh Avenue, she turned north and joined the next onslaught of pedestrian traffic, craning her neck, searching for a taxi. She spotted one. A miracle! Fleet of foot, she cut across the crowds to the curb and, lifting her purse hand, waved to get the taxi driver's attention.

At that moment, a teenage kid, with sharp eyes and scissor-fast legs, charged her, his steely eyes focused on her purse.

A man at the curb, using a two-finger technique, whistled for a taxi, the pitch loud enough to shatter store windows. There was a squeal of tires, and the kid seized the hectic moment, launching himself toward Kate's purse, reaching, twisting his body like a seagull swooping to grab its prey.

And then everything seemed to happen in slow motion. A tall man spotted the kid as he left the curb, the kid's arm outstretched, hand open, fingers snatching the purse from Kate's wrist. The man, only three feet from Kate, his eyes sharp, had anticipated the attack.

Just as the mugger grabbed the purse, the man was there, his reflexes lightning fast. He kicked the kid's right leg hard. The leg buckled. The forward motion pitched the kid headlong, arms flailing, mouth open, Kate's purse flying through the air and crashing to the street.

Off balance, the kid stumbled, and thumped head-first into the side of a waiting taxi, dropped like a sack, and rolled onto his back, his face set in a painful grimace.

Horns blared, crowds gathered, and two cops on their beat hurried over, the female cop having witnessed the event from a distance. She was already on her radio calling for backup, the crackling static loud.

Kate stumbled back onto the sidewalk, shaken

and disoriented, immediately comforted by a woman who had retrieved her purse and handed it to her. Kate thanked her while she looked around for her hero, spotting him by the still-waiting taxi. He stood over the kid, who was cursing and holding his head in pain. Traffic snarled, car horns blasted, a police siren whined, and a semi-truck's brakes sounded like the trumpeting call of an elephant.

The cops flipped the mugger onto his stomach, cuffed him, then jerked him to his feet. They yanked him off to one of the two squad cars that had just bounced to a stop, lowered him down into the back seat, and closed the door.

The man smiled as he approached Kate. "Are you okay?" he asked in a deep, concerned voice.

Kate nodded. "Yes, I think so."

She looked him over. He was in his 60s, and no spring chicken, but he was in good shape, the body of an ex-athlete, with a broad face and brush-cut, gray hair.

"Thank you, sir. I didn't see that coming."

"I used to coach college football. I saw him coming on fast, like a running back."

The man gestured toward the cops. "They'll probably want a statement from us," he said.

"Oh, yes, I suppose so."

"By the way, my name's Frank. Shall we stand over there out of the way? Here, let me help you with your bag."

Thirty minutes later, Kate and Frank had given their statements and contact information to the female cop, and they were free to go.

As Frank was saying his goodbyes, Kate said, "Frank, can I take you to lunch or something? Coffee and a snack, at least? I'm so grateful for what you did."

Frank gave her the "aw shucks, ma'am" grin, and with a tilt of his head, he said, "Well, I am a little hungry, but then, as my wife likes to say, I'm always hungry. I'll just need to call my buddy and tell him I'll be a little late. He won't mind. He's with his grandkids."

They found a touristy diner near Eighth Avenue on 35th Street and settled into a comfortable booth, the lunch crowd lively, the waitress friendly.

Frank ordered a sandwich, big enough for two, and a beer. Kate chose a grilled cheese and tomato and a ginger ale.

"I didn't get your name," Frank said, folding his meaty hands on the formica table top.

"Kate Clarke."

She offered her hand, and he shook it.

Frank thought about that. "That's a familiar name. Why is that?"

"I hardly think you'd know my name, Frank."

"No, I've heard it. I'm sure of it."

Kate shrugged casually. "I'm a writer, a novelist. Maybe you've seen my books in airport bookstores."

He drew back and snapped his fingers. "I knew it!"

She shook her head. "Now, don't tell me you've read any of my books. They're mostly written for women."

"No, I haven't read them, but my wife has. There are at least ten of your books in the bookshelf back home."

Kate lifted an eyebrow. "Well, how nice. I'm flattered."

"She loves your books. I bought her one for her birthday a couple of years ago. I don't remember the title or anything, but she loved it."

He reached into his pocket for his cell phone. "I've got to text her and say, 'Guess who I'm having lunch with?' She'll never believe it."

"Why don't we ask the waitress to take a photo of us?" Kate asked. "It might be fun for your wife."

Frank lit up. "Great idea!"

The waitress snapped three. Frank chose the best one and sent it off.

"I can't wait to hear from her," Frank said, grinning. "She won't believe it!"

"Where is your wife?"

"In Grand Rapids. That's where we live. I flew down to hang out with an old college buddy who lives in New Jersey."

"I hope I'm not pulling you away from anything?"

"No, no. Like I said, he won't care. He's having lunch with his daughter and grandkids. I would have been crashing their party, anyway. We'll hook up later this afternoon, watch some football, and hit some bars tonight."

When their food arrived, Frank ate voraciously. "Sorry," he said, after swallowing some bites. "I eat like a bear."

"So, eat away."

A text dinged in. Frank wiped his mouth with a napkin and reached for his phone. He read the text and laughed. "She can't believe it! Angela, that's my wife. She says, 'No way you're with Kate Clarke.' But then she wants me to get your autograph. Sorry. Hope that's okay?"

"Of course. I'll be more than happy, Frank, after what you did for me. Give me your address and I'll sign a book and send it to her."

"Now that's a nice thing to do, Kate. Real nice. She'll love it and show all her friends and family."

After Frank finished most of the sandwich, he asked, "So, you must have some kids and a husband hanging around someplace."

Kate reached for her glass of ginger ale. She sipped it thoughtfully. "I was married once, Frank, a long time ago. We didn't have children, and it didn't work out."

Frank wiped his mouth with the paper napkin, his face dropping into sadness. "Oh, I'm sorry to hear that, Kate. You're a nice-looking woman, and I'm sure you were a knockout in your day."

Kate laughed a little. "Thanks, Frank. I'm seventy-four years old, I have a lot of friends, including a man I see now and then, and I've had a full, good life."

"How many books have you written?"

Kate glanced up at the ceiling. "Oh... Well, let me see... Forty-eight, I think."

"Holy geez, Kate, I haven't even *read* that many books. Maybe I read six in college, but I don't remember any of them. What the heck does that say about me? A big jock dumbass, for sure."

"You didn't need to read so much, Frank. You did other things. Coaching must be very rewarding."

"Yeah, I loved it. I bet you read a lot in college," Frank said. "I bet you were the smart girl that all the girls were jealous of, and all the guys, like me, wanted to date."

Kate laughed again. "I like you, Frank. You have an open, enthusiastic way about you. I bet you were a great coach."

He took a deep breath of consideration. "I hope so. I tried to be. Those guys made me a better man than when I started. That's for sure. I was too cocky and too stubborn when I was a kid, and sometimes, I still am. But I guess time matures you, if you let it. But I'm still a pain in the ass sometimes. Just ask Angela. She'll tell you."

"And where did you and Angela meet, Frank?"

"In college. I played football and she read books, just like you. She's as smart as they come, and I still don't know why she married a bum like me. Hey, I'm not complaining any, you know? We have two kids, a boy who doesn't like football, but likes computers, and a girl who's into boys, big surprise. Anyway, Angela and I saw each other and... well, I don't know exactly what happened. We just knew we should be together. Did you ever have that, Kate?"

Kate dropped her head in a slight nod. "Yes... I did.

Once, but it was a long time ago, when I was just a silly girl, back in Ohio, when I was in college."

"So, what happened?"

"I was too late. He fell for another girl and moved to Arizona."

"Geez... that's too bad, Kate. Did you ever see him again?"

"See him? No, I never did, but I heard from him a few times... years ago, now. He congratulated me on my second novel. It got good reviews and I guess he read about it somewhere."

Frank waited for more. "Is that it?"

"He married a girl from a wealthy family and had two daughters. Unfortunately, the marriage didn't last."

"So, maybe you two should have gotten back together?"

Kate's smile held sorrow. "I was married by then, and after my marriage fell apart, he was married again."

"Oh, geez, Kate, bad timing."

"Yeah... Well, it was many years ago."

"Do you still keep in touch?"

"He died four years ago. I found his obituary on the internet."

"I'm sorry, Kate. Really sorry to hear that."

Kate lifted a hand, made a vague gesture, and let it fall. "I was, too. It was just as you said, about you and Angela. We saw each other, and we knew we should be together... or maybe it was just me."

"Well, let me tell you what my Grandma Hazel

used to say. 'If two people are really meant to be together, then some way or the other, they'll get together.'"

"It's a nice thought," Kate said, looking away.

Frank swallowed the last of his beer, then stared down at the table. "You know, it's funny how life goes, isn't it? Your timing was as bad as mine was in football. Back in the day, I played college football at Penn State and was heading to the Pittsburgh Steelers after college, in the 1992 NFL Draft. But then I got into a car wreck and busted up a knee and a foot. That was it. No NFL career."

Kate frowned. "That's awful, Frank."

His smile held resignation. "Yeah, it was that, all right. So, I felt sorry for myself for a while, and then one of my coaches said to me, 'Hey, you big crybaby, use the difficulty to your advantage.'"

Kate sat up. "That was a little harsh."

"Yeah, maybe, but it snapped me out of it, and I was able to move on and become a teacher and a football coach. I was okay after that. Yeah, it was okay. Don't get me wrong, though. If I could go back in time, you can bet I'd never climb back into that car and never drive too long in the night, until I fell asleep behind the wheel and smashed into the rear-end of a pickup truck at a stoplight. Thank God the pickup driver was okay."

Frank fixed his eyes on her. "I'm sure you know what I mean, Kate... you and your guy. I'd bet that sometimes you think, 'Hey, maybe I'd like to go back and change some things. Do it again, you know?'

Who doesn't want to go back and change a few things that went sour on them?"

Kate's voice was sad, her voice soft. "Not anymore, I don't, Frank. It was all too long ago."

Frank shook his head, unconvinced. "Come on, Kate, don't tell me about the long-time-ago years. I can think back on the days when I was a kid, throwing that football like a bullet, feeling good, and strong, and invincible. I can smell the sweat and the grass, and I can still feel the high of playing football in the cold air and winter snows. And then I'm right back there, in the flesh, and no time has passed. No time at all."

Kate looked at him, holding his firm stare. "Yeah, Frank. You're right about that. There are times when it seems like it all happened only a week ago, and not a lifetime ago."

Frank made a fist, then released it, staring at it. "What I'd give, Kate, to go back. God forgive me, but I'd give almost everything to go back and do it all again, only better."

Kate and Frank parted on Eighth Avenue after he'd put her in a taxi. They exchanged addresses, he kissed her on the cheek, and they waved farewell.

"I'm gonna read one of your books, Kate!" he said, pointing a sure finger at her. "You can bet on it!"

In the taxi, heading uptown, Kate eased back into her seat and closed her eyes. Frank was right. She could see Paul Ganic standing before her, his eyes warm. And she could smell the damp wind of Cove Lake, view his trailer, and remember the day they traveled to the book auction sale, and later, had a picnic. It had been a lovely day, an unforgettable day. She'd longed for him to kiss her, and he nearly had, and how she wished he had. Kate was certain that the kiss would have been the magical moment, joining them in love that would have lasted a lifetime.

Kate had often pondered her instant and constant love for Paul, a love that had never waned. How was it that their relationship had seemed much more than it had been in reality? She always thought she'd forget him, but she never had, and she knew she never would.

She recalled the last thing Paul ever said to her on the phone, all those years ago, when Kate's husband was sitting in the living room, watching television.

"We just had bad timing, Kate, and I have to say it, even though I shouldn't. I shouldn't have left Paxton and gone to Arizona. I should have never left you. We could have had a great life together. A perfect life."

CHAPTER 29

I t was the second week in October when Kate
drove her rental car to Paxton, Ohio, and by
then, the leaves were blazing with autumn colors.
For the entire two weeks after she'd met Frank, her
mind had hummed with memories and images of
Paul, and every kind of "what if?" about Paul that
she could imagine.

At first, she'd ignored them. She told herself
she'd clung to those memories of Paul because her
marriage had failed. Over time, she had realized
she wasn't in love with her husband, and he'd been
cheating on her, so there was nothing to mend; no
hope that they could save the marriage. Thankfully,
they hadn't had children, and they'd divorced and
stayed friends. He'd married again, and he was
happy, and had a child. Well, good for him. She had
not found another.

Kate had never been with a man she truly loved.

Therefore, she rationalized that her obsession with Paul had to have been a girlish infatuation. After all, they had never even kissed or slept together; it was not a deep, rich relationship; they'd spent only one day together, so why had she been convinced that he was Mr. Right?

As she passed a sign that read **PAXTON, OHIO - 32 MILES**, she thought of *You Can't Go Home Again,* a novel by Thomas Wolfe. Is that what she was trying to do? Go home in order to escape back into memory? She'd read the novel twice; it was a psychological journey which explored serious social and emotional themes.

Her own novels were not so literary or profound, but she was okay with that. Her main goal had always been to tell a good story, with some romance, some likeable characters and an entertaining plot. Obviously, she'd succeeded in doing that, in creating characters and plots her readers could relate to, because she had sold a lot of books.

But how and why, exactly, had she decided to take this journey back to Paxton? Instantly, she remembered.

In a dark mood one rainy night, soon after the failed mugging and her meeting with Frank, Kate had left the television and its lousy nightly news. She'd stood by the window for long minutes, pulling the curtains aside, staring out at the ghostly street lights and wet streets.

Her laptop was on, a half-written novel waiting at the kitchen counter, but for the first time in a long time, she had no enthusiasm for it. The wandering thing strained under the weight of a dreary plot about a woman who fatally falls in love with a younger man, who reminds her of her first and only love.

Kate realized she could never finish it. It was too depressing, too indulgent, and too pathetic.

Later that same evening, Kate had sipped a glass of white wine, seated in her deep, comfortable chair, with her knees drawn up beneath her. There was a crack of thunder, and, just like that, she knew she had to return to Paxton. After fifty years, she suddenly had the compulsion to see the town again, to remember, and to walk the streets, to drive beside Cove Lake and see the spot where Paul's trailer had been.

Haunted by the past, a past that seemed unfinished and waiting for her, she had to return, and breathe the air again, remember the old characters again, and face the old ghosts.

She had been running away from a love that still pursued her, a love that had been like a thin thread, like a tiny bud that had never blossomed into an actual relationship. And yet, it was deep and resonating, and she had written about that lost relationship, in one form or another, in all of her most successful novels.

Driving her rental car, Kate approached Paxton, leaning forward, her gaze straight and her eyes wide. Anticipation swelled as she drove along Main

Street, feeling both the simple joy of returning and the angst of returning, and then she frowned in disappointment when everything around her was changed and unfamiliar.

The Towne Grocery and The Busy Bee Restaurant were gone, and so was Kip's Bar and the bowling alley. The Aurora Theater had morphed into a bland looking Marshalls, and a Starbucks seemed alien and out of place.

She was cheered to see that the Greek revival library was there, thank God, but Mackay's Books New & Old, where she'd worked part time for three years, was an AT&T store.

What had happened to Art Mackay, the vigorous, cranky old man, who'd been younger than she was now, who'd worn faded overalls, tennis shoes and wired spectacles? She'd lost track of him years ago. There wasn't the convenience of texting and social media in those days, and it was easy to lose track of friends.

It was a sun-bright day, so Kate parked near the village green and wandered the streets, finding a wooden bench near the white gazebo. She eased down with a weary sigh, feeling her tired legs and sore feet.

She sat in uneasy reflection, her mind rolling over old thoughts and feelings. Before she'd left New York, she'd had a yearly physical. Dr. Olson had advised her that she'd developed an irregular heartbeat, which needed monitoring, and her blood pressure remained too high, despite medication. It seemed absurd to hear such things, even though she was often fatigued and needed more sleep. But, as with many older people, she still felt like a young woman on the inside, even if she was seventy-four on the outside.

Kate tugged up the collar of her olive-green, autumn jacket and crossed her legs, reaching into her pocket for the black French beret cap, and tugging it snuggly over her short, gray hair.

Sitting there, it was easy to remember the past, 1968, when everything sparkled and danced; when all things appeared new and possible, and the future waited with a smile and open arms.

Grinning with pleasure, she recalled those late study nights, when she and her friends drove into the A&W Root Beer parking lot and ordered burgers, fries and root beer from the carhop. Kate chuckled to herself, thinking, *I wouldn't be able to digest that now.*

Her thoughts always returned to Paul Ganic and, as she sat there, feeling the cool wind across her face, his name was a whisper in her head.

Throughout her life, she'd often dreamed about Paul, about them being married, and about her being pregnant; about planning their future together. But at least twice a year, she'd also had a persistent nightmare that woke her from sleep, screaming.

She and Paul are driving at night, she behind the wheel. The headlights are tunneling through the darkness, needle rain falling, rain drumming the roof and hood of the car. She's in a manic mood, high with the adventure of racing across the single lane road, the tires splashing through puddles, the engine a comfortable whine. She gives the accelerator a boost, and the car shoots ahead.

Paul says, "Maybe you want to slow down a little, Kate. There's a bridge coming up, and it might be slippery."

Over the sound of the car engine is a rushing wind, rain splattering the windshield, the windshield wipers frantically slapping back and forth like out-of-control pendulums. The headlights find the bridge, lighting it up, and she bears down on it, her shoulders hunched forward, her face fixed in a thrilling challenge.

"I'm going to shoot across that thing like a rocket!" she says, with a fixed grin.

"Slow down, Kate!" Paul shouts, sliding over, ready to grab the steering wheel.

When the tires hit the bridge, they skid. The steering wheel whips left, and the back tires slide away. She fights the wheel, jerking it right, but she feels the car go. A hot panic stops her breath as the car slams through the wood railing, sails over the water and plunges into the black, surging lake. The car smacks the water hard and sinks.

In the black, cold water, Kate wrenches, gulps for air, twists and struggles to scream out for Paul. But there is only blackness, and cold, and death.

Kate hated the dream. She always assumed that its meaning had something to do with her and

Paul's doomed relationship, but why did it repeat in exactly the same way, and why did it have to be so terrifying?

The Comfort Inn, where Kate booked a room, had a firm bed, a large screen TV, a bright clean bathroom and windows that looked out on the now University of Paxton campus. It was not the campus she'd known. While looking at the website photos a few days before, she'd counted five new resident halls, a chapel with a lovely white spire, and at least two new administration buildings. From the map she'd found downstairs in the lobby, she also learned that there was a new football field, student center, alumni house, and library extension.

Kate ate dinner at an Olive Garden, ordering the salmon special, eating slowly, while skillfully listening to nearby conversation, something she had begun to do when she was in college. It was entertaining, interesting and helpful, a great way to capture authentic dialogue for her novels.

At a table close by sat a family of five. The mother was pretty and well-dressed. The father, a business type with a serious Mt. Rushmore expression, seemed preoccupied. The late teen daughter, a prom-queen type, who loved to gab about clothes and her *TikTok* Likes, said, 'Oh. My. God,' whenever possible. Her two younger brothers stared into their cellphones, ignoring everyone, until their father curtly told them to put them away. They did so, sulking.

The father said, "The secret to life does not lie in

your phones, boys. Put your mind on something else for a change before you permanently damage your brain cells."

The daughter said, "My classes are so boring. I mean... like I know everything. I learned all that in high school. And my teachers are so, I don't know, boring and everything."

"You can always learn something new," the mother said, blandly, as she sipped a martini.

"I'm not paying all that money for you to be bored," her father said gruffly. "Open your ears and stop talking so much. You kids today are always on your phones or gabbing away—when you should be listening or studying. Start listening once in a while instead of blabbing about nonsense, and you won't get so bored. Your generation are a bunch of lazy whiners, who are always asking, 'What has the world done for me lately?'"

The daughter stiffened her neck in insult. "Oh. My. God. Daddy, that's so uncool."

"Uncool or not, your grades don't reflect the fact that you know everything."

The daughter sulked. The sons sulked, and the parents ate in aloof satisfaction.

Kate's smile was inward. She recalled what Art Mackay had said about her 1960s generation. "Your generation are all draft dodgers, hippies, and druggies. God help this country."

That night, Kate had difficulty sleeping. Her dreams flitted about, flashing images of a girl and a boy. In that dream world, she recognized them as her children, a son named Greg and a daughter named Ellen, and she loved them with a passion she'd never felt during her waking life.

The next morning, Kate sat upright in bed, straining to remember those kids' faces, but they swam away from her and faded, and all the emotion of being a mother melted away into the silence of her room.

While she showered, Kate reasoned that the dream had been inspired by the family of five she'd overheard the night before. She thought, *How the mind plays tricks, and then forgets.*

Breakfast at the Lemon Tree Café included scrambled eggs, seven-grain toast, a fruit cup, and strong, black coffee. The yellow walls and white ceiling were cheerful and the young waitress friendly. Kate quickly realized that the old photos hanging on the walls were of Paxton in the 1960s, when she'd lived there.

After paying her check, Kate wandered over to the photographs, put on her reading glasses, and studied the framed photos up close, with nostalgia and a smile.

There was the old Busy Bee Restaurant, and the record shop, and the gift shop, where Connie Poe had sold some of her art work. On the far wall, near the bathrooms, was a faded, black-and-white photo of Mackay's Books New & Old. Outside the shop, near a rack of books, was old Art himself, standing stiffly, with a tolerant smile, his pipe in hand. Kate's throat tightened with emotion.

And then she saw it! Standing in the door's shadow was a figure. Nosing forward and narrowing her eyes, Kate could just make out who the fuzzy, out-of-focus figure was. It was herself! She stood just inside the door, peering out at Art! A thrill sang through her, and she stepped back, clasping her hands in delight. How wonderful! What a lift!

Outside in the chilly morning, Kate walked to her car, climbed in and drove to the train station. She was surprised to see that the old train station was gone, having been replaced by a two-story, blond brick building with plenty of glass, tall hedges and a manicured lawn. The blue and white office sign advertised doctors, lawyers, and a real estate company.

Kate found an empty space and parked. She shut off the engine and sat for a time, her hands resting on top of the steering wheel. Why had she come back? There was nothing to come back to. The past was gone, vanished, as if some magician had waved a magic wand and said, "Abracadabra!"

She inhaled a deep breath and blew it out, fluttering her lips. Lifting her eyes to the distant hills, she recalled that she and Paul had picnicked up there all those years ago. A lifetime ago. It now seemed as if it had been a dream.

Minutes later, Kate was traveling a dirt path that led through a brown grassy field, winding through sparkling autumn trees. She climbed a grassy hill and trudged down the other side to a meadow, moving to some boulders, where she and Paul had spread out their picnic. It had been a wonderful day and one she'd never forgotten.

While they had eaten, and talked, and laughed, Paul had mentioned a hidden cave further up the hill, in the shelter of trees. He'd often played there as a child, he'd said, and he'd wanted to show it to her. For some reason, she'd been uncomfortable about exploring it, and refused to go.

Maybe she'd climb the rest of the hill and search for that cave. Why not?

CHAPTER 30

K ate climbed the hill, moving through trees and low brush, then across a ravine to a trail that led toward a sandstone cliff. She paused to catch her breath, feeling her heart pounding.

"It's okay," she said to her heart. "Hiking is good for you."

Kate searched the area for fifteen minutes but didn't find a cave. After another rest, she was about to give up the search when she spotted crushed cans of beer, cigarette butts and tossed paper cups.

She paused, looking about. And then she had a déjà vu moment. She would have sworn she'd been here before, and suddenly, in a mental flash, she knew exactly where the cave was.

Kate approached the cliff, certain that the entrance to the cave lay hidden by the overhanging branches of a tree. She crept forward, kicked the beer cans away, and then hesitated, hearing birdsong and the cawing of a crow. The wind was chilly and the sun bright, and her ears picked up the sound of a distant siren coming from town.

Inhaling a breath for courage, she reached and parted the tree branches that obscured the cave entrance. There it was, the mouth of the cave. Her pulse quickened.

Morning sunlight lit up the entrance, revealing shadowy depths beyond. Still holding the branch, Kate swung it up and hooked it over a protruding, jagged rock, allowing sunlight to brighten the cave's interior.

She stood entranced. She had no doubt that she'd been in this cave before. No doubt at all. But when? Staring in wonder, she ducked her head and inched forward, squinting, allowing her eyes to adjust to the dim light of the depths.

She screamed when a rabbit leapt from the darkness, burst into sunlight and went darting off, vanishing into thick brush.

Catching her breath, Kate concentrated on the darkness beyond the sunlight, wishing she had a flashlight. She was about to turn away when the impulse to move deeper into the cave tempted her. After all, Paul had escaped here as a child, so how dangerous could it be? And, anyway, she was curious. Crouching, she crept forward, her body taut, her lower back registering dull pain, her left foot stiff. Still, she pushed on. The ground was damp, the moldy smell wrinkled her nose, and the silence was ringing in her ears.

There were three more crushed beer cans and some cigarette butts, indicating that someone had been there recently. Her footsteps were deliberate and careful as she examined the immediate area, the damp cave walls with streaks of moss, jagged rocks and water marks. She decided not to go any deeper. Who knew what lay beyond? Racoons? Snakes?

Kate took a minute to imagine Paul as a kid hiding away, flashlight in hand, his adventurous spirit exploring every part of the cave.

As she turned, maneuvering herself back toward the opening, she grew dizzy, and white spots swam across her eyes. A sharp stab of pain grabbed her heart, and she stumbled, called out and fell to her knees, gasping for air, reaching out a hand toward the entrance, desperate to crawl out into the freedom of sunlight and fresh air.

A wave of exhaustion slapped her, and she tumbled onto her side, her chest heaving, her eyes wild. Her blood ran cold as she thought, *I'll die here and never be found.*

The sunlight vanished, her body pulsed, and she sank onto the wet ground, in clouds of rolling fog and whirling blue light.

Kate stumbled out of the cave, her eyes stabbed by the glare of shining sunlight. Covering her eyes with a shaky hand, she dropped to her knees, disoriented and terrified. She cast her eyes left and right, her breath coming fast. She heard echoing birdsong and glanced up through autumn leaves into a deep blue sky. What had happened?

Her grappling, rattled mind took minutes to settle and remember. She had been in the cave and had passed out. Too little air? Was she all right?

She inhaled a breath and blew it out. It felt good. Very good, and her raw nerves cooled, and her mind cooled, and her skin cooled. She was okay. Fine. Feeling just fine. *Nothing to be scared of*, she told herself. She thought, *Calm down and look for your purse and your cellphone.*

Glancing about, she saw neither. Turning back toward the cave, she swallowed. Did she really want to go back inside? Hadn't her phone been in her right back pocket? Yes, that's where she'd often kept it. She felt for it, but it wasn't there.

She pulled herself up, and her legs were strong, her body vital, her breathing easy. A gust of wind whipped her long hair across her face, and she raked it away, startled. Long hair? She didn't have long hair. She seized the ends, staring, incredulous. Black! A glance at her hands brought a shock. Young hands! No age spots. No blue veins.

Kate tottered away in a confused haze, forgetting about her purse and phone. She reached for a sturdy sycamore tree, leaning back against it, mouth-breathing, patting her face, her chest, her legs. What was going on? It was some kind of pretend—a dream so powerful she couldn't wake up!

She pushed away and went rambling through a maze of trees, emerging into full sunlight, the expansive valley and a forest of trees spread out around her. She stared intently at the town below. It wasn't the town of 2022! It was the town of her college youth—the town of 1968!

Kate stood there, unmoving, in the everlasting morning, trying to fight off these crazy visions and dreams, sure she had slipped away into insanity. Her teeth chattered from shock, and she made a hopeless sound.

Her vision went liquid and wavy. She blinked, and her mind fumbled in a fever of déjà vu scenes and fleeting faces. A big rock with a flat top came into her blurring vision and she grappled for it and sat, while she seemed to be floating, as if in a mist, like a ghost.

She wasn't sure how much time passed, but as the sun warmed her and the wind stirred her hair, she gradually settled and felt anchored to the earth. To this new earth. To her new reality. She sat with her hands beside her for a while, and then she pressed them into the rock. It was solid. She felt solid. Her fingers gripped the rough, hard surface. Her feet pressed into the earth of grass and leaves and twigs. She felt her face and hair and legs. Yes, she was there. She was real.

Minutes later, she rose, willing herself into motion. She moved tentatively down through the long hill grass, her pants damp and too big, her jacket loose, sweat forming on her neck and back because of the long hair she didn't previously have.

At the base of the hill, she found a dirt path and followed it, remembering the area. She leaped a bubbling stream. She skirted a grove of trees and skidded down an incline, across the railroad tracks, and stopped, staring at the train station—the train station that wasn't there in 2022!

What the hell was happening? She quickly assessed her situation, feeling more energized and alive than she'd felt in years. Her eyes were clear and focused, sharp with vision. Her ears seemed brand-new, her mind was quick, and she'd just descended that hill with little effort, hardly winded.

Hallucination? Possible. Stroke? Maybe. Dead? Doubtful. Time travel? Impossible, especially because she was young again. That wasn't possible, was it? Was time travel even possible? And how old was she? In her early twenties? Barely twenty?

She had to know how far this reality would stretch and what it was going to throw at her. She hurried toward the train station, climbed the outside stairs to the wooden platform, and glanced about.

Travelers waited for the train, two men seated on benches, one smoking a cigarette, the other with his nose in the morning paper. An older couple, simply dressed, stood stoically, their tattered suitcase between them. Three women in fancy dresses chatted with animation, and a young woman paced, licking an ice cream cone.

Kate started for her, pausing about five feet away. "Hello," Kate said in an uncertain voice.

The girl wore frayed bellbottom jeans, a faded yellow T-shirt, a faded jean jacket, and flat leather sandals. Her long, dishwater-blonde hair was pulled back into a braid, and she regarded Kate with dull interest as she continued licking her ice cream cone. She said nothing.

Kate continued. "I've been... well, I haven't been feeling so well and I've sort of lost my way. Can you tell me what day it is?"

The girl's slouching posture lifted, her tongue stopped, and her face pinched in feisty suspicion as she looked Kate up and down. "You must have had a bad trip."

Kate seized on that. "Yeah... well, yeah. Some bad stuff, you know. My boyfriend."

Understanding dawned. "Yeah, well... bastards, you know?" Her tongue flicked at the sides of the melting ice cream.

She stopped, a thought lighting up her eyes. "In another lifetime, I mixed some pills with the whisky my boyfriend gave me. It was like, far out, and it knocked me on my ass. Cops came, and they were fat, ugly and pissy, and they tossed me in jail for a night. 'What the hell?' is what I said to them. They said I needed a bath, and my boyfriend needed a haircut. Pigs, all of them, you know? But that was so, so long ago."

The girl shrugged, and a closer look told Kate that the strange girl, who'd said something about another lifetime, was older than she'd first thought. She might have been about Kate's age—that is, if her current reality really *was* a reality, and she had returned to her twenties.

Kate's smile was fleeting, her nod a girlish,

decadent agreement. "Yeah... That's me right now. I'm like, out of my head or something. So, what's the date?"

After the girl glanced toward the tracks, she turned back, the sunlight bathing her. "It's 1968. Tuesday, September 24."

Kate ceased to see anything clearly.

The girl's voice lowered to a threatening whisper. "You can't change the past, you know."

Kate's spooked eyes expanded on the girl's sudden cruel and cold expression.

With a sneering, crooked grin that made her ugly, she said, "You silly fool."

Kate wavered and staggered back, away from the platform to a wooden bench, and sank down. The girl kept her mouth working on the ice cream cone. She watched Kate with a frosty gaze, and didn't move to help.

While her heart raced and her head throbbed, Kate wrestled with the stark reality of what she'd just heard. The train came thundering into the station, but Kate was only vaguely aware of it as passengers disembarked, as others climbed aboard.

Minutes blurred by. People blurred by. The sun cast shadows and threw planks of yellow light across the platform, while Kate bent over and put her face in her hands.

A voice startled her, and she sat up, dropping her hands, squinting up at him. It was a conductor.

"Are you all right, young lady?"

Kate swallowed and found her voice. "Yeah...

Yeah. I just…"

"Are you a student at the college?"

The question confused Kate. "A student?"

"Yes. Are you a student at Paxton College?"

Kate stared at him, her eyes moving in restless confusion. "Is this 1968?"

The conductor's eyes narrowed, his voice stern. "Do you want me to call the police? What's the matter with you?"

Kate forced herself to sit up, running a hand through her wind-blown hair. "No… No. I just. I'm fine. I just, well, you see, I got lost, but I'm fine now," she said, pushing up. "I'm leaving. Thanks. I'm just fine now."

Kate lowered her head and moved across the platform to the stairs, not looking back as she descended them and started for town.

CHAPTER 31

K ate hurried up the steep sidewalk, past Chamber's Drug Store and out onto Main Street. She knew the way because she'd walked it countless times; she could have walked it blindfolded.

On Main Street, she stopped, stared, then blinked. She saw a 1965 red and white Mustang, a black Ford Fairlane 500, and a blue and cream-colored 1967 Buick Skylark, the same year and model as her father had driven.

The street was lively with traffic, pedestrians, and children waiting on the far corner for a yellow school bus.

Regal's Record shop was there. The Towne Grocery, Kip's Bar, and the bowling alley, all just where they were supposed to be—that is, where they were in 1968, when she was a junior at Paxton College.

Kate wanted to laugh out loud, and she wanted to cry, and she wanted to scream, and she wanted to pray for help. In the morning sunlight, she squinted, searching the street for reasons and answers.

When a well-dressed man approached, wearing a dark suit and tie, a cigarette dangling from his lips, Kate was seized by an impulse, and she waved and hurried over. He stopped.

"Can I please look at your newspaper?" she asked, desperation in her voice. "Just for a minute. I'll give it right back."

He gave her a curious once-over, pulled the paper from the crook of his arm, and handed it to her.

Kate fumbled with the paper, opening it to the front page, her eyes lighting on the date. Tuesday, September 24, 1968. The headline read **VIETNAM WAR BECOMING COSTLY**.

With trembling hands, she returned the newspaper, and the man continued on his way, with a little shake of his head.

From deep in the folds of her brain, Kate recalled a quote from Thomas Wolfe's novel *You Can't Go Home Again*. She'd used it as the opening quotation in one of her novels. It was uncanny how much it applied to her own life right now.

"*They lived like creatures born full-grown into present time, shedding the whole accumulation with the past with every breath, and all their lives were written in the passing of each actual moment.*"

She overrode her doubting mind and set out

along the streets, walking aimlessly, certain the past vision would soon melt away, or that some illumination would reveal the truth, whatever that truth was.

At the corner of Main and Maple, a dinged-up, green and white Ford two-door pickup came clanking and chattering over to the curb and stopped. Kate turned to see the thing, a prominent marijuana leaf decal stenciled on the door.

The driver leaned in her direction, stretched an arm and rolled down the passenger window, his loopy grin and glazed eyes suggesting he'd taken a couple of puffs on some weed with his morning coffee.

"Hey, Kate. What are you doing in town this early? And what's with the clothes? Have you been wrestling in the dirt or something?"

Kate nearly did a double take. It was Luke Parker, the guy her old college roommate, Vicki Allen, had dated.

Luke stared, his shoulder-length, wavy blonde hair trimmed severely at the bangs, the start of a beard not yet successful.

"Want a ride back to the apartment, Kate?"

There was a prolonged interval while Kate struggled to step into Luke's reality. She noticed he waited with contentment, and seemed to live in the NOW, even though that expression wouldn't be popular until many years later.

"Are you just kind of groovin'?" Luke asked, unperturbed.

Kate took a step toward the truck. She couldn't keep hovering on the periphery of craziness any longer. It was time to let go and jump in with both terrified feet.

"Yeah... Yeah, Luke, just kind of hanging out," Kate said stiffly, wiping a strand of hair from her face.

"Okay, yeah. Good, Kate. Yeah, you know? So, do you want a ride to the apartment?"

Kate straightened her spine, glancing around. She had nowhere else to go. "Yes, I would."

"Okay, then get in and let's ride the wild surf, Kate."

The front seat was lumpy, the fabric creased, peeling and tattered. The whole inside of the truck smelled of gasoline and needed a good cleaning, just as she remembered.

As the truck rattled up Main Street, and Luke went grinding through the gears, Kate's right hand gripped the seat so tightly that her knuckles turned white. It had nothing to do with Luke's driving. She was questioning her breakout from the cave, from darkness back into daylight. In those few astounding moments, had she'd experienced a birth into the past, or a death into the past, where everything appeared the same, but nothing *was* quite the same?

Had she been given a new free will to choose a different path from the one she'd chosen the first time around? Or had the story already been written by an unseen novelist, and she would only seem to play her part until the story ended?

It was the mind of the seventy-four-year-old who asked these questions, and not the twenty-year-old, who lacked the life experience to create such thoughts.

The adventure seemed insane and curious and, of course, the outcome was completely unknown. So, she determined to put one foot in front of the other, make her choices—or her apparent choices—and then let the chips fly where they may. What other *choice* did she have?

"So why are you out so early, Kate?" Luke asked.

"I don't know… I mean, what time is it? I don't have my watch."

"It's a little after nine, and I know you're a late sleeper because you like to write late at night. So, what's shakin'?"

Kate fished around for a lie. "I just couldn't sleep, so I did a Charles Dickens."

Luke glanced over, not comprehending. "A what?"

"The author, Charles Dickens, was an insomniac. He used to walk around London all night."

Luke flashed his white teeth with a broad, impressed grin. "Oh yeah, the *Christmas Carol* guy! I know him."

"What's your major, Luke?"

"You know, business stuff and some philosophy."

"So, what are you doing out this early?"

Luke chuckled. "I was doing a Dicky Dickens, too, Kate. I was out by Cove Lake with some buddies, you know, drinking and smoking stuff."

The words Cove Lake struck Kate's ears like a gong. She blurted out, "Cove Lake?"

"Yeah. The cops only patrol it once or twice a night. We took turns on lookout, so it was real smooth and copesetic."

When the truck drove by Mackay's Books New & Old, Kate glanced over. The CLOSED sign still hung in the window and Art was nowhere to be seen. He was probably upstairs in his apartment, late again.

"How's Vicki?" Kate asked, aware that her mind was alive and jumpy. "Is she still singing?" As soon as she'd said it, Kate wanted it back.

"What do you mean, still singing? You must be joking. You know she's singing all the time, like a morning bird high in a tree, she's singing. You know it better than anybody else."

"Yeah, yeah, I know that," Kate said, recovering. "I only meant... well, *where* is she singing?"

Luke flicked her a look. "Whoa, Kate, you are, like, far out this morning. We talked about this a couple of days ago at the apartment. Maybe you need some shut eye. Your mind's all mush or something. You know that Vicki is singing at the Candlelight Coffeehouse this Friday night."

"Oh, yeah! That's right! Yeah, of course. I was just... Yeah, I just need some sleep."

Kate's mind stumbled. What had Luke just said? Two days ago? If she didn't remember what had happened two days ago, but Luke did, then where was the Kate of two days ago? Was she suffering from a weird form of amnesia? Was there another

Kate roaming around somewhere, or had she merged into past Kate, future Kate and present Kate? It was too much to grasp, and she shook the thought away as she glanced at Luke.

"So when's your first class today?"

He checked his watch, winced, and struck the top of the steering wheel with the heel of a hand. "Mother duckie! I don't have time to get a shower. I've got statistics at ten and I can't be late. I hate that class and Professor Bower. He's like a tight-assed drill sergeant or something, you know? The way he paces around the class with his hands locked behind his back, and his flattop haircut, from like the last decade, it just gets to me. He gets all uptight about nothing. I mean, you'd think that those numbers are like his kids or something, and he doesn't want them insulted when you don't know the answer, or just don't give a shit about the answer because it's too damn early. I mean, I can do the work and everything but, I don't know, the guy just gets on my nerves, and you know, most people don't get on my nerves, Kate."

Kate looked at him, nodding. "Yeah... I get that, Luke."

Thoughts of Cove Lake and Paul's trailer distracted her. Would the trailer be there? Would Paul be there?

At the apartment, fortunately, Luke had his key and he let them both in. He hustled off to Vicki's room to change his clothes and then dashed off to his class.

Kate stood in the center of the living room, and the smells triggered memories. There was stale cigarette smoke, the whiff of old pizza from a closed pizza box, which sat on the rickety coffee table, near empty cans of beer. The ashtray was an ugly mound of cigarette butts, sheet music lay scattered on the floor, and Vicki's Martin & Company acoustic guitar was propped on the couch.

Kate moved to the pizza box and lifted the lid, finding a dried-up slice of cheese and pepperoni, long dead. She closed the lid and stood in amazement, her hands on her hips, remembering those days, those overly emotional, improvisational and experimental days.

Inside her bedroom, Kate closed and locked the door, leaning back against it, scanning her room. It was smaller than in her memory, neater than she recalled. And she'd forgotten the 30" x 45" black-framed poster of the writer Flannery O'Connor, which hung on the wall above her single bed.

Then Kate's eyes focused on her portable typewriter, sitting in the middle of her desk. Her smile started small and then expanded. On the right was a stack of blank typewriter paper. On the left was the draft of a short story. The desk was perfectly situated by a window, which looked out on a back yard. How she remembered sitting there! On good writing days, her fingers flew across the keyboard, her mind flooded with plot ideas and character descriptions. On bad days, or whenever she was stuck, she'd stand up and part the cream-colored curtains, letting her mind settle on something outside: a tree, a cloud, a star, a shadow, until an idea struck, and she could return to her writing.

Three years later, in 1971, she would complete her first novel on that typewriter, a novel that had been published when she was twenty-five. Would the same thing happen this time around?

At her tall, pinewood bureau, Kate opened the top drawer and peered inside. There they were: her wallet, her apartment keys, her car keys and the black savings account passbook from the Union National Bank of Ohio. Opening the passbook, she learned she had $238.28 in the bank, at an annual interest rate of 7.5 percent.

Kate held the car keys in her hand—the keys to her light blue and white 1963 Ford Falcon Sprint. She looked up at the ceiling, and then toward the window, feeling anticipation and mystery grow in her. If Paul Ganic was living in his trailer near Cove Lake, then she was in for a shock, or perhaps a life rewind, and a miracle. She'd drive there, but not now. Now she was bone-weary, feeling exhaustion rolling over her in waves.

The bed felt good. It was soft, the pillow deep. Sleep came reaching up for her, pulling her down into currents of watery dreams.

CHAPTER 32

The road to Cove Lake was steeper than Kate remembered, with more curves and trees and potholes. The trees were also closer to the lake than she'd recalled, and their vibrant, multicolored leaves were reflected on the water's surface, creating abstract art.

Kate's Ford Falcon swerved around potholes and thudded over flattened patches of struggling weeds poking out from crevices of old asphalt.

So goes memory, Kate thought. The mind distorts, or forgets, or makes up the past world, so autobiographical nonfiction morphs into fiction.

Kate's every nerve was on alert, her stomach in knots, her mind alive with old thoughts of Paul and Myra, his 'cowgirl' girlfriend, who later became his wife. Myra had a lot of poise, and a smooth confidence that impressed, like a prized thoroughbred.

Kate might have even called Myra's confidence an invincible arrogance, but, then again, Kate's jealousy and her author's mind might have made that up to turn Myra into an antagonist. In fact, the girl was model-attractive, statuesque and intelligent, and she looked fantastic in her cowgirl hat, and cowgirl boots and artistic makeup.

Myra was the reason Kate had scrambled out of sleep on Wednesday morning, disoriented, scared and bewildered, determined to see if Paul was living in his trailer by the lake.

Vicki had pounded on Kate's locked door at seven o'clock that morning to learn if she was dead or alive. Kate hadn't seen her Tuesday afternoon when she woke up from her nap, or that evening, before she dropped into bed again at 10 p.m.

"Are you alive in there?!" Vicki had shouted. "Wake up!"

Ten minutes later, Kate's sleepy, blurry eyes had found Vicki at the kitchen table, smoking and drinking coffee. Kate stared at her old friend, amazed to see her again in the flesh and looking prettier than Kate recalled.

Kate knew that Vicki was going to marry Luke and have three kids. Although it hadn't been the happiest of marriages, they'd made it work. A week before Vicki passed away, at sixty-six years old, from lung cancer, she had told Kate, "Luke is an absent-brained philosophy professor, but he was the best thing that ever happened to me, and it was you who kept us together, you know."

"Me?" Kate had asked.

"You were the one who convinced me to transfer to Ohio State with Luke. If I hadn't, I just know we would have separated."

But to Vicki, who didn't know the future and didn't know that Kate had already lived it, Kate standing in the kitchen with vague, sleepy eyes was normal. It happened every day.

Vicki had a hangover, and she was grumpy, and she had to get ready for class, so Kate kissed her on the cheek.

"I'm glad we're roommates," Kate said, standing back with a smile. "It's nice."

Vicki looked at her as if she had two heads. "What the hell's up with you this morning?"

After a quick bowl of cereal, Kate showered, dressed, bolted out of the apartment and piled into her car.

She was heading to Paul's trailer, hoping to see him before Myra showed up and swept Paul off his feet again, and off to Tucson again. No, not this time!

When Kate rounded the last curve, the Ford Falcon's tires popped across the gravel, a temporary solution to a lousy road, and Kate craned her neck, her pulse rising, her eyes searching. And then, just off to the right, nestled in a clump of trees, she saw it. The trailer! Paul's trailer.

Her excitement was quickly replaced by a tense dread. What if it wasn't Paul living there? What if he was already married? What if she'd gone back in time and Paul Ganic didn't even exist?

But his car was there! It was the same black and white Pontiac! How could she ever forget that?

There was only one way to find out if Paul was real. She nudged the car forward, about thirty feet from the trailer, and pulled over onto the shoulder of brown grass. Kate had a plan. It was a silly plan and a simple plan, but she was sure it would work, that is, if Paul was in his trailer.

Before leaving the car, Kate checked her makeup in the rearview mirror. Lips red, not too red. Not too much eye makeup. A hint of blush on her cheeks. Her teeth? Pearly white. Good.

Kate got out of the car, gently closed the door, and stepped to the rear. She crouched at the right back tire and removed the tire's stem cap. Glancing about, she gently depressed the tip of the valve and listened, as the whispering air escaped, and the tire deflated.

When she was satisfied the tire was flat enough, she replaced the stem cap, pushed up, rubbed her hands together and softly patted her newly washed, 1960s, flip-style hair.

She was pleased with her outfit. The bellbottom jeans hugged her tight tummy. The cranberry cotton blouse was a trim fit. The hip-short woolen jacket showed off her slim hips. The black, blunt-toed boots with two-inch heels gave her height.

Kate started for Paul's trailer, shoulders back, chin held high, feeling an agile body and a sharp mind. But by the time she started up the concrete trailer stairs, she was a doubtful wreck.

Facing the screen door, she saw that the inner door was open, revealing a couch, chair, and table, but no one was about. She swallowed and knocked on the screen door frame. It sounded loud. A male voice called out, "Yeah, who is it?"

And then a head poked out from around the kitchen entrance.

Kate pushed out her voice. "Hello! Can you help me?"

Paul Ganic emerged fully, wiped his hands on a rag, stuffed it into his back pocket, then started toward her.

The impact of seeing him again stopped her breath. He opened the screen door, looking down at her, and her heart set sail.

Kate studied his hero body, the broad shoulders and muscular forearms, the narrow hips, the flat stomach. Even dressed in jeans, a loose, black T-shirt and work boots, there was an aristocratic look about him.

"Hi," he said, his smile friendly and curious. "Did you say you need help?"

Kate's eyes were on his handsome face, absorbing it, trying to absorb the impossibility of the moment.

When Kate didn't speak, Paul did. "Do you need... help?" Paul repeated.

Kate snapped out of it. "Yes... Yes, I need help. Yes, I do."

"Okay... What kind of help?"

"Oh, yes, well, it's my car. I've got a flat. Just outside. I was driving down here and the next thing I knew, the thing must have hit one of those potholes or something, and a tire just went flat, I guess. I mean, yeah, I think that's what happened."

Paul nodded, checking her out. "Okay... Yeah, well, that happens on that poor excuse for a road. I'll tell you what. I was working on my kitchen faucet, so I'm a bit grimy. Let me wash up and I'll meet you out there in five minutes. Okay?"

Kate nodded and smiled, as a beam of morning sun lit up her face.

Paul hesitated, his eyes focusing on her full mouth, moist and red. Her pretty face and her fit, slender body surprised him, and aroused him. He quickly recovered his eyes, aware they had lingered on her much too long to be polite, or so his mother would have said.

"Okay, yeah, well, thanks. I'll be standing over there near the car then," Kate said.

Standing by the Falcon, she waited, paced, and worried. What words could she use to interest him? Should she try to be funny? No, she wasn't so funny. Should she ask a lot of questions? No, nobody liked a blabbering, nosy girl. Paul was twenty-five, and he'd been to Vietnam. But she was seventy-four years old, as weird as that sounded, and she had tons of life experience.

The problem? She was fighting the hormones, impulsiveness, and desires of a twenty-year-old, and the twenty-year-old was winning.

Paul came from the trailer and started toward her, a man of easy grace, with an easy smile. When he saw her car, his eyes widened in pleasure.

"Well, look at this! What a beauty!" Paul said, reaching out to stroke the body. "It's a 1963 Ford Falcon."

"Do you like it?" Kate asked, knowing the answer, but anxious to get something started.

Paul stepped back and pocketed his hands, appraising it. "Back in 1960, Chevrolet had the Corvair, and Plymouth had the Valiant, but they were a little more expensive, and for my money, the Ford Falcon was the best car, and the best-looking car. Oh, I see it's leaning a bit over there. Let's have a look."

At the right back tire, Paul lowered to his haunches, running a hand over the tire. "There's no damage that I can see."

He squinted up at her. "You say you hit a pothole?"

"Yeah, right over there," Kate pointed. "Yeah, over there somewhere. I mean, there are a lot of potholes so... well, I don't know which one," she said, hearing her stupid, scatterbrained words, and hoping Paul didn't think she was a bimbo.

"Well, it looks to me like you're just low on air. The tire looks fine. In fact, the tire looks new."

Paul rose, putting hands on his hips. "Simple. You just need some air."

Kate glanced about, playing dumb. "Can I drive it like that to a gas station?"

"No, you shouldn't. Tire pressure *that* low can lead to a blowout, which isn't good. Do you have a spare? I can change it for you."

Kate batted her eyes, looking befuddled. "Oh, yeah, I think so."

Kate opened the trunk and, sure enough, a good spare waited under the carriage bolt, retaining plate and nut.

"Looks good," Paul said. "I'll have it changed for you in no time. Then take the low-pressure tire to Pete's Texaco Service Station up the road, about three miles."

Kate stood by with crossed arms and a fluttering heart, while Paul quickly jacked up the car, replaced the tire, and had the old tire bolted inside the trunk in about ten minutes.

"Wow, that was fast," Kate said, as Paul closed the trunk, then wiped his hands on a rag he'd pulled from his back pocket.

"Yeah, easy. By the way, my name is Paul Ganic," he said, with an outstretched hand.

Kate took his big hand and shook it, and, at the touch, she felt faint, and all those fifty-odd years just melted away.

She breathed in. "I'm Kate Clarke. Nice to meet you, and thank you so much. I owe you something. Money?... I don't know, or maybe a burger and a beer? My treat."

Paul thought about it, while Kate was sure her tight, hopeful grin looked goofy.

Paul nodded. "I might just take you up on that, but it will be *my* treat."

"No. No way," Kate said. "You helped me."

"Yeah, but I'm kind of old-fashioned."

"This is the 1960s, Paul," Kate tossed back. "It's a whole new world, and I'm a whole new girl... even if I didn't know how to change a tire."

Paul's steady eyes evaluated her. "Do you think so? I mean, about the whole new girl thing? I've never heard that expression before."

Kate was at a loss for words, so she shrugged a shoulder.

They stared, eager strangers, their uncertain eyes moving.

"Okay, Kate. I'll let you pay this time, but then I'll owe *you* one."

Kate wanted to leap up and scream out, "YES!" But she didn't. Her smile was measured, a bit flirtatious. "Are you a student?"

"Yeah? You?"

Kate nodded. "Yeah."

"Fancy meeting like this."

"Yeah. Fancy," Kate said, holding him in her eyes. "Real fancy."

Paul smiled at her. "And you with this Falcon. A real beauty."

"When?" Kate asked, falling under the dreamy spell of his probing eyes.

"What about tomorrow night? I have to work until seven. Say about 7:30?"

"Sounds good," Kate said, her smile widening. "Should we meet at the Pizza Place in town?"

Paul allowed his gaze to focus on her parted lips, and he had the sudden impulse to pull her into his arms and kiss her.

"Pizza Place?" he asked, distracted. "Yeah, sure. Why not? Are you of age... to drink?"

"I'm twenty. I can drink the Near-beer stuff."

Paul glanced toward the river and then back at her. "Okay, Kate Clarke. I'll be there. Be sure to get that spare tire inflated."

She saluted him. "Yes, sir! Right away, sir."

Paul laughed low in his throat, cocked his head right, and slanted a smile. "I think I like you, Kate."

Kate had waited more than fifty years to hear those words, and they nearly brought tears.

Her smile was shy. "Yeah... me, too."

"By the way," Paul said, his forehead wrinkling. "Why were you driving way down here?"

Kate had an answer. She pointed. "The lake. It's my quiet place when my head gets all messed up."

Paul waved as the Falcon drove away, the distant sound of the car engine fading into the breathing wind that encircled the trees.

Paul whispered to himself. "Kate Clarke, why does it feel like I've known you before?"

CHAPTER 33

O n Thursday afternoon, just as Kate was leaving her literature class and heading to work, she met Connie Poe in the hallway. Connie had been Kate's dorm mate during her sophomore year. She was a good artist, but very insecure about her work, and so Kate had always tried to encourage her.

"Your work is good, Connie. You should get out there and show it around," Kate had said more than once, but Connie was too petrified to do so.

"It's ordinary, Kate. It isn't original or anything."

"It's original to me, and if it's original to me, then it will be to others. Just take a risk and get your work out there. What have you got to lose?"

"What if people hate it?"

"Some will love it, and some won't. That's just the way things are, Connie. You can't please everybody. Just do it."

In the hallway, Connie took Kate by the elbow and

led her over to a bank of windows that looked out on manicured walkways and a stalwart bronze statue of William Paxton himself.

Kate hesitated. "I've got to get to the bookstore, Connie. What's up?"

Connie's large blue eyes filled with angst. "I need you to go with me."

"Go with you where?"

"To the gift shop."

"Why the gift shop?"

"You said I should take a risk and show my paintings, so I thought I'd take a few to the gift shop in town and see if the owner will agree to display and sell them."

Kate leaned back, staring into Connie's freckled face, at her wide, scared eyes and at her mouth, moving side-to-side, as it always did when she got nervous.

"Okay... why the gift shop? Why now?" Kate asked.

"Because I've been thinking about what you said... about getting out there. Well, I was in that gift shop yesterday, and I saw some seascapes on the wall. They're just one notch above those paint-by-number paintings, with seagulls and puffy clouds, and the ocean waves sliding up the beach. I figure, if he's selling those, maybe he'll sell mine."

Kate glanced at her watch, the one she'd found in her desk drawer only that morning. A wonderful morning! She had sprung out of bed like an Olympic gymnast and dashed over to her typewriter and written two pages of awful, gushing prose, describing her excitement about her upcoming date with Paul.

"Connie, do you really need me to go with you? I'll be late to the bookstore, and I haven't seen Art in fif..." Kate stopped when she realized she was about to say she hadn't seen Art in fifty years.

Lost in her own anxiety, Connie didn't notice. "I need your strength and support, Kate. You said you'd go with me."

"I don't remember saying that."

"Okay, so you didn't say that, but will you please go with me? Please? I can't do this alone."

Kate saw the pleading, puppy-dog look in Connie's eyes and recalled the times, early in her career in the future, when she'd sent manuscripts to countless agents and received countless rejections. It had been demoralizing.

Kate blew out a sigh. "Okay, Connie, but let's hurry."

"Right on, Kate! The paintings are already in my car. You always were my best friend."

That surprised Kate, since she'd lost track of Connie in the future, when they were in their forties. Connie had not succeeded as an artist. She'd ended up marrying an older man, moving to St. Louis, and working as a restaurant manager.

As they climbed into Connie's orange Volkswagen bug, Kate remembered that the first time around, she hadn't accompanied Connie to the gift shop. She'd said she was too busy. This time, she could make it up to her. And maybe this time, if Connie could gain some confidence, she would succeed as a professional artist.

The New World Gift and Stationery Store was painted sea blue and white. It had large front and side windows to let in natural light, and the generous room was artfully designed with glass shelves exhibiting handmade jewelry, unique gifts, one-of-a-kind pottery sculptures, mugs, vases and bowls. In the back area, shelves were meticulously arranged to display greeting cards, wrapping paper, fountain pens, boxes of pencils, journals, sketchpads, notebooks and diaries.

And as Connie had said, there was a variety of seascape paintings hanging on the walls, lit by natural light. Kate noticed how incongruous they were with the autumn Ohio countryside spread out around them.

The owner, Noel Cross, was a small, thin man in his late fifties, with short, white hair and a Sigmund Freud white goatee. He wore dark, creased pants, a crisp, white shirt, and a light blue tie. His wingtip shoes were polished to a fine gloss, and his wire-framed glasses gave him a professorial appearance.

Kate and Connie entered the store, Connie toting two 16" x 12" paintings wrapped in brown paper. Kate carried two larger paintings, 24" x 18".

Although Kate had shopped in New World in her past life, she didn't remember it being so refined and tasteful, and she was impressed. But Connie was looking up and scowling at the inflated prices of the generic seascapes.

Noel approached them haltingly, sensing something distasteful was about to unfold; something that wouldn't make him money. His thin, tight mouth and moving, observant eyes suggested frugality. "May I help you, ladies?" he said crisply, his flat gray eyes settling on them.

Connie trembled, and her throat worked, tension making it hard to swallow or to speak, so Kate spoke up. "Hello, sir. Are you the owner?"

He nodded, keeping his hands at his sides and his sharp nose upturned. "I am."

"Well, first, let me compliment you on your lovely shop."

Noel didn't respond. He reluctantly lowered his eyes to the wrapped paintings Kate and Connie had propped against their legs. He frowned with suspicion. He didn't look at Kate, but around her, as if avoiding her eyes.

"My friend here, Connie, is a wonderful artist," Kate said. "Her paintings are artistic, but they also have commercial appeal, and I think the people in this town would love them. People of all ages, and from different backgrounds."

Noel's eyes hooded over. "Well, how nice, but I'm afraid that I'm..."

"... Here, take a look at one," Kate said, cutting him off. She removed the brown paper and held the painting high into the light. "See how familiar and yet unique this is? Artistic but approachable. Comforting, even. I know it will sell."

Noel held up a hand. "I'm sorry. I'm just not interested." He indicated toward the walls. "I already have a shop full of paintings."

Kate was undaunted. "But this is an oil painting of an early morning on Cove Lake, sir, with wild geese, autumn trees and moving, gilded skies."

"Yes, I can see that. I have excellent vision, notwithstanding my glasses."

Undaunted, Kate continued. "Cove Lake is local, and I think people will love that. It's particular to Paxton, and not just any old generic ocean, beach, and seagull. Connie would give you whatever percentage you want. Could you please just hang a few of her paintings for a few months and see if they sell?"

Noel shook his head vigorously. "No, I'm sorry. I won't. I'm not interested. Not at all."

Just then, Noel's attention was diverted by the opening front door. Two older women entered and turned to examine a piece of pottery displayed in the front window, a light blue and purple, curvaceous, textured vase. One reached for it and held it up to the light, turning it this way and that.

Noel started toward them, his mouth tightening. "Ladies, please be careful with that vase. It is an original. Very expensive."

The two ladies glared at him, and one spoke indignantly. "We are *always* careful. We are retired school teachers!"

Mr. Cross sighed and turned back to Kate, just as she hoisted another unwrapped painting of

Cove Lake. It featured a glorious, golden sunset, a rowboat on placid, glittering water, and a fisherman hunched over his fishing rod. In the background, nestled in the shadow of trees, was a distant trailer. Kate straightened, suddenly realizing the trailer was Paul's!

"Hey, wait a minute. That's Paul's trailer!" Kate exclaimed. "*I'll* buy this one."

Connie glanced at Kate. "What? Who?"

"You must have painted this near Paul's trailer."

"Who's Paul?"

At that incredible moment, Kate glanced out the window, seeing Paul walk swiftly past the shop, obviously in a hurry, his hands deep in his pockets, his expression preoccupied. On impulse, Kate thrust the painting to Connie, and was about to dash off after him, but then stopped, thinking better of it. If he had an appointment, he wouldn't have time to talk, and, anyway, she hadn't finished the business with Connie and Noel. Still, it was odd—that synchronistic moment!

Noel turned irritable. "Ladies, will you please take your paintings and go? I tell you, I'm not interested." His jaw was set. His arms folded. His dark, bird-like eyes said, "No."

As Connie's shoulders sagged, one woman who'd been admiring the vase ventured over, staring at the painting which Connie was holding.

She was a heavy woman, with stony features and perceptive eyes. She looked at Connie. "Will you hold that one up, please?"

Connie lifted the morning Cove Lake painting with both hands, her face hidden.

"It's good, isn't it?" Kate said enthusiastically.

"Did you paint this, young lady?"

"No, my friend Connie did."

The woman inclined her head forward, scrutinizing the painting. "Well, I like the composition and your choice of colors. The wings on the geese are quite expert. It's difficult to paint wings, and I like the foam-like clouds and the glazed autumn leaves. Yes, I like that very much. I have sat beside that lake many times in my life."

Connie lowered the painting, her eyes filled with burning hope. The woman looked directly at Connie. "This painting is not like the average paintings you find in this kind of shop. It's got originality, and yet it looks familiar."

Noel scowled. "Ladies, will you please conduct your business somewhere other than in my shop?"

The second lady drifted over, her thin body and moving eyes suggesting a nervous nature. She presented the vase to Noel with a little lift of her imperious head, and, in a commanding voice, she said, "Gift wrap it!"

Noel stammered. "You... You want to buy it?"

"I wouldn't ask you to gift wrap it if I didn't want to buy it, would I?!"

Noel's annoyed expression fell into boyish pleasure. "Well, of course, I'll wrap it for you. Yes, right away."

"And put it in a sturdy box, with white or blue

wrapping paper," the woman said. "And use a fine, generous ribbon. I love a good, generous ribbon."

"Yes, ma'am," Noel said, offering a head bow, and then retreating to the glass counter.

The woman turned to her friend, who was now appraising two of Connie's other paintings. "What have we got here, Helen?" she asked.

"I like these, Margie. They speak to me. What do you think?"

"Yes, they've got something. A touch of the whimsy. A little different."

Helen said, "Could you ladies hold those two up a bit higher, and into the light?"

Connie held one up, Kate the other.

Helen twisted up her lips in thought. "Margie... What do you think? I think they would be a perfect addition to my sitting room."

Margie nosed in closer. "I like the blue boat on the bank, and the girl waving on the dock. Yes, I like that one. It reminds me of my daughter."

Helen added, "And those ducks flying into the sunlight, with those storm clouds coming in. Very dramatic."

Helen took a step toward Connie, her mind made up. "How much do you want for the ducks and the storm clouds?"

Connie stammered. "Oh... I... Well, I'm not sure."

Noel Cross called from the counter. "It's worth fifteen dollars."

Helen shook her head. "Too much. I'll give you ten."

Connie lit up. "You mean you'll buy it?"

Helen jerked a nod. "For ten dollars I'll buy it."

Mr. Cross paused his wrapping. "I tell you, that painting is worth fifteen dollars."

Margie glared at him in a challenge. "A minute ago, you were about to send this girl and her paintings packing. Now you say the painting is worth fifteen dollars?"

Connie spoke up, excited. "You can have it for ten," she said, handing it to Helen.

Helen's face held a pondering, fixed grimace. "Do you know what? I'll take the other three as well. Fifteen each for the two larger paintings and ten each for the smaller ones."

"Helen... at least let me have the blue boat and the girl," Margie quipped.

Noel Cross' voice took on force. "This is my shop. If you are going to conduct business in my shop, you will pay the price I dictate."

Margie lifted her chin in defiance. "Then we will conduct our business outside and I will not purchase that one-of-a-kind, very expensive vase!"

Mr. Cross wilted in defeat. "All right... All right. Do it and be done with it."

Margie strolled over to Noel. "Sir, I believe you would be doing yourself a favor if you hang this young woman's paintings in your shop. I, for one, will tell my friends, and they have friends and family. And Helen and I have many former students. You appear to be a smart and practical man, and I say, there is money to be made in these paintings."

Noel gave her a considering sidelong glance and then scratched his cheek. His smile was strained, his manner polite. "Well... perhaps, on your very generous and knowledgeable suggestion, I will hang some of the paintings. Not many, mind you, but some, and then we'll see how they sell. No promises."

Kate and Connie exchanged muted triumphant glances, and Connie wanted to scream out in joy.

As they drove back to the college, Connie was happier than Kate had ever seen her.

"Thanks, again, Kate. I can't believe it. I can't believe how high I am. Oh, and I have another painting of the lake for you at my apartment... and it has the trailer in it."

"Is it like the one you just sold?"

"It's better. It has this big, oozing yellow sun hovering over Cove Lake trees, washing the world in yellows and bright orange. White popcorn clouds are edged with purple and pink, and the lake is cobalt blue, with reflecting shards of sunlight. And the trailer's even bigger in this painting."

Kate faced her. "Really?"

"Yeah. And it's kind of lit up from within, and there's a woman, from the waist up, peering out the picture window, with golden blonde hair in a halo around her pretty face."

"Blonde?" Kate asked, troubled.

"Yeah, when I was painting it about two weeks ago, that's what I saw, a blonde. And she wore a cowgirl hat. But I didn't paint that."

Kate stiffened, turned, and stared straight ahead. Was Myra back in town? Is that who Paul was rushing off to see? Was it already too late? Again, too late?

CHAPTER 34

When Kate entered Mackay's Books New & Old, Art was standing by the coffee station, his pipe in one hand, a Styrofoam cup of coffee in the other. Wearing his spectacles and the usual overalls and sneakers, and with his hair pulled back in a gray ponytail, he stared at her with a snide expression.

There he was, clear, present and alive again. He studied her and she studied him. Kate detected an unarticulated sadness in Art that she'd never noticed before. She'd always assumed he was just a cranky old guy who took the world as it was, espousing sardonic witticisms to entertain and shock. The older Kate saw much more going on behind Art's mischievous eyes. She saw a troubled, scared and lonely man, who used words and a crusty exterior to protect himself from the world. But Art also possessed a quiet strength, along with an internalized complexity that the 20-year-old Kate had not been aware of.

Art said, "Well, as my old, cantankerous, whiskey-drinking, loud mouth of a father used to say, 'It's better to arrive late than to arrive ugly.'"

Art took a sip of his coffee. "And you, Kate, certainly ain't ugly."

Kate smiled, a beautiful smile that transformed her face from tense worry over Paul and the cowgirl, to pure joy at seeing Art again. "So, am I forgiven?"

"Always. Hey, I'm just glad you show up at all."

Kate went to him in a rush, going for a hug. With an astonished expression, he spread his arms wide, coffee cup in one hand, pipe in the other, letting her wrap him with her arms.

"Whoa, what's this all about?"

Kate squeezed him with joy, thrilled to see him again. When she released him, she stepped back, looking him over with a big grin. "You smell the same and look the same, and you make me happy, just as you always did."

Art leaned his head back and looked at her narrowly. "What in the hell have you been drinkin' or smokin' or ingestin' there, kid?"

"Nothing, Art. It's nothing I can explain to you."

"We have time. It's been slow. We've got one customer, somewhere in the back, in non-fiction, and she's been back there forever."

Kate glanced in that direction. "Maybe I should go see if she needs help?"

"So go, and help away," Art said, with a push of his

hand. "Go and earn your keep, you crazy girl in the good mood."

Kate started off, passed three aisles and turned right, stopping dead in her tracks. A girl lay sprawled on the floor. "Art! Art! Come quick!"

By the time Art hurried down the aisle, Kate was kneeling beside the girl, staring into her sickly, wan face, the girl's breath shallow and uneven.

"What's the matter with her, Kate?"

Kate made a sound of anguish and threw a hand up to cover her mouth. "Oh, God!"

"What!?" Art exclaimed, lowering to his knees.

Kate looked at Art with alarm.

"Do you know her?"

Kate did know her, or, at least, she'd seen her. It was the same girl she'd seen at the train station on Tuesday, after she'd left the cave. She'd been licking an ice cream cone. And she was dressed the same, in frayed, bellbottom jeans, a faded yellow T-shirt, a faded jean jacket, and brown leather sandals. Kate had asked what the date was, and the girl had stared at her coldly and said, "You can't change the past, you know."

Art placed two fingers at her neck. "Damn! She's got a pulse, but it's faint. Call an ambulance. I think she's overdosed."

Later, after the ambulance jumped away from the curb, siren wailing, Kate and Art stood near the front door of the bookstore, watching the curious crowds slowly disperse. Two stern-looking cops had arrived, taken down Art's and Kate's statements and left without saying much. Kate told them she didn't know the girl, and Art shrugged and said, "What do I know? I guess she overdosed on Jack Kerouac."

The cops weren't amused, and neither was Kate.

When they were back inside, Kate sat in the high-back chair near the door and Art went to the counter, reached beneath it and tugged out a half-drunk pint of whiskey. Two paper coffee cups were handy, so he unscrewed the whiskey bottle cap and splashed some in. He took one cup to Kate and held the other to his lips, his eyes staring ahead.

"What is it with your generation, Kate? Head-in-the-clouds ideas. Music full of protest and anger. Tripping out and dropping out."

Kate tossed back the booze in a gulp, then held the cup in both hands, staring into it. "In the future, things won't look as radical as they were described. Believe me, things get worse."

Art grappled with her words. "What are you talking about? You're acting strange today."

Kate made a vague gesture with her hand. "Nothing... forget it. I don't know what I'm saying."

"But you knew that girl, Kate. You recognized her."

"Not really. I met her the other day, on the train platform. We exchanged a few words."

"And?"

"And nothing. That's it. Have you ever seen her before?"

Art sipped his drink. "Nope."

Kate rose. "I've got to go see her."

"See her? Why?"

"What if she doesn't have anybody?"

"The police will take care of that. They'll find her family. Those cops said there's been a lot of this kind of thing going on lately, with kids out of their heads on junk."

Kate tossed her cup into the wastebasket. "I have to go, Art. You're not that busy, anyway, so I don't think you really need me, right?

He shrugged. "So, go, already, but before you do, I want to say something."

Kate's eyes opened fully on him. "Okay... Shoot."

"You're different."

Kate didn't answer.

"Can't put my finger on it. But you're different from the last time I saw you, which was on Sunday."

"I changed my hair."

"Yes, but that's not it. By the way, the flip style thing makes you look older."

"So maybe I am older."

"Okay, maybe you are. But you've changed... something."

Kate stuck her nose in the air. "What's that smell?"

"What smell?"

Kate grinned and winked. "*It smells like the left wing of the day of judgment.*"

Art went into thought, staring down at the floor. "Wait a minute, I know that quote."

A minute later, his head jerked up, eyes flashing with recognition. "Got it! *Moby Dick*! Melville!"

Kate rushed to him and went to tiptoes, kissing him on the cheek. His eyes went wide with surprise. Kate whirled about and started for the door. Turning back, she said, "I've missed you, Art. No one else in my entire life recognized that quote."

"Yeah, and don't think I didn't notice how you skillfully changed the subject and how you just kissed me on the cheek."

He pointed at her. "Never before have you done that, Kate Clarke. Now get out of here, you crazy kid."

Paxton Medical Center was a three-story brick structure with a parking lot on one side and an ER entrance/exit on the other, where two ambulances were parked. The smell of freshly cut lawn, mixed with the scent of fallen leaves, caused noses to lift as people entered and exited the building. Two window washers on scaffolding worked the wide windows, which glinted in the late afternoon sun.

At the wide lobby desk, Kate explained to a uniformed nurse who she was and why she was there. The nurse had no news and told her to sit in the waiting room while she investigated. Kate snuggled down into a comfortable chair and was floating on the surface of sleep when a silver-haired doctor appeared, wearing a white coat and a stethoscope around his neck.

Kate sat up, then rose.

"I'm Doctor Gosser. I understand you found Jodi Sayers unresponsive in the bookstore?"

"Yes... I'm Kate Clarke."

"I saw the police report. You said you don't know Jodi? Is that correct?"

"That's right."

Dr. Gosser had a thin, peering face and a bit of a paunch. "And you want to see Miss Sayers?"

"Yes... Were you able to find any family?" Kate asked.

"No. She had no identification on her. No purse, wallet, or money, but in slurring speech she managed to give her full name when she was admitted to the ER."

"May I talk to her?"

"I'm afraid not. She overdosed on Librium. We pumped her stomach, and she's sleeping. She was lucky you found her when you did. Another ten minutes and she would have died. What do you want to talk to her about?" Dr. Gosser said, cocking a wary eye.

Kate glanced away. "I just thought she might need a friend, that's all."

"She might indeed, in a day or so, especially if we can't find any next of kin. And she'll have to have a psychiatric evaluation."

Kate stared down at the gray tile floor, wishing she could be in the room for that. Would Jodi mention time travel in her evaluation, since she seemed to know that Kate had time traveled?

"Are you a student at the college?"

"Yes."

"Well, I'd give it two days, maybe try again on

Saturday afternoon. By then, Jodi might be ready to see visitors."

Kate nodded, thanked the doctor, and left the hospital. In the car, the breeze moved Kate's hair as she drove back to the apartment to shower and dress for her date with Paul. She swallowed a heaviness. What was Jodi doing in the bookshop? Looking for her? Why?

Kate had so many questions, but she focused on one, as painful as it was. Had Paul already decided to move to Tucson and marry Myra? Connie had painted Myra two weeks before, so she and Paul had already been together by then. Events weren't unfolding as they had previously in 1968, but would the ending be the same? Would Paul leave?

CHAPTER 35

The Pizza Place was a bustling spot, with interior colors of rust and yellow, a thumping jukebox, and college kids munching pizza and reaching for pitchers of beer. There was a front square room, where the main ovens were, and a larger back room, where one wall displayed a burnished metallic gold fresco of a quaint Neapolitan village, where hooded women with toothy grins hauled baskets of glistening red tomatoes.

Paul was in the crowded back room, and that's where Kate found him, flipping through a newspaper, seated at an orange plastic table for two. For just a second, Kate wondered why he wasn't staring into his cell phone. The thought swiftly vanished when he glanced up at her, giving her an alluring, slanted smile, tipping her world slightly out of focus, as if a dream had come to life.

Paul set his newspaper aside and rose when Kate approached.

"Hi, there," he said, his deep blue and black flannel shirt setting off his blue eyes.

Kate wore jeans, a blouse in a soft shade of gold, an open forest green jacket and platform shoes. After they were seated, she sought to calm her nerves and racing heart.

"So, you're early," she said, filling up the sudden silence.

"The Marines and my father," Paul said, with a little shrug. "Both good teachers who insisted that the early way is the only way."

Kate glanced at her watch, then exhaled an exaggerated breath of relief. "Whoo. Then I just made it. No demerits."

Paul grinned. "And with seconds to spare. No KP for you tonight."

"The music's pretty loud," Kate hollered, but she recognized the song and started moving her body to the beat, humming along until the refrain started and she remembered some of the words. "*Lonely days...* da,... da da da da da da... *My baby* da da da *letter.*"

"*The Letter* by the Box Tops," Kate said, smiling. "I remember."

Paul looked surprised. "Remember?"

"Well... It was a while ago."

"Last year."

Kate shrugged. "Seems like a long time to me."

Paul laughed. "Okay, Kate Clarke. I'm going to

agree with you on that one. I was still in Vietnam, and that seems like years ago, and it seems like days ago."

Kate leaned forward so she wouldn't have to shout. "Time is crazy, isn't it? Fast, slow, young, old."

"Okay. Sure... I'm twenty-five years old and I wonder where the last three years of my life went."

"You're not so old, Mr. Ganic."

A whooping cheer came from the front room, and then gales of laughter.

Paul nodded toward the sounds. "I'm not *that* young anymore."

"They haven't been to war," Kate said, more seriously than she'd meant to.

"Good for them. I'm glad. Drink up, boys, and don't worry about the snipers and the mines."

Paul rearranged his mood. "Okay, enough of that kind of talk. Let's have fun. What should we order?"

She looked at him with a question. "Were you a good soldier?"

"I tried to be, but it wasn't so easy over there. Now, let's focus on pizza."

Kate gave him a keen appraisal. "Any brothers or sisters?" She couldn't remember, and she wondered why.

"A sister. Older. Left the nest young and moved to Alaska. She doesn't stay in touch with any of us, Mom, Dad, or me. And you? Brothers? Sisters?"

Kate spread her hands. "Just me. Only child." She made a funny face of apology. "Maybe a little spoiled..."

Paul thought, *Why does she seem so familiar? Why do I feel so attracted to her?*

And then a bright flare of white light exploding behind his eyes startled him. In a watery vision, he stepped out of glass doors into a vast, fragrant and familiar world where he and Kate knew each other intimately, their wishes, their moods, their bodies. They were together, close and touching, lying on a thick carpet of green grass, golden sun lighting up the surrounding trees. He heard Kate's gentle, caressing voice in his ear, and he was aware of her scented skin and the erotic touch of her fingers, stroking the tension out of him.

And then they were making love, naked and hot, she above him, her body yielding to his. Her mouth came down on his silken lips, the tenderest of flesh, a thundering pulse, a mounting desire to join. Their bodies curved and rose and cushioned and loved. For soaring moments, he was suspended in passion, and then he fell off the edge of the world.

The vision shattered, and Paul shook it off, his forehead damp with sweat, his body warm and pulsing.

He saw Kate gazing at him from across the table, slowly coming back into focus. He stared at her, bewildered, feeling awkward, wondering what had just happened to him. It hadn't been just a sexual fantasy. It had seemed like a real memory.

"What's the matter?" Kate asked. "You just kind of tuned out. Are you okay?"

Paul recovered, pushing a hand through his short

hair, forcing a twitchy grin. "… Yeah. Nothing. Just… Nothing."

After he'd returned from Vietnam, he'd had nightmares, but what he'd just experienced hadn't been a nightmare, and he wasn't asleep. He shook it off, running a hand across his mouth, resetting his shoulders. "We should order. I think I'm hungry… I haven't eaten since breakfast, and I'm a little light-headed."

They ordered a pitcher of Near-beer, a large pizza with extra cheese, mushrooms and pepperoni, and, at the last moment, Kate decided on a salad, something she would have never eaten with pizza the first time she was twenty years old.

While they ate and shared small talk, Paul fell under Kate's spell, and he had no other word to describe it. There was an energy about her that comforted him, attracted him, but also confused him.

They left the Pizza Place, falling into silence as they strolled the sidewalk, eventually ending up at the town square, sitting on a bench inside the gazebo. The town lay before them in shop lights, in mild traffic, and in kids playing tag on the green. A black-and-white dog joined the kids, snapping at their heels, romping and circling.

"I missed all this when I was away," Paul said, leaning forward, his hands folded.

Kate did a little fishing to learn more about Myra. "Would you ever leave… move somewhere else?"

"I've been thinking about it."

Kate unconsciously put a hand on her cool cheek, troubled. "And where would you go?"

"Arizona, maybe. I haven't made up my mind."

"Why Arizona?" Kate asked, knowing the answer.

Paul looked at her. "After I was discharged, I drove around the U.S., to sort of restore myself and forget the war. I met a girl in Tucson, and she came for a visit a while back."

Kate turned her eyes away. "I've never been to Tucson."

"Nice place. Nice people."

"When would you go?" Kate asked, already feeling a mood come on. Already feeling a little panicky. Had she come back in time just to repeat the same events? Why? For what purpose? Was there anything she could do to change the outcome?

"Like I said, I haven't decided."

And then Kate heard herself say, "I wish you wouldn't go."

She hadn't planned to say it, and it wasn't like her to say it, but she wasn't sorry. Time was not on her side.

Paul's eyes came to hers. "We've just met."

"I know... Don't care."

He didn't turn away. "I want to see you again, Kate. I mean, after tonight."

Kate's lips curved into a meager smile. "Me, too. See you again, I mean."

"And I'd like to read some of your stories you talked about at dinner."

Kate pulled up the collar of her jacket. "I don't

know…"

"Shy?"

"Maybe. My writing gets better later on."

"What does that mean? Later on?"

Kate laughed a little. "It means I've written about you."

Paul sat up. "About me?"

"Yeah. Why not about you?"

"I hope I'm not the bad guy, and I hope I get the girl in the end."

Kate laughed again. "So, maybe you *are* the bad guy. Bad guys are sometimes the most fun characters to write about."

"So, I don't get the girl?" he asked, his meaning personal.

Kate's eyes warmed, her voice as soft as silk. "Oh, yes, you get the girl, all right."

Paul offered a teasing smile. "And does that girl and me live happily ever after?"

Kate felt hope and anxiety in equal measure. "I think so. I hope so. I'd say it's a mystery. You're a mystery."

Paul clapped his hands. "Oh! Great! Good! I've always wanted to be a mystery. And, incidentally, you're a mystery to me, too."

Kate's anxious attention turned toward two boys rolling in the grass, and a dog darting about, barking at them.

"Two mysteries, we are, Paul Ganic."

"Can I see you this weekend, Kate?"

"Yes."

"What should we do?" Paul asked, fixing his eyes on her.

"Anything. Maybe a picnic."

"Good. I've got the perfect place."

"Up near the cave?"

"The cave?"

"There are caves around here, you know."

"Yeah, I know, but I have a better idea. There's a pretty little town about fifty miles from here, near the Ohio River, called Cane Creek."

"Okay. Works for me."

Paul walked Kate back to her parked car near the Pizza Place, and their bodies drifted ever closer, each feeling the magnetic pull of attraction. They lingered at the car, neither wanting to part, their conversations touching on classes and teachers, and movies and music.

Did she like classical? Yes, Mozart and Chopin. He liked Bach and Brahms. They both liked Simon and Garfunkel, Bob Dylan and Diana Ross.

Two girls passed, licking ice cream cones, and Kate thought of Jodi.

Paul pointed to the Paxton Sweet Shop, across the street. "Want an ice cream?"

Kate smiled and nodded, grateful not to part. "Yeah. I do."

They strolled, Kate with two scoops of chocolate chip in a cup, Paul with two mounds of strawberry on a sugar cone.

When there was a pause, Paul blurted out. "I could ask you back to my trailer."

They stared eye to eye.

"And I'd go," Kate said.

After another silence, Paul said, "This is going to sound like a line, Kate, but I feel like I've known you before, and I don't know what it means."

Kate stared ahead. "You're right, it does sound like a line. But I don't care. This feels right, doesn't it? It feels right and good and safe. I feel safe with you, and I feel... well, I feel at home with you."

Paul stared at his ice cream. "Yeah... but I feel mixed up."

"Who doesn't?"

"You, too?"

"Yeah."

"What is it?"

"You and me."

He stopped, gazing at her meaningfully. "Like I said before, we've just met, Kate."

"I don't think so."

"Then what? What are you saying?"

"That I've waited a long time for this night."

He shook his head. "I don't know. There's something going on here and I just don't get it."

"Then don't get it. Feel it. Go with it."

By the time they reached Kate's car, Paul had finished his ice cream cone.

"What time Saturday?" Kate asked.

"Ten o'clock, rain or shine."

"Okay. I'll meet you at the trailer?"

He nodded.

Kate ran a hand through her hair, still not

wanting to part. "I had fun."

"Yeah, me, too. And don't worry about the food for the picnic. I've got it covered."

Kate drove away, hearing thunder. By the time she reached her apartment, rain pelted down. She watched the rain wash the windshield, and something in her remembered a rainy night and she remembered a car and a bridge. She remembered dark, cold water, and she shivered.

A kind of wildness moved inside her, and the nudge of a warning that she should run for her life. But run where? No, she wouldn't go anywhere without Paul.

CHAPTER 36

On Saturday morning, Kate shook awake and braced herself up on her elbows. A dream still hovered in the air around her. She'd been an elderly woman, a successful novelist, and she'd lived in New York. The dream had seemed so real and so eerie. Her books had been in bookstores and in airports, and on the internet, but she wasn't quite sure what "internet" meant. And she'd traveled to book signings, and she'd even been on several national talk shows.

An idea for a story seized her—one that had taken shape the night before, while she sat in her car during the rain storm. Kate scrambled out of bed and checked her bedside clock to see it was only a little after eight. She had plenty of time before she had to meet Paul at his trailer at ten o'clock.

Still wearing her long cotton gown, Kate slid into her desk chair, scrolled a piece of paper into her portable typewriter and began typing, her hands flying across the keyboard.

Over the sound of the car engine was a rushing of wind, rain splattering the windshield, the windshield wipers frantically slapping back and forth like out-of-control pendulums. The headlights tunneled into the dark night, found, and lit up the bridge. The car raced toward it, her shoulders hunched forward, her face fixed in a thrilling challenge.

"I'm going to shoot across that thing like a rocket," she said, in a gleeful voice.

"Slow down," Steve, her boyfriend, said. "You're going too fast!"

When the tires hit the bridge, they skidded, and the back tires slid away. The steering wheel whipped left, and she fought it, feeling the car go. A dreadful panic stopped her breathing as the car slammed into the wood railing, sailed, and plunged into the surging black lake. The car smacked the water hard and went under.

Kate leaned back in the chair, sighing out pleasure. She liked it. It had good, tense action and drama. After she finished writing the entire story, maybe Mr. Conning would have her read the story to the class.

After a shower and a speedy breakfast of Cheerios, banana and cinnamon toast, Kate swept from the apartment into the overcast chill of morning and drove to Paul's trailer, arriving fifteen minutes early.

He emerged from the trailer, wearing jeans, a dark blue shirt and an old Army jacket. Descending the stairs, he held up a wicker picnic basket, grinning broadly.

"It's all in here," he said. "Including a bottle of white wine."

"I'm impressed," Kate said, squinting a look at him as he drew up. "I bet you got it at Vans."

"Hey, how do you know about Vans? I thought only locals knew about that place."

Kate thought about it. How *did* she know? The name just jumped out. "I don't know. I guess somebody told me about it."

"Aren't you something, Kate Clarke, writer of stories about guys like me?"

Paul looked skyward. "The weather people promised there'd be no rain."

"I brought an umbrella just in case. Some of those clouds look pretty dark."

"Want to take my car?"

"Sure. It's bigger."

As Paul backed the Pontiac from the carport, Kate turned to him with a rueful expression. "I have a favor."

Paul straightened the car and drove off along the gravel road. "Fire away."

"Would you mind taking a slight detour to the Medical Center?"

Paul glanced over. "Friend? Family?"

"I didn't tell you about it yesterday. I was going to, but... I didn't."

Kate described the bookstore incident and how Jodi Sayers ended up in the hospital.

"I went to visit her, but the doctor said I couldn't see her until today. It won't take long."

"Okay, let's go. Sounds like she could use a friend."

Twenty minutes later, Kate and Paul were at the medical center front desk, where they were told what elevator would take them to Jodi Sayers' room on the third floor.

Kate stopped at the nurses' station on the third floor and learned that Jodi hadn't had any visitors and that she hadn't made or received any calls. The kind nurse added that Jodi had improved, but that she was depressed.

Kate and Paul entered room 305 to see two beds, each separated by privacy curtains. Jodi lay in the bed to the right, her curtains partially open, revealing Jodi under a light blue blanket, her eyes closed. A hefty man with a buzz cut sat in a chair nearby, leafing through a magazine. Kate assumed he was an orderly, assigned as a suicide watchman.

He glanced up sternly as Kate and Paul stepped quietly toward Jodi's bedside. He rose and approached them. "Are you family?" he asked, with some hope.

"No… a friend."

"Do you know her family?"

Kate whispered. "No… we just met the other day. How's she feeling?"

The orderly's voice dropped its hopeful tone. "Quiet. Hasn't said much."

"We won't stay long," Kate said.

The orderly nodded and returned to his chair and

magazine, and Kate and Paul moved toward Jodi's bed. Her breathing was light, her face drawn and sallow.

Kate and Paul exchanged a "What now?" glance.

Since morning, Kate had been struggling to separate fact from fiction, although that wasn't unusual. When she was immersed in a story, she often got distracted. But there was something about Jodi that was different. She recalled meeting her on the train platform on Tuesday, but her memory was foggy as to why she was even at the train station. And then she also remembered that Jodi had spoken to her in a dream, a weird dream about a cave and about the future. Jodi had said, "You can't change the past."

During her shower that morning, Kate's mind had flashed back to her date with Paul. She'd known about Paul's girlfriend, Myra, and that she was from Arizona. But how did she know that? Paul hadn't told her.

Jodi's eyes fluttered open, blinked, closed, and opened again. They slowly slid to the right, focusing first on Paul, and then on Kate, and they widened in recognition.

"You?" Jodi said in a weak, scratchy voice.

"Yeah. Me. I found you unconscious at the bookshop."

Jodi's eyes closed, and she let out a heavy sigh. "Yeah... well. I came to tell you, but you weren't there. The owner said you were late."

Kate shifted her purse from her right hand to her

left. "Tell me what?"

Jodi's eyes opened on Paul. "Do you want me to tell you, with him standing there?"

Kate stared, confused. "Yeah… I guess."

"No, you don't."

Paul looked at Kate. "I'll be outside."

After he was gone, Kate stepped closer to the bed. "How are you?"

"Lousy. Why didn't you leave me there, in the bookstore?"

"Because you would have died."

"That was the point, dumb shit."

Kate drew back a little, fighting offense. "Okay, Jodi. I came by to see how you are, and to see if I can get you something, or call someone for you."

Jodi looked away. "What's your name?"

"Kate."

Jodi turned her stony, dark eyes on her. "I came from the cave, too."

Kate felt a quivering in her knees, as an image of the cave shot into her mind. The smell of it. The chill of it. The terror of it.

"Don't tell me you're already forgetting?"

"Forgetting what?" Kate snapped.

Jodi's mouth sagged. "Damn… I see it in your eyes. It's fading."

"What are you talking about?"

Jodi's voice took on strength. "Time travel, you silly bitch."

And with the words "time travel," the sting of memory returned like a slap. Kate vice-gripped her purse as the scenes of past, present and future tumbled through her mind like moving storm clouds.

Jodi's lips parted, forming a dark, crooked grin. "There you go, baby doll. Now you remember again, don't you? All you needed was a little reminder, right? Well, one day you won't remember, no matter what anybody tells you."

Kate reeled, saw a chair against the wall and groped for it, dropping down. She spoke more to herself than to Jodi. "Then it wasn't a dream... They weren't dreams," she said, in startled recognition.

"You only wish, right?"

Kate's eyes jumped to hers. "No, I don't!"

The orderly lifted his wary eyes from the magazine, checking them out. "Everything okay over there?"

Jodi glanced at him with a snide grin. "We're just fine, nursie boy."

His face darkened, his voice deepened. "I'm an orderly, okay? And my name is Clay."

"Yeah, yeah, whatever," Jodi said, tartly.

Jodi lowered her voice as she spoke to Kate. "Like I said, you will completely forget, sooner or later. All of it. Everything, and that's our problem, Kate. We'll both forget, and then who knows what the hell will happen to us and where we'll end up?"

Kate's eyes were riveted on Jodi. "Where did you come from?"

"Where do you think? From the future, like you."

"What future? When?"

"From 2005. I was sixty years old. Now, I'm twenty-three and I'm starting to forget, and I'm going out of my mind. It's a kind of amnesia, isn't it? So maybe some people remember things longer, and some remember shorter. Who knows why or how."

Kate's throat tightened and she tried to swallow but failed.

Jodi's face hardened. "I wanted to save my little brother from going off to war. He was killed... a week ago, somewhere in Vietnam, in some rice patty. But things weren't the same as the last time, and I know you get that. This time, Don was already dead when I got here. Not like the last time. The last time I saw him off on the bus. Understand? I was too late. The timing was off. All those years wasted."

Jodi pounded the bed with a fist. "Dammit! You can't change the past. It will stop you, and it laughs at you."

Kate shot up, keeping her eyes on Jodi, her expression agonized. "Have you gone back to the cave?"

"Of course, I went back after I got the news that Don was killed, but nothing happened. It doesn't work like that. It doesn't just throw a switch and let you try again. It doesn't send you back to the future. I'm stuck here, with no one. Nothing. My parents are both dead and now my brother, my good, sweet brother, is gone, too. And... it's all starting to fade. I'm starting to forget everything."

Tears glistened in Jodi's sad eyes, and she turned her face aside. "Why didn't you let me die?"

Kate's shoulders were hunched as though she expected an unanticipated slap. "Jodi... I can help. I'll give you some money. I'll help you find a place to stay and then you can get a new start."

Jodi sniffed and coughed, and it was minutes before the emotion drained away. When she finally spoke, her voice held restraint and despair. "We played in that cave when we were kids, Don and me. I was sick in 2005. The doctors said I was going to die in a few months, so I came back here to remember Don and the past. I returned to that cave and ducked inside, and drank a few beers, and remembered and laughed. And then... well... you know what happened."

Paul entered the room, silent, remaining a few steps from the door. Kate turned to him, then back to Jodi. "My friend, Paul, fought in Vietnam."

Jodi sat up and wiped her eyes. "Does he know?" Jodi whispered. "I mean, about time travel?"

Kate shook her head.

Jodi raised her voice so Paul would hear her. "I'm glad you made it."

Paul nodded, but stayed quiet.

"My little brother didn't make it."

"I'm sorry," Paul said.

Kate leaned closer to Jodi. "I can help you."

Jodi shook her head. "No... I don't want anything. I'll figure it out."

Kate opened her purse, removed her wallet and reached for two twenties, all she had, and laid them on the side table. "It's not much. I'll come back tomorrow with more."

Jodi's lower lip trembled. "No… please… no more. I'll be okay. I'm a survivor. You've got to think about yourself now, and what you're going to do, before you forget it all."

Kate stared blindly.

And then Jodi tried to smile. "Hey, I get another chance at my life, don't I? Maybe I'll do better this time."

Kate lowered her trembling voice to a soft whisper. "How many times have we done this?"

Jodi shook her head, and Kate felt the painful force in Jodi's gaze. "I don't know," Jodi said. "And that's what's been making me crazy."

Kate tried to show a brave face. "I'll see you tomorrow."

Jodi leaned her head back and shut her eyes. "Tomorrow? Hell, forget tomorrow. I'll probably forget where I came from, and who I was way out there in the future. And you'll forget too, Kate. How does the saying go? Something about a blessing and a curse?"

CHAPTER 37

A fter Kate and Paul left the hospital, Paul drove east to Cane Creek, Ohio, to the historic home of John Franklin Stanish. Kate switched on the radio, found a 1960s rock station and made small talk, hoping to push away the disturbing thoughts about Jodi and time travel.

Paul turned northeast off State Route 52 onto Dutch Lane, then drove up a steep road that approached the town from the south.

The Stanish House sat on the crest of a high hill above the Village of Cane Creek, with a commanding view of the historic town, a grove of trees, and the extensive river valley.

Kate rolled down her window and inhaled the fresh air. "Wow! It's so open and beautiful. I feel like I can breathe."

"Yeah, I don't know how they've managed to keep the builders out, and I've heard it won't be long before new houses go up over there on that next hill. With that river view, they'll cost a fortune."

The Stanish House was painted a dark green with brown trim. It was relatively small, although the second-story porch offered a pristine view of the Ohio River and the distant shoreline of Northern Kentucky.

Paul parked in the lower parking lot, and they left the car under a white sun, moving in and out of thin, gray clouds. With picnic basket in hand, Paul and Kate climbed the hill toward the house, pausing often to view the vast expanse of colorful autumn trees, rising hills and winding river. Kate gazed up into the bowl of the October sky and took a big breath, blowing it back into the heavens.

"It's heaven," she said, feeling free, turning in a circle. "By the way, who was John Stanish?"

"A Presbyterian minister back in the 1840s and '50s, who gave food and shelter to runaway slaves during his time with the Underground Railroad."

The couple found a spot under a circle of trees and sat on a soft blanket Paul had brought from the car. They spread out their picnic items and, by then, the afternoon sun had broken from the clouds, casting shimmering light across the Ohio River.

While Paul popped the wine cork, Kate removed the ham and cheese sandwiches, the two slices of apple pie, the chips, and the pretzels.

"Hungry?" Paul asked.

"Yeah, I am."

"It's a little colder than I thought it would be."

"It's just the river wind. I don't mind," Kate said, spreading her arms, presenting her face to the sky. "And the sun's out. It's perfect."

Kate sipped the wine and nibbled on a sandwich, while she gazed out past the river to the shadowy Kentucky hills. In her vivid imagination, she could almost feel the air of struggle and terror that the slaves must have felt as they ran for their lives—ran for freedom from vicious slave owners and heartless bounty hunters.

Running and searching for food. Running with rubbery, exhausted legs, running away from a life of hell, and risk being caught and beaten, or killed. Running and praying for help, throat dry, body cold, every snap of twig an alarm, every cry of an animal a warning, every step ahead a little closer to that most cherished of all words: Freedom. Freedom to live. Freedom to flourish. Freedom to love without fear.

It had all happened long ago, and yet, had it really been so long, in the grand scheme of human existence? The conversation with Jodi had jarred Kate's memory loose, shaking out visions of the future and memories of another past.

In a sense, she was a kind of prisoner; a prisoner in time, seeking her own kind of freedom. If Jodi was right—and Kate knew she was—Kate would soon forget who she was and how she'd returned here. The clock was ticking.

Paul noticed Kate's thoughtful expression. "A dollar for your thoughts."

Kate rearranged her legs so that she faced him. "A

dollar, not a penny?"

"Inflation."

"I was thinking about slavery, and freedom and time."

"So many thoughts for a young woman."

"Yeah, well, sometimes I think my head will explode."

"I know that feeling," Paul said. "Life is a big mystery, isn't it?"

"It is that, all right, but I'm glad you brought me here. It's easier to think, or not to think. It's easy to just be."

Paul took a drink of his wine. "I brought you here because I want to tell you something, and I wanted us to be alone and in a beautiful place."

Kate reached for a potato chip and looked at it. "Good news, I hope?"

But she wasn't so sure. Had Myra returned?

Paul cleared his throat. "I've decided. I'm not going to Arizona."

After a long deliberation, and after she'd munched a few potato chips, Kate looked straight at him. "Then you've just changed my life... and I'll never be the same."

Paul swirled the wine in his paper cup. "When I was in Vietnam, I knew guys that had girls back home. They carried photos and talked about them, and they made plans for when they got back. One guy, Ted, was head-over-heels in love. He had three photos of his girl, and she was pretty. From Pittsburg. A couple months before his tour was up, he got a Dear John letter."

Kate stilled, her sandwich half eaten.

"So, Ted was broken up. I told him the usual stuff. 'You'll find another girl even better', you know, that kind of thing. Anyway, all of us were worried about the guy; thought he might do something crazy and get himself killed. But he didn't. He didn't say much, but he was okay. He caught the Freedom Bird out of 'Nam around the same time I did."

"What's the Freedom Bird?" Kate asked.

"It's the airplane that flies you home after your tour is over. Anyway, I told Ted to stay in touch. He didn't. So, when I was driving around the States clearing my mind, I went to see Ted. Guess what?"

Kate lifted her head. "Was he okay?"

"Ted married the girl next door. He said that after he got the letter, something in him snapped, and he knew the relationship with the 'Dear John' girl wouldn't have worked out anyway. Then he said, a few days after he got that letter, he remembered the girl next door, and when he got home, he realized he'd always loved her. He told me, 'She was always the one. Thank God I got that Dear John letter. It was the best thing.'"

Kate waited for Paul's point.

"I didn't have a girl over there. I could have, but I didn't. I broke up with a girl I had been dating because I didn't know if I'd come back. Turns out, she married another guy while I was gone. Then I met Myra, and I thought she was the one. I was going to move to Arizona because I thought she was the one, and I thought it was time I changed my life. But then you came into my life, knocking on my trailer door, and you said, 'I need help.'"

Paul shook his head in wonder. "There you were, with two big, bright eyes, thick black hair, beautiful red lips and a smile like spring."

Kate's heart fluttered and her cheeks flushed. "Wow... you're a poet."

Paul took a swallow of wine. "Like I said, it's all a mystery, isn't it? How time works. How love works."

Kate gave him a playful smile. "What happens if you meet someone tomorrow and you think she's the one?"

Paul knee-walked across the blanket, putting his face close to hers, his eyes close, his lips close. "You're the one, Kate. I knew it from the first. Just you, Kate. You."

He kissed her, deep and warm, and she shut her eyes and drifted. She lay on her back, letting herself go, falling into heat and passion, their parted lips moist and hungry. Kate felt the exciting weight of him, and the hard strength of his arms and hands, and she kneaded the muscles of his back, and shoulders, and the nape of his neck, with anxious fingers.

Paul looked down into her eyes, and Kate pulled him closer, an urgent desire building. They kissed and explored, and drifted into timeless moments, neither aware of the storm clouds that had rolled in fast from across the Northern Kentucky hills.

Kate and Paul ignored the grumbling thunder,

and a gathering wind that fluttered their blanket and blew away their white paper napkins, which went skipping across the lawn, then up, sailing away like white birds.

A gray curtain of rain charged across the river, climbing, low clouds shrouding the Ohio hills, the wind thrashing trees, the storm changing the quality of sound and light.

A thunder roll, a crack of lightning, and the first taps of a pounding rain finally startled Kate and Paul from their embrace. They rolled away, Kate screaming with shock and delight, Paul scrambling to grab the remnants of their picnic and toss them into the basket.

Kate gave the blanket a jerk, rolling it up into her arms, and she and Paul grabbed hands and made a dash down the hill, drenched, laughing and winded, heading for the car.

Paul opened the trunk and tossed in the blanket and wicker basket, while Kate yanked open the passenger door and piled in.

With the trunk closed, Paul started for the driver's side, then stopped, his attention drawn to a big puddle already forming in the center of the parking lot.

Kate watched, incredulous, as Paul darted over to the pooling puddle, even as thunder boomed and sheets of rain came sliding across the countryside, drumming on the roof of the car and bouncing off the asphalt.

Paul waded into the middle of the puddle, turned

to face Kate, and then, with a wide grin and silly face, he wiggled his fingers, inviting her to join him.

She watched as he lifted his right foot high and then stomped the water flatfooted, something a kid would do. Water exploded from his foot amid a crackle of lightning.

And then he leaped into the air and came down, both feet making great geysers that soaked him. Paul spread his arms wide, head back, palms to the sky, and he hopped, and stomped, in a kind of weird, splashing, circular dance.

Seized by the crazy, spontaneous moment, Kate shoved the door open, boiled out, and ran to him, rain pelting down, her hair plastered to her head, her wet clothes clinging.

Giggling, she waded into the puddle, seized Paul's hand and, with goofy grins, they sprang up into the wet, gray day, and came down hard, smacking the surface, spraying jets of water, their faces scrunched, their eyes shut, sheets of rain drenching them.

Paul shouted. "Hey, Kate Clarke, are you a rainy-day girl?"

Kate kicked water, smashed water, and splashed water, laughing her head off. "You're crazy, you know?!"

Paul pulled her into his arms and kissed her, their lips cold, their bodies shivering. A thunder clap shook the world, but they didn't break the kiss.

PART 3

CHAPTER 38

Paul was hauled out of sleep by Gus, Kate's gray tabby cat, who bellowed a mellow "MEOW," then climbed onto Paul's chest, crouched, and stared him down with big, round, green eyes.

It took Paul dull seconds before he realized Kate wasn't lying beside him on the bed. It was after nine o'clock on Saturday morning, March 22, 1969.

"Okay, okay, Gus. I'll get up and feed you, since your best friend and mom obviously didn't."

Paul gently shrugged Gus off his chest, tossed back the blue quilt, and swung his feet to the floor, noticing sunlight lighting up the curtains. He ran a hand through his tousled, thick, reddish-blonde hair, grown long because Kate liked it that way, and stood up. He performed a full body stretch, culminating in a cavernous yawn, and then he padded off barefoot, wearing only his undershorts, to the trailer kitchen.

Gus waited, alert and focused, while Paul reached into the cabinet for Gus's red, paw-print cat food bowl. Kate had found it at the pet store in Paxton, and bought three of the bowls in assorted colors: yellow, blue, and red.

"Hey, buddy, on the breakfast menu this fine, sunny morning is chicken and egg with broth, your favorite, so don't snub it and walk away. Okay, pal?"

Paul scooped the food from the can, dropped it into the bowl, and mashed it up, as per Gus's finicky preference. Paul stooped, set the bowl on the floor and stood back, placing his hands on his hips, his expression hopeful.

"Okay, Gus, bon appétit."

Gus bowed to the bowl, examined the food, sniffed it, lifted his head, and glanced up at Paul as if he were the enemy. He turned away and went striding off, insulted.

"Ah, come on, Gus," Paul pleaded. "It's Friskies, for heaven's sake, your favorite. I paid a lot of money for it. What's the matter with you?"

The phone rang and Paul moved into the living room to answer it. "Hello?"

"Hey, it's me," which meant it was Kate.

"Yeah, well, your cat won't eat the chicken and egg in broth. I mashed it up, too, and garnished it with a sprig of parsley, like all the chefs do."

Kate laughed. "My cat?"

"Well, yeah. You were the one who found him out by the lake."

"Hiding in *your* boat."

"So that makes him mine?" Paul answered, amused.

"Yeah, at least that's the way I see it. And you, my handsome husband, will never admit that you love Gus as much as I do."

"And you, Kate Clarke Ganic, have a way of creating your own reality. It's the writer in you."

"And another reason you love me."

"No argument there. Well, look at that! Gus just poked his head around the corner and scowled at me. I'm telling you, he doesn't like me, and I knock myself out for him."

"Just ignore him. He's just trying to show you who's boss."

"Well, we know the answer to that. Okay, why did you call?"

"Something silly."

"Silly can be good. So what is it?"

"Dr. Burnett said I wouldn't feel the baby move until between sixteen and twenty-four weeks of pregnancy, remember?"

"Yeah, I remember."

"Well, it's only been fourteen weeks."

"Okay... has the baby been kicking?"

"Not kicking, but I swear I can feel it."

"That's normal, isn't it?"

"I called Dr. Burnett right after I got to the bookstore, and he said I might feel flutters."

"And are you feeling flutters?"

"I think so."

"Well, that's good then, isn't it?"

"I told you it was silly."

"Not silly. I'm glad you called. How's Art?"

"Ironically, he's off to see the doctor. He pulled something in his back, lifting a box of books. I told him he needs to hire a high school kid to do the heavy lifting, but you know Art. Stubborn and cheap."

"And you love him."

"Yes, I do."

"Okay, well, don't *you* lift any heavy boxes."

"No way. Oh, and I called my parents this morning when I got here, collect."

"How's your mother?"

"Not so good. I know she's drinking again. I could hear it in Dad's voice."

"Your dad's voice, but not your mother's?"

"No, you'd never hear it in hers, but I'm worried about her."

"We can go see them."

"That's a nice thing to say."

"I like them. Your father and I get along, and your mother's a good conversationalist."

"To you... not to me."

"Well, we can go, if you want."

"Yes, I'd like that," Kate said, quietly. "Oh, and by the way, I love you."

"I'll take that. And you're not sorry you married me? A guy who carried you off to my trailer near the lake?"

"No way, but I'm not sure about your mother. I think she's sorry you married me."

"It will take her a little more time, Kate. We got married fast, and you got pregnant fast. It all happened fast, and she's a woman who came from a different time, and a slower time. The 1960s craziness upsets her. She thinks we're all too impulsive and rebellious."

"Well, at least your father likes me."

"My father loves you, and you know it. He said marrying you was the best decision I ever made."

"Ahh... how nice. When did he say that?"

"You know. I told you. How many times?"

"I don't mind hearing it fifty or a hundred times."

"He said it the first time on that cold November day, two days before Thanksgiving."

"Our wedding day," Kate said warmly.

"Yeah, and around the same time you found Gus in my boat on the lake."

"Now we're back to Gus and we've come full circle, and I have to get to work. Three people just walked in. What are you going to do today? Clean the trailer?"

"I'll give it a lick and a promise. The new carpet feels good on my bare feet."

"Not dressed yet?" Kate asked.

"Nope. Just underwear."

"Damn... Why am I here when I need to be there?"

"I think I know what that means."

"You know what I mean, all right, you sexy guy. What time are you going to work?"

"Early. I'm going to polish up the beautiful '62 Bel Air Sport Coupe, with the bubble top, and finish the checklist. By the way, did I tell you that there were only about six hundred of these beauties ever made?"

"Yes, my darling, you did tell me, and I know it's your new favorite baby doll."

"Yeah, and I'm excited. In six months, I've done a complete mechanical restoration, including rebuilding the powertrain, the suspension/steering, the brakes and the fuel system. It's ready for a test drive and I want you to be the second after me, of course, to give it a go."

"I'm honored, sir, but I still don't know what a powertrain is."

"Never mind. How about tomorrow?"

"Super, duper. Gotta go."

"Love you, Kate Ganic."

"As I do you, mon chéri. Study up for your biology exam."

"I've got it in my hip pocket. See you about five."

Paul hung up the phone and glanced about the trailer. He was newly amazed how Kate had transformed the place from a bachelor hangout to a married nest, complete with a new sofa, matching chairs, a new TV, phonograph, a claw foot coffee table from a yard sale, and white lace curtains.

There was even an original oil painting on the wall, painted by Kate's artist friend, Connie Poe. It featured a big, yellow sun hovering over majestic Cove Lake trees, bathing the world in yellow and bright orange. White puffy clouds hung in a cobalt blue sky, and shards of sunlight glittered the water.

Paul's trailer was featured in the foreground, lit up from within by an unseen spray of golden light, and one could see a woman, from the waist up, dressed in a red top, peering out the picture window in deep reflection. The woman had been a blonde, but, as per Kate's instructions, Connie had painted over the blonde and painted Kate in, with her raven black hair.

Paul turned toward the kitchen. There he was, Gus, chomping away at his breakfast, a ray of sunlight showering him in a kind of cat glory.

Paul sprawled on a deep curve of the brand-new sofa and smiled with contentment. Now that Gus was happy, all was right with the world.

CHAPTER 39

On Sunday afternoon, under a gunmetal gray sky and chilly wind, Kate and Paul stood outside Pete's Texaco Service Station and Auto Repair. They were near the garage, where Paul had parked his new pride and joy, his light green Chevy Bel Air Sport Coupe. Paul ran a hand along the body, wearing the proud expression of a new father.

Kate circled the car, making little nods of approval. "It's lovely."

Al Haynes approached them from the pumps, wearing a baseball cap turned backwards. His blue jumpsuit showed grease stains, and an old rag dangled from his back pocket.

"What do you think, Al?" Paul asked.

Al licked his lips. "Pretty as a picture, Paul. Damn good-looking lady."

"The Bel Air or Kate?" Paul joked.

Al kept his serious expression. "Both."

Kate bobbed a little bow. "Thank you, Al."

Al pointed to Paul. "And he's going to let you drive this thing? His new lady love?"

"Yeah, why not?" Kate asked. "I'm a good driver."

Al leaned a little to his left. "I betcha a hundred bucks you wouldn't let me drive it, would you, Paul?"

Paul squinted a look. "You're a motorcycle guy."

"You're dodging the question there, Paul."

Paul's hand rested on the front hood. "Anytime you want to take her out, Al, have at it."

Al chuckled. "No way, Paul. I'd be so nervous that I'd run the thing into a tree. By the way, you got any moonshine on you?"

"No, I'm off it. We've got a baby on the way. Go see my father. He's always got some stored in his work shed."

A car pulled into the station. Its tires passed over the black rubber hose that snaked across the pavement and rang a bell, signaling for an attendant. As the car snuggled up to the pumps, Al waved at Paul, turned about and went to work.

Paul looked at Kate. "Okay, now the full lecture. It's a two-door, bubble top Sport Coupe, 409 V-8 engine, 360 horsepower with a 4-speed shifter. And get a look at the tachometer, mounted on the steering column. Is it a beauty or what?"

Kate faced the car, crossed her arms, and nodded. "I love the light green color, but I don't know anything about engines and carburetors. And what's a bubble top?"

Paul placed a hand on the roof of the car, his

enthusiasm growing. "Notice the rounded roof. See the curved glass and smooth lines? It makes the roof appear similar to a bubble. Get it?"

Kate cocked her head left and right, thinking about it. "Yeah, I guess so. I mean... bubble? I don't know."

Paul rubbed his hands together. "Yeah, well, whatever. Let's go for that test drive."

Kate glanced up into the gray, moving sky. "It might rain. Do you really want this brand-new car to get wet?"

"I'll take my chances. I heard the weather report this morning. Cloudy skies, but no rain."

Kate climbed behind the wheel and Paul slid into the passenger side, closed the door and gave her last-minute instructions on the 4-speed shifter. "Just shift her nice and easy, and she'll do the rest."

"Aye, aye, captain."

Kate inserted the key, gave it a gentle turn, and the engine engaged, settling into a soft purr. Paul grinned, patting the dashboard. "Listen to that. It's music, Kate. Pure music. Let's go!"

Kate shifted to low, touched the gas, and the car rolled out of the station, as Paul gave Al a final wave.

"Where to?" Kate asked.

"Let's drive down to Lake Road. It should be quiet today, and you can open her up a bit."

Kate drove for five minutes, past sprawling, two-family homes, and turned left onto a narrow road that traced the Cove Lake shore. While she drove under a canopy of trees and took a curve, starting down a hill, she had a flash of memory. She saw an out-of-control car jump off the road and plunge into the lake, and she tasted the mineral lake water.

Two crows sailed by, and a car approached, fast, from the opposite lane. Kate snapped back to reality, and, on reflex, she whipped the car to the shoulder of the road and slowed down, just as the on-coming car whooshed passed.

"He's going too fast!" Kate shouted, her shoulders stiff.

"Just relax, Kate," Paul said calmly. "It's okay. It looked like a couple of high schoolers out on a Sunday joy ride."

Kate's face tightened, her eyes squinted, and she drove slowly.

Paul glanced over. "Want me to take it?"

"No… I'm okay."

More visions flashed in, and Kate struggled to shake them off.

"Kate, what's the matter?"

"I don't know."

"You're sweating. It's sixty degrees out there, and my window's half open."

And then Kate recalled last October, when she and Paul had gone to a Paxton College football game. It was 41 degrees by game time, with a quick, cool wind, and she'd snuggled in close to him.

The packed bleachers held noisy fans from Paxton and their arch rival, Dearborn. Darkness had settled in, enclosing the field under bright lights and burning excitement, and the field seemed to sparkle, a fine, green carpet of manicured perfection.

And then Paul had turned to her, and made a fist, smiling. When he opened his hand, she was stunned to see a golden wedding band. "Will you marry me?" he'd asked.

Kate blinked fast, her pulse rising. Yes, that was true. That had happened. But what about the car? What about her visions of living in the future and of having two children, a boy and a girl? Had that been a dream?

But it was the car dream that kept boomeranging back, a nightmare she couldn't shake. She saw herself driving a car, just like this one, the same color, the same stick shift, and Paul was seated beside her. She saw it clearly, and she felt the terror and the cold truth of it.

"Pull over, Kate," Paul demanded.

Kate's face was pallid and taut with stress. She shook her head, and her eyes cleared.

"Kate… Pull over!"

Kate took a sharp intake of breath, turned onto the narrow shoulder, and braked to a stop. Keeping her hands squeezed tightly on top of the steering wheel, she lowered her head, resting her forehead on them.

"Kate, are you sick? What's the matter?"

Kate cleared her throat. "I don't know. Sometimes I have dreams, like flashbacks. I've told you about them. I've told you how they seem so real. I just had another one. Weird."

"Okay, let's switch sides. I'll drive us home."

Minutes later, Kate was sitting on the passenger side, with her head back and eyes closed. Paul took the old asphalt road that curved around Cove Lake, driving slowly, dodging pot holes and tar patches, tossing occasional, concerned glances toward Kate.

"Feeling better?"

"A little."

"Any pain?"

"No… It's nothing like that."

"We'll be home soon."

Buck Miller was astride his wicked-looking, silver and black Harley Davidson, his hands gripping high handlebars, his meaty forearms flexed. He wore his horned riding helmet, goggles, black leather jacket, jeans and heavy boots.

The Harley roared along Lake Road, Buck leaning, taking the sharp, bending turns at a thrilling speed. He went bursting across the aging asphalt, flying, sinking and snarling past blurring trees and the lapping water of Cove Lake. Fresh air filled his lungs, as quacking ducks went flapping across the water, fleeing.

The Harley climbed a steep hill, angled left away from the lake, and plunged down a winding side road, Buck's eyes wide and bold, his mouth set into a grimace of pure pleasure.

Paul's Bel Air approached the twenty-foot wooden bridge that crossed a narrow portion of the lake. Just as his tires reached the broad boards, Paul saw the motorcycle charging him from across the opposite side. Paul was fully committed to crossing the bridge, with no time to stop, back up, and retreat.

There was no time to think. With barely four feet to spare, Paul reacted expertly, nudging the car to within only inches of the guardrail.

Buck Miller was coming fast. When he saw Paul's car, he knew he was in trouble. His keen eyes spotted a sliver of opportunity to shoot past the car to safety, and he took it.

Paul tapped the brakes, and that's when he heard it. A cracking, squealing sound. Kate screamed as the bridge sagged to the right, the guardrail snapped, and the Bel Air slid off the bridge and plunged into the thirty-foot water.

Buck was about to shoot past the Bel Air when the bridge groaned and gave way. As it collapsed, the Harley pitched violently left, slamming into a section of the remaining wooden guardrail. It bounced off, flinging Buck away in a somersault. Man and machine sailed, splashed, and vanished.

Paul was vaguely aware of being submerged, as cold, churning water gushed in around him. Disoriented and tangled in objects, his slow-motion arms reached, and his hands searched for Kate. Bubbles boiled from his mouth, and he fought raw panic. He felt a hand touch him for just an instant, and he twisted toward it, but it was gone.

His chest swelled and strained for air, his heart kicked, and a bright crackling explosion in his brain stunned him, and he drifted.

A police car on the far side of the bridge skidded

to a stop, both officers startled by what they'd witnessed. One officer grabbed his radio and called for help, as the driver burst from the car. He skidded down the shoreline to the lake, conflicted, feeling helpless, as bubbles rose to the surface where Paul's car had sunk.

In desperation, the officer yanked off his cap, removed his gun belt and jacket, and went wading into the cold water, wincing. He dived, disappearing under the surface.

Minutes later, the wail of an on-coming siren and the chop of an approaching helicopter shattered the silence. From across the lake, two boats rushed to the scene, white foam trailing behind them.

A fine mist fell, the wind kicked up, and the broken, sloping bridge was a grim-looking skeleton, sinking beneath the slate gray, rippling tide.

CHAPTER 40

November 2017

Seventy-three-year-old Paul Ganic pushed through the glass revolving doors at Macy's Department Store and stepped out onto 34th Street. Anxious shoppers nudged, bumped, and edged around him.

With only a week before Thanksgiving, sale signs were everywhere, as were shoppers. There were early Christmas shoppers seeking one-day bargains, women pursuing kitchen deals, and grumpy fathers toting kids, scouting the upper floors, looking for Santa.

And there were the elderly, who still distrusted online shopping, who donned hat, coat, and gloves and patiently climbed aboard buses to take their annual journey to the Mecca of all department stores, Macy's.

New York City lay cleaned and washed from an early morning rain, and it was bright and glowing in the cold, November sunshine.

Paul turned up the collar of his black woolen overcoat and started uptown, deciding to walk for a while before flagging down a cab.

At seventy-three years old, Paul was fortunate to have all his hair and to be in good shape, thanks to a local gym membership. He also took frequent, two-mile walks in Riverside Park, which was across the street from his two-bedroom condo on West 84th Street.

Paul carried a large, red, Macy's shopping bag. Inside was a two-piece frying pan set, a Christmas present for Molly Stivers, the attractive, fifty-two-year-old woman who lived upstairs. They were friends—nothing more—although she wanted more.

It's not that Paul felt old, but he was too old to begin a relationship with a woman who hobnobbed with the wealthy, the connected, and the political. She had the energy of three people, and if she was nice and intelligent—and she was—she was also a bit pushy and restless. And she had three cats. Paul liked cats but, unfortunately, two of those cats didn't like him. But then, from what he'd seen, they didn't like Molly either.

Paul was a confirmed old bachelor, and he intended to stay that way, an old dog who had mastered all the new and old tricks he'd need for the rest of his life.

At the corner of 41st and Broadway, Paul turned to search for a yellow cab. When a young woman approached him, he ignored her, certain she was looking for someone else.

She faced him fully, her expression sad. "I didn't get it."

Paul glanced about, but there was no one around him. "Are you talking to me?"

"Why not? You have a good face."

Paul didn't know how to respond. She was a pretty girl, somewhere in her twenties, with a tall, trim body, like a Rockette dancer. She wore an elegant, doubled-breasted, Edwardian style coat, and a white, smart hat, her long, blonde hair resting on her shoulders.

"I'm having a really shitty day."

"I'm sorry…"

The girl inhaled a frustrated breath and blew it out in a white vapor cloud. "I'm a triple threat, you know."

Paul knew what that meant. "So, you're a performer? Singer, dancer, actor?"

"Only if I work in the theater. If I don't work in the theater, I work at Roland's."

"Restaurant?"

"Rooftop bar."

"It's a little cold for that, isn't it?"

"It's enclosed, and it's heated, and it gets hot with the free-standing fireplace."

A taxi approached, its dome light on, indicating it was free for hire. Paul was going to flag it down, but he didn't. The girl just stood there, looking glum and dejected.

"Auditions..." she said bitterly, looking skyward, lifting then dropping her shoulders. "I hate them."

"What show did you audition for?"

"*Hello, Dolly*."

"I saw it a while back."

"Yeah, well, they're doing an updated version. More modern, with big, fancy, moving sets."

"I'm sorry you didn't get a callback."

She looked at him. "But I did. I got called back three times. That's why I'm so pissed off. It was down to me and one other girl, and I'll tell you this for sure: I can dance a whole helluva lot better than she, and I sing better, too."

"Well, maybe she knew somebody."

The girl crossed her arms, staring up into the sky. "I don't know. You never know what type they're looking for, do you?"

Paul extended his gloved hand. "I guess not. By the way, I'm Paul."

She looked at him, took his hand and gave it a little shake. "I'm Mandy. Like I said, you've got a good face. A kind face. I know you think I'm nuts, but I'm not. I've never just walked up to a perfect stranger and started bullshitting like this. I just needed somebody to talk to right then; right at that moment, back there when I saw you. My boyfriend didn't pick up his phone, and he hasn't answered any of my texts. My mother's not around or not picking up her phone, and I've texted everybody and anybody else I know. Nothing. Zip. Then I saw you."

Paul searched for words. "Well... that's one of the good things about New York. You can talk to a perfect stranger and not worry, because you'll probably never see them again."

"Yeah, but maybe that perfect stranger is a nut job, too. But I'm pretty good at judging people, and I didn't think you were a nut job."

"Thanks. I try not to be, although I have my moments."

The corners of her mouth turned up and nearly formed a smile. "Will you have coffee with me? There's probably a Starbucks around here somewhere. I mean, if you want to. I mean, if you don't have to be anywhere else? I don't want to be alone right now."

Paul gazed at her, and he saw a pretty girl having a really bad day.

"You don't have anything else, do you?" Mandy asked, her eyes hopeful.

"No, I don't. Okay, let's get a coffee. Better yet, it's almost time for lunch. How about I take you for lunch and buy you a glass of champagne?"

Mandy's mouth quivered, her eyes misted up, and she lowered her head.

"Mandy... I didn't mean to..."

She held up a hand and made a vague gesture. "No, no... It's okay. It's just that... It's just that... it's just such a totally awesome and nice thing to say, and I guess I needed it. Real nice."

"Okay. So?" Paul said, lifting a hand. "Shall we?"

Mandy looked at him warmly, wiping away tears. "You're a cool guy, Paul."

Paul shrugged. "Thanks. Now let's do lunch with champagne."

Mandy's expression changed, a beautiful smile lighting up her pretty face. "Where have you been all my life, Paul?"

Mandy linked her arm in his and they went striding off.

They sat in quiet elegance in Peter S Café, just off 44th Street. The tablecloth was linen, the white tapered candle fluttered, the atmosphere was dark-wood-dim and subdued, and the Moët & Chandon Impérial Brut Champagne was bubbly and golden in crystal flute glasses.

Mandy had retreated to the bathroom to freshen up, sweeping back to the table with luscious blonde hair, red lips, dreamy blue eyes and a smile of delight.

She tasted the champagne and sighed with pleasure. "Oh. My. God. This is awesome, Paul! Will you be my sugar daddy?"

"No, Mandy, but I'll be your friend."

"Your wife is lucky."

"Not married."

"No way."

"Way," he said, lifting his left hand, ringless, to prove it.

Mandy glanced about, lowering her voice. "Are you gay?"

Paul smiled. "No, I'm not."

Mandy leaned back. "Then, I don't get it. You're a really handsome man, like Cary Grant or something."

Paul looked at her doubtfully. "And how do you even know who Cary Grant was?"

"My grandmother loved him. She had pictures of him in a scrap book, and she made me watch his movies. I liked them. Well, some of them."

"I bet you liked *An Affair to Remember*, right?"

Mandy twisted up her lips in distaste. "No way. That was so, I don't know, like sugary sweet. No, I liked the one where he played the thief."

"Ah, yes. I liked that one, too."

Mandy sipped her champagne, not taking her exploring eyes off Paul. "Seriously, Paul, were you ever married?"

Paul stared into his glass. "Yes. Once, a long time ago."

"How long?"

"Long before you were born."

"When?"

"The late '60s."

Mandy stared, her eyes not blinking. "Oh, wow. Yeah, like that's a long time ago, all right. So, what happened?"

"I don't talk about it."

She lowered her eyes. "Oh… Okay. Sorry."

Texts "dinged" in, but Mandy didn't reach for her

phone.

"Answer those if you want," Paul said.

"I don't want to. I'm having fun and I don't want anything to spoil it."

Their entrees arrived, hers the pan-roasted chicken with figs and smoked mushrooms and Paul's, the pan-seared halibut, with grilled asparagus and charred shallots.

"When did you start dancing?" Paul asked.

"When I was six."

"Have you been in any Broadway shows?"

"Three, all as a dancer/singer, never a lead."

"You'll get there. Keep at it."

"I have two auditions next week. Who knows?"

"Well, I have a good feeling about you, Mandy. Why don't you audition, just as an actress, for some TV shows? You have a good look for that."

"Tell my agent. He's only got me one audition for some TV show I've never heard of, and I didn't get the part."

"Maybe you should look for a new agent?"

"No more about me, Paul. I want to know what you do."

"I'm retired, although I still do consulting jobs when I want them."

"What kind of jobs?"

"To make a long story short, I'm an environmental engineer."

"Whoa... what is that?"

"Simply put, an environmental engineer helps to improve recycling, waste disposal, public health, and water and air pollution control. We also study ways to minimize the effects of acid rain, global warming, automobile emissions, and ozone depletion."

"So, you're like an environmentalist?" Mandy asked, draining her flute of champagne.

The waiter appeared and quickly refilled her glass and topped off Paul's.

Paul sliced into the halibut. "Part of it, yes, but the day-to-day stuff is also focused on what the state and federal regulations are and how you're going to meet those regulations, while considering costs and timelines."

"Wow... so, you're really making a difference in the world."

"As are you. When I go to the theater or the symphony, the performers and musicians make a big difference in my life. I got a consulting job here in New York about twelve years ago, and after a few months, I moved here, so I could see people like you perform."

Mandy gazed at him with admiration. "Do you know something, Paul? Guys like you aren't around much anymore. You're like the best."

"Oh, I don't know about that. I just seem that way because you've had a glass and a half of champagne."

Mandy turned serious. "What was your wife like?"

Paul laid his fork aside and glanced out the window. "Without sounding too cliché, she was as close to me as my heart. The best thing that ever happened to me."

He stared at Mandy with a detached, emotionless gaze. "She was killed in a car accident, and she was pregnant with our child."

Mandy slouched, her eyes filling with grief. "Oh my God, Paul, I'm so sorry."

His gaze was stuck in the distance, as if he were seeing the past. "It was a very long time ago."

"Don't take this the wrong way, but you never fell in love with another woman? I mean, that was a long time ago."

"I've had lady friends but, no, I never did fall in love… like that first time with Kate."

The voices at tables around them seemed to stop, as if they were waiting for the next word.

Paul blinked the memories away and returned to his lunch.

Mandy readjusted herself in the chair and lowered her voice. "Paul… *will* you be my friend?"

His smile was faint. "How about I be another grandpa? I could use a granddaughter."

Mandy stretched out a hand. "You've got it."

They shook.

At Broadway and 48th Street, Mandy kissed Paul on the cheek, and he put her in a cab, handing her twenty dollars.

"Text me and let me know how things are going, Mandy."

She smiled up at him. "Thanks for everything, Paul. I'll be in touch. Let's do this again."

"Anytime."

When she was gone, Paul walked aimlessly, and the only thing he knew for sure was that he had to go back home to Paxton. Talking to Mandy had brought it all back. He wanted to walk the streets again and see the lake again and remember Kate again.

How many years had it been? Not since 1987, when his father died, and Paul sold the house. Yes, it was time, even if the grief tore at and shredded his heart.

Perhaps Kate's breath still lingered by the lake, in the trees and in the sound of the lapping water. Maybe the ghost of her wandered and searched for him.

Yes, speaking with Mandy had shaken something loose inside, and he felt the pull to return to Paxton. After all these years and the lonely nights and the bad dreams, for whatever the reason, he was going to fly to Columbus, rent a car and drive to Paxton.

CHAPTER 41

On Saturday morning, two days after Thanksgiving, Paul sat on a hill overlooking Paxton, Ohio. It was dawn, and the town began to awaken around him, with twinkling lights, the murmur of traffic, and the flyover of a single-engine airplane. Paxton was a much larger town than the one he and Kate had lived in all those years ago.

Paul gave a tug on his black ski cap to cover his ears, and he buttoned the top button on his blue parka, feeling the crisp morning air seep into his bones. He tipped his head, deep in thought. He thought of Mandy and, once again, he calculated how old his child would have been if Kate hadn't been killed in the car accident back in 1969. He had hoped for a girl. She would be forty-eight years old, and by now, he'd surely have a grandchild, who would probably be about the same age as Mandy.

It had been another reason Paul had taken to

the girl, and the thought of playing grandpa to lovely Mandy brought a smile and a small sense of satisfaction that he'd been able to cheer her up on one of her dark days. She'd left him recharged and optimistic. *It's the small things*, Paul thought.

There were still a few stars in the brightening sky, a low moan of a freight train whistle and some ground mist below. Friday had been a long day, and when he'd arrived at his motel room after ten o'clock, he'd looked forward to a shower, a spot of bourbon whiskey, and a long, deep sleep.

Sleep had not come easily, and he was awake by four a.m., splashing water onto his face and gazing at himself in the bathroom mirror. Not so many wrinkles, but some loose skin and plenty of gray hair. And there were his tired eyes, or sleepy eyes, or sad eyes. Why had he come? What did he hope to gain? What kind of fool was he, anyway?

He'd snubbed the motel coffee, dressed, said good morning to the pleasant desk clerk, and left the burgundy and gray motel, seeking a Starbucks, but he came up empty. It was too early, even for the early birds.

Paul had driven through the quiet, sleeping town of Paxton in a semi-doze, not impressed by the changes: the chain stores, all with the same-sized, generic signs; the put-'em-up-fast cell phone stores and fast-food joints; and the ever-present new bank branches, offering credit cards with loan shark interest rates.

Well, he was an old man, wasn't he? Grumpy old

man? Yeah, probably. Cynical old man? He hoped not.

He found a pastry shop that was open, and it had a cheerful, yellow and tan interior. The heavy woman behind the counter was friendly and energetic, and she insisted he sample the freshly baked raisin scone. The warm bite cheered him, and he bought two, along with a cup of dark roast coffee.

Paul drove toward Lake Road, sipping the coffee and snaking his hand into the white bag where the scones were. Pinching off pieces of the warm, crusty thing was fun.

The streets were eerily quiet, since the students were on break for Thanksgiving Day weekend, and other residents had left town for the holiday.

In the 1980s, when Paul had returned to sell his parents' house, he'd seen the beginning of inevitable change. Big houses were already sprouting up near the lake, with longer boat docks stretching out into the water. There were outboards, and speedboats, and an expanded marina for rowboat and dual paddleboat rentals.

As Paul turned onto a smoothly paved road, he touched the brake and slowed down. He crept along in dread, draining the last of his coffee, absently placing the empty paper cup in the cup holder. Yes, he'd returned to Paxton to visit his parents before their deaths, but he had never allowed himself to drive by Cove Lake or revisit the area where his trailer had been.

There it was, the spot where his trailer had once

sat, that old relic of a thing even in the 1960s. But he'd grown to love it, and after he and Kate had married, she'd insisted they live there and fix it up instead of moving to an apartment.

The new owners of the property had bulldozed the entire area, and the land had been graded to maximize space and expand access to the lake. The road had been widened, and tall trees hid other big homes near the lake and further up the hill.

Where Paul's trailer once sat was a sprawling, four-bedroom house, complete with a two-car garage and a thirty-foot aluminum boat dock.

Paul felt depression creep into his soul. He didn't linger. Driving away, he heard old voices, old laughter, and the old regrets that come from a place in the head where memories live.

When the first spray of rosy dawn appeared in the eastern sky, and the trees took shape and the houses emerged from shadows, Paul drove to the other side of town and parked. He glanced up into the surrounding hills and set his mind adrift, recalling boyhood days of baseball, chores with his father, and roaming the hills, searching for fun and hidden caves.

Sitting on the hill with his knees up, Paul recalled tumbling down the weedy slope into high grass, falling into the wildflowers of spring, and into the warm and endless days of summer.

Age had come on him swiftly, like a time thief in the night. He'd never thought of age so much. He'd remained vital and enthusiastic about his work.

Fortunately, he'd been respected and in demand—and he was still in demand, if he wanted to work.

But then he'd taken a tumble during a ski trip in Colorado seven years back, and he'd badly injured his right knee. Three years ago, he'd caught a bad cold that had turned into pneumonia because, as his dear neighbor, Molly Stivers, had scolded, "You don't look after yourself and you don't have a woman to bully you into seeing a doctor."

The pneumonia had taken a toll on his energy, and as he slowly recovered, that's when he heard the tolling of the age bells, and he realized he wasn't thirty-five years old anymore, and he never would be again.

Getting to his feet, Paul inhaled the cold morning air, and it revitalized him. He rambled, and kicked at the brown grass, and glanced up at the sky, and he made silly wishes that blew away in the wind.

When he found himself at the cave—HIS cave, as he used to call it—he ambled over, his hands deep in the pockets of his parka. He'd spent many autumns, springs and summers ducking in and out of that cave. Two racoons lived in it for a while. One autumn, Paul wrestled with a brown snake or two, and he'd won, but they'd returned a month later, and he'd let them have it for a while.

One hot summer day, when he was fourteen, he'd gotten into a fistfight with Mark Lynch to see who'd be king of the cave. He'd won, and Mark said he'd never forgive him. They laughed about it thirty years later, when Paul ran into him in Columbus.

Mark had become a state congressman by then and had wanted to help Paul. "But you're on the wrong side, Paul. Get with it. I can get you some jobs if you switch your political team."

"I'm on both sides, Mark," Paul had said. "That's how everybody wins."

Mark had called him an idealist.

Paul approached the cave and frowned at the crushed beer cans, scattered potato chip bags and cigarette butts. Low brush and two heavy tree branches covered the cave entrance.

Still standing well over six feet, Paul parted the branches, stepped over a thicket, and lowered his head. Morning light filtered in, a dusty, foggy light. Crouching, Paul ventured inside into shadows, the dank, earthy smells filling his nose with nostalgic pleasure.

A hot breath of a breeze startled him. Then a current of cold wind rushed across his face. He heard a humming noise, or was it the wind creaking through some crevice in the rear of the cave? Odd sounds. Unfamiliar sounds.

Paul shut his eyes, then opened them, adjusting to the dim light. A sharp flash of blue light nearly blinded him, and he threw up a hand to cover his eyes. Windchimes. What? Where? There was the squeal of wind—the loud bang of a branch against the cave door.

A dizzy, whirling feeling made him clumsy. It was time to back out. Get out! His bum leg buckled, and Paul dropped to his knees, pain cutting sharp through his leg and foot. He gulped in air. Flat, stale air. A slap of heat walloped his face, shoving him onto his left side.

"Heart attack," Paul gasped. "Stroke?"

Paul gulped in one last breath of air before everything went black, and his head struck the earth, his mouth open.

CHAPTER 42

P aul lunged from the mouth of the cave with momentum and intensity, spilling to the ground, skidding on his stomach, his chest heaving. Panic was loud in his head, like an unbearable shrill alarm. He sat up, mouth breathing; big, scared eyes moving; brain working; heart thumping.

He saw an open place in the trees ahead, and he sprang up on strong legs and sprinted for that open place, like a wild animal running for its life.

The open place was the crest of a hill surrounded by glittering autumn trees, a towering blue sky, and the town of Paxton below. Paul stood with scrambled thoughts, sweaty palms and damp face, staring down at the town he'd known in his youth; a town long ago erased by time and progress. Goose bumps rippled up the back of his neck to the top of his head.

In the full flood of afternoon sunlight, Paul saw

his new hands, and he felt his face with them. He flexed his arms and his legs. His bum knee was strong. No pain. No numbness. Both legs were ripe with robust energy, ready and waiting for his command to send them leaping and racing off across the grass into the fresh, afternoon wind.

In that moment of confusion, Paul gazed out across the wide fields, at the surrounding trees and the town below, and he recalled late night talks when Kate had shared her dreams and visions about caves and time travel, amazing stories about the future and the past.

Paul slowly brought a shaky hand to his mouth, and swallowed, in a desperate effort to clear his mind and truly see what was spread out before him. Was it possible that Kate's dreams had not been dreams at all? Several times, she'd said, "Sometimes I don't know if they happened or not. Some of them seem so real, and I dream them over and over again."

He knew now, with the certainty of death, that these dreams had not been just dreams, but that Kate had lived her life before—as it seemed he was about to do. It was impossible, and it was terrifying, and it was stupendous.

In a kind of trance, Paul started down the hill toward town, recalling something he'd memorized in American History when he was a student at Paxton College. Thomas Paine had said, "*We have it in our power to begin the world over again...*"

Paul heard his mind talking too much, bantering, tossing out sneering words of doubt. He saw that his mind was that of a twenty-five-year-old man. He shut it off, set his determined jaw, and descended the hill, shedding his ski cap and stuffing it into his unbuttoned parka, lengthening his strides.

In some odd way, it all made sense. He and Kate and time travel, or whatever you wanted to call it—their immediate attraction, their love at first sight. Well, it wasn't first sight, was it? They'd known each other before. Okay, how many befores? How many times were there?

Paul didn't really care what the phenomenon was called, or how it had happened, or whether his beliefs and concepts had been smashed to pieces. He couldn't deny his young, strong body and what was in front of him: a world he'd known fifty years ago.

Paul had two goals: find out the date, and find Kate. If her dreams had been actual events, then Paul's here-and-now reality, his brand-new life, was real, too. But he knew from Kate's "dreams," that soon he'd forget what had happened before. That meant he had precious little time to change the past so that his and Kate's life together would not end tragically.

He made a vow: he would not lose Kate again. Not this time. Never again!

Paul crossed the railroad tracks and stopped, staring at the old train terminal with fond astonishment. He climbed the stairs to the platform and hesitated. Passengers wore the hats and clothes of the 1960s. Billboards on the terminal walls advertised Winston Cigarettes, Avon for men, and the Clint Eastwood movie, *Coogan's Bluff*. Paul recalled those posters. All of them.

He released an uneasy breath as the world of his youth stared back at him, challenging him once more to believe it or to deny it. It took seconds for him to pull himself together. As he did so, a man approached. He was weathered-faced, wearing brown, corduroy trousers, a railway-striped, long sleeve shirt, black suspenders, and a worn, faded, brown felt hat, tugged low over his brow.

He drew up to Paul and stopped. "Good afternoon," he said, looking Paul over.

Paul gave him a single nod.

The man looked to the hill where Paul had come from. "You know, friend, you can't change the past."

Paul felt his skin crawl as he eyed him suspiciously. "Who are you?"

The man shrugged. "Let's just call me a time watchman."

Paul didn't like this time watchman, and he stared coldly at him. And then Paul spoke as a seventy-three-year-old man who'd lived a long life, the man who'd lived a lonely, regretful life, the man who'd fought bitterness and rage for most of that life. This was the man who answered the time watchman in an acid tone.

"I'm not going to change the past, friend. I'm going to change the future. Now, get away from me and leave me alone."

The man's face darkened, and his wrinkles deepened. He touched two fingers to the brim of his hat. "All right then, young man, I'll bid you a good day, and wish you good luck. You'll need the luck."

The man turned and shambled away, exiting inside the train station.

Shaking off the encounter, Paul drew up to a prim, middle-aged woman, with a black purse and matching clunky shoes, wearing a dark coat and a stylish hat.

"Pardon me, ma'am. Could you please tell me the date?"

She regarded him warily. "What? What did you say?"

"I know how it sounds, but I've been away. Please, what's the date?"

She leaned a bit toward him, trying to smell his breath.

"Please, ma'am. I'm not drunk."

She turned her head, hugging her purse tightly to her chest, and then said, curtly, "It's Thursday, October 17, 1968."

Paul lit up, turned on his heel, hurried across the platform, and bounded down the stairs. As he went striding past Chamber's Drug Store and out onto Main Street, he tossed an anxious glance toward the clock tower next to the National Bank of Ohio. Had that clock been there before? He didn't remember it.

It was 4:05 p.m.! Kate was scheduled to work at Art's bookstore at four o'clock!

Traffic was heavy, the beautiful model cars of the 1960s rolled by, and women in beehives and smart, fashionable coats window-shopped. And there were men in dark suits, hats and polished shoes, exiting the bank and entering the smoke shop.

The Regal Record Shop was pounding out rock music by Jimi Hendrix, and bustling with long-haired, hippie wannabes and local teenagers. Feisty students from Paxton College crowded the Paxton Sweet Shop and shouldered into the Pizza Place and Kip's Bar. It was all just as Paul had remembered it.

When he saw Mackay's Books New & Old only a block away, he hurried, as anxiety reasserted itself. He felt the adrenaline impact his breathing, and his throat tightened. If Kate was alive again, if she was in there, then a lifetime of despair, guilt and anger would lift and blow away in the autumn wind.

Paul stood facing Art Mackay's two-story bookstore, and he thought, *My life ends here. My life begins here.*

He stepped forward, reached for the brass doorknob, and turned it. The door swung open and a little bell above "dinged." Paul entered and closed the door behind him, feeling jittery nerves and a wild sense of expectation. He looked to his right, his throat dry, his pulse racing.

Perched on a stool, reading, waiting for the next person or thing to irritate him, was Art Mackay. He lifted his eyes from the paperback book he was reading. He wore faded overalls, a dingy white shirt, black Keds tennis shoes and wire-rimmed spectacles.

Paul wanted to rush to Art, grab him up in a bear hug, and tell him he was the best thing he'd seen in fifty years, but he didn't.

How many times had Art come for dinner at the trailer, back in the day? Five, six times? The three of them had cooked together, drunk wine, and laughed easily. They had talked music and politics, argued over the war, and read portions of Kate's stories and poems. Art was a good and generous friend, who had died at sixty-seven in the bookstore, the place where he'd wanted to die.

"I bet you're a student, aren't you?" Art said, with mild disgust. "You've come down from Paxton College on high to find a book that some damned professor said will change your life, right?"

Paul made a vague gesture, wanting to laugh out loud.

Art closed his book and removed his spectacles. He spoke in the voice of an orator, flinging out the soaring words, as if they were standing in a Greek amphitheater.

"Well, young man and student friend, the Earth continues to turn round and round, despite spasms of violence, mystery and injustice, shuddering its way toward that inevitable day of cataclysmic destruction. But it will rise again, despite itself—mark my words—like a great, soaring phoenix."

Art's voice changed, falling in volume and resonance into his every day, conversational, scratchy baritone. He tossed his book down on the counter, pushed his hands into his overall pockets, and stared pointedly at Paul. "All right, now that we have that out of the way, what book can I find for you?"

Paul battled emotion, the sudden fear that Kate wasn't there, that she wasn't in town, that somehow, she had never been born.

Art bored into Paul with his eyes. "Out with it, young man. Time and tide wait for no man... or woman."

"Kate..."

"Kate?" Art asked.

"Kate Clarke."

Art inhaled a breath, his face opening to Paul's meaning. He could see it on the young man's face. Attraction. Love. Desire.

"She's here, isn't she?" Paul asked, his voice tight and small with fear.

Art twisted up his lips, then jerked a thumb toward the rear of the store. "She's in the stock room, working."

"Can I... see her? Talk to her?"

"You want me to go get her, young man, or can you find your own way?"

"I can go."

"Then go... You appear to be a man who knows what he wants. And maybe you even look a little familiar. So, on your way."

Paul turned left and started up the middle aisle, passing towering shelves of books. The stockroom door was open, and he heard Kate humming a tune as she passed across the doorway, carrying an armful of books.

Paul waited outside the door, unsure of what to do

or say. Finally, he took a step forward and knocked on the open door.

A moment later, Kate appeared, without the books, and his heart jumped. Her raven black hair was tied up in a yellow bandanna, and the tip of her tongue was poking out from the side of her mouth, just as it always did when she was lost in her work. All those years ago, he'd kissed the tip of that tongue.

She placed her hands on her hips, and her lovely eyes expanded on him.

"Hello..." Paul said, softly.

Kate blinked and gave him a vague smile. "Hello? Can I help you?"

Paul had waited so long. "Kate... I'm Paul Ganic."

"Yes?" Kate said, with polite confusion. "Did Art tell you my name?"

"No, he didn't."

She searched his face, his eyes lit up by a strange intensity. She grew uneasy. "Okay... Can I get you something?"

"Have you had dreams about the past lately?"

Kate drew her head back. "Dreams?"

"Yes, dreams about the past and the future?"

Kate took a step back, seeing a curious depth in his eyes that awakened something in her she couldn't comprehend.

"Don't be scared... It's just that I... I mean, do you recognize me?"

Kate cocked her head right, frightened, searching for Art.

"I'm not trying to scare you, but please try to

remember your dreams. Please… it's important that you remember."

Kate looked at him strangely. "Who are you?"

"We used to know each other."

"I don't know…" Kate's voice trailed off, and something flickered in her eyes, suggesting a new thought, an old memory. She took another step backwards and was stopped by stacked boxes filled with books.

Paul softened his voice. "It was a long time ago, Kate. I lived in a trailer down by Cove Lake. I had a boat. We had a cat named Gus. I went to school here. We knew each other. Please… you must remember. Those dreams… They're not just dreams. They happened. *We* happened."

Kate's face fell into confusion. Her eyes moved left and right, as memories struggled to rise to the surface of her mind.

Art drifted over, and stood to Paul's left. "Is everything all right, Kate?"

Kate looked at him with bold, frightened eyes. "Do you know this guy, Art?"

Paul looked at Art. Art looked at Paul. "No, but he knows you."

Kate stilled, putting a fingernail to her lips. Her mind went wandering in search of her old dreams, recalling diary entries about those dreams, and about the man she'd seen in her dreams, and how she'd described him. How she'd kissed him and loved him.

Kate stared directly at Paul, her face vivid with

conflict. The man standing before her, staring down at her with pleading, loving eyes, was the man in her dreams!

In that startled moment, Kate sprang forward, brushed by the two men, and hurried to the front door. When she was gone, Art turned to Paul.

"Who the hell are you? What did you say to her?"

"I'm sorry, Art. I didn't mean to upset her. I'll go."

Paul left the shop, searching for Kate, seeing her sitting on a bench near the public library, her head down. With easy, careful steps, he wandered over, stopping ten feet away.

Kate didn't look at him for a time. She didn't move. She stared down. When she spoke, it was at a thoughtful whisper. "Dreams... Yes, so many dreams... And you were there. You were there in all my dreams, but I had forgotten."

In a remarkable instant, Kate glanced up at Paul, and her face brightened, and her eyes sparkled in the sun. She rose and stood before him, tentative.

"I saw it in your eyes, Paul. In those few seconds, I saw everything."

"How many times, Kate? How many times have we searched for each other?"

Kate shook her head. "What do we do now?"

Paul's expression was urgent. "We can't stay here. We have to break the cycle. We have to go and never come back. We have to leave here before we forget... before we lose each other again."

Kate fell into his arms, pressing her head into his shoulder, feeling as though she'd finally come home after a long, long journey.

Paul held her, kissing her hair, glancing up into the sky, grateful to be alive and to have Kate in his arms again.

"Why that cave, Paul?" Kate asked. "What's in that thing?"

"I don't know, but I've been thinking about it. When I got back from Vietnam, there were storms, bad lightning storms that struck all along the hills and the caves. My father said they were the worst storms he could ever remember. My mother said they were from the devil."

They looked at each other and tried to smile, but failed, each feeling the anxiety of the unknown.

"Where will we go?" Kate asked.

"It doesn't matter. We'll be together, and this time, nothing will separate us. Never again."

EPILOGUE

November 2015

U nder a dazzling sun and deep blue, New York City sky, there was a gentle breeze and a temperature of thirty-nine degrees. The giant helium balloons went bobbing over the streets for Macy's Thanksgiving Day Parade, and there were big smiles, cheers, and shouts of "Happy Thanksgiving!" echoing down Central Park West, all the way to Herald Square.

Kate, Paul and their two grown kids, Ethan and Diana, along with their spouses and five kids, sat in the bleacher seats on West 77th Street. They were joined by spectators bundled in hats, scarves and winter coats, all enjoying the festive day. Kids waved, pointed and shouted, and some toddlers wore big mittens and turkey-shaped hats.

There were baton twirlers, stilt walkers, and high energy dancers, and the thunder of drums and the shrill brass of marching bands. The celebration included seventeen giant character balloons, twenty-seven floats, twelve marching bands, 1,000 clowns, and guest appearances by Pat Benatar and Mariah Carey.

Kate linked her arm into Paul's and drew him close. "It's a perfect day, isn't it?"

He kissed her nose. "Yeah, but you have a cold nose there, Mrs. Ganic. And you look cold."

"Yep, but I don't care. You'll keep me warm."

"I'm cold, too," Paul said, with a dramatic shiver. "Whose idea was this, anyway?"

"Yours. This is our tenth time, and they were all your idea."

"Rhetorical, Kate. You know I love this. But I wish I hadn't forgotten to bring that thermos of hot chocolate."

"You had a senior moment there, my darling," Kate said, with a big grin. "Join the club. I forgot to put the turkey in the oven."

Paul looked at her with mock accusation. "No... Say it's not true? Not you, the famous author who's written twenty-five books, one play and two screenplays? You forgot to put the turkey in the oven?"

Kate held up her hand as if swearing an oath. "Yep. Guilty as charged. Dinner's going to be late."

"We could go out."

"No way. Not on Thanksgiving."

"We could eat the pumpkin pie first," Paul said, with a wide, delicious grin, and a sweep of his tongue across his upper lip.

Kate narrowed her playful-severe eyes on him. "Don't even think about it, Paul Ganic."

He smiled, drawing her closer. "Having fun?"

"The best."

Paul glanced to his left. The parents were having as much fun as the grandkids.

"Hey, Kate Clarke, we did okay, didn't we?" Paul said. "We've got good kids, and plenty of grandkids to entertain us in our old age."

Kate laid her head on his shoulder. "Yeah. Want to do it all again? We could drive to Paxton, Ohio, climb that hill and duck into that cave. Who knows, we might even do it better next time."

Paul was motionless for a thoughtful moment. "No... don't want to, and I thought you didn't dream about the past anymore."

"It's all in my diary, so we don't forget."

"Maybe I want to forget. I don't want to go back and do it all again. I'm having fun, and I've had a blast. I want to keep on going and see where this life adventure leads."

Kate looked up at him. "We know where it will lead... unless we go back to that cave."

The Charlie Brown float drifted by, and the kids cheered and waved.

"Could you really leave this?" Paul asked. "Our kids? The grandkids and all the great times and memories, with more to come?"

Kate leaned forward, turned her head left and watched her grandchildren. Their hands were waving at Charlie Brown, their faces were bright with joy, their parents—Ethan and Diana and their spouses—all smiles.

Kate returned her head to Paul's shoulder. "No, of course, I couldn't leave them. Never. And, anyway, who knows if, when we entered that cave, we'd return to 1968? We might miss each other, and then you'd run off and marry somebody else."

"Or you…" Paul said, kissing her nose again.

"No, not me. Never. You're my guy. My only guy, in the present time, past time or any future time."

A high school band marched in, with a sharp rat-ta-ta-tat of snare drums, the sun glinting off the brass. They burst into the song *Over the Rainbow*, and Kate lifted her head, turning to Paul, her lips puckered, waiting for a kiss.

After they broke the kiss, she shouted over the music. "Is that our song?"

"I don't know. Do you want it to be?"

Kate gave him another peck on the lips, holding him in her warm and loving eyes. "Yeah. I do!"

Feeling a spreading contentment, Kate leaned her head back and stared up into the blue dome of sky. In her head, words came, and she mentally wrote them down.

Above us is the entire sky, timeless, with no boundaries, immense and glowing. And here are the past and the present, intermingled, in an ever-changing dance.

And here are crowds of people, and the day is wonderfully cold, but full of warmth, and filled with children, the promise of new life.

And there is the enduring hope that no matter what happens, in the end, love, caring, and friendship come together, and the world is a better place. And the world celebrates.

THANK YOU!

T hank you for taking the time to read *Time Past,* a Time Travel Novel. If you enjoyed it, please consider telling your friends or posting a short review. Word of mouth is an author's best friend, and it is much appreciated.

Thank you,
Elyse Douglas

❊ ❊ ❊

HERE ARE EASY INSTRUCTIONS for how to leave a book review for *Time Past* on *Amazon.*

Log into your *Amazon* account.

Find the book title - *Time Past* by Elyse Douglas

On the upper right hand corner click on Returns & Orders.

Locate *Time Past*, and on the right side, select

"Write a Product Review."

Select the number of stars you'd like to rate the book. If you'd like to just rate the book without leaving a review, go to step five.

If you wish to write a review in the Customer Reviews section, the review should be a minimum of 20 words.

Click submit. *Amazon* will usually send you an email that lets you know your review was accepted.

Again, many thanks for reading *Time Past*. We hope you enjoyed it!

* * *

Other novels by Elyse Douglas you might enjoy:

The Christmas Diary (Book 1)

The Christmas Diary – Lost and Found (Book 2)

The Summer Diary

The Other Side of Summer

The Christmas Women

Time with Norma Jeane (A Time Travel Novel)

The Christmas Eve Letter (A Time Travel Novel) Book 1

The Christmas Eve Daughter (A Time Travel Novel) Book 2

The Christmas Eve Secret (A Time Travel Novel) Book 3

The Christmas Eve Promise (A Time Travel Novel) Book 4

The Christmas Eve Journey (A Time Travel Novel) Book 5

The Speakeasy Series – Time Travel Novels

The Lost Mata Hari Ring (A Time Travel Novel)

The Christmas Town (A Time Travel Novel)

The Summer Letters

Time Change - A Time Travel Novel

Time Visitor – A Time Travel Novel

Daring Summer - Romantic Suspense

The Date Before Christmas

Christmas Ever After

Christmas for Juliet

The Christmas Bridge

Wanting Rita

www.elysedouglas.com

Subscribe Here for Updates

Editorial Reviews

THE LOST MATA HARI RING – A Time Travel Novel
by Elyse Douglas
"This book is hard to put down! It is pitch-perfect and hits all the right notes. It is the best book I have read in a while!
5 Stars!"
--Bound4Escape Blog and Reviews

"The characters are well defined, and the scenes easily visualized. It is a poignant, bitter-sweet emotionally charged read."
5-Stars!
--Rockin' Book Reviews

"This book captivated me to the end!"
--StoryBook Reviews

"A captivating adventure..."
--Community Bookstop

"...Putting *The Lost Mata Hari Ring* down for any length of time proved to be impossible."
--Lisa's Writopia

"I found myself drawn into the story and holding my breath to see what would happen next..."
--Blog: A Room Without Books is Empty

Editorial Reviews

THE CHRISTMAS TOWN – A Time Travel Novel
by Elyse Douglas

"*The Christmas Town* is a beautifully written story. It draws you in from the first page, and fully engages you up until the very last. The story is funny, happy, and magical. The characters are all likable and very well-rounded. This is a great book to read during the holiday season, and a delightful read during any time of the year."

--Bauman Book Reviews

"I would love to see this book become another one of those beloved Christmas film traditions, to be treasured over the years! The characters are loveable; the settings vivid. Period details are believable. A delightful read at any time of year! Don't miss this novel!"

--A Night's Dream of Books

Editorial Reviews

THE SUMMER LETTERS – A Novel
by Elyse Douglas
"A perfect summer read!"
--Fiction Addiction

"In Elyse Douglas' novel *The Summer Letters*, the characters' emotions, their drives, passions and memories are all so expertly woven; we get a taste of what life was like for veterans, women, small town folk, and all those people we think have lived too long to remember (but they never really forget, do they?).
I couldn't stop reading, not for a moment. Such an amazing read. Flawless."
5 Stars!
--Anteria Writes Blog - To Dream, To Write, To Live

"A wonderful, beautiful love story that I absolutely enjoyed reading."
5 Stars!
--Books, Dreams, Life - Blog

"The Summer Letters is a fabulous choice for the beach or cottage this year, so you can live and breathe the same feelings and smells as the characters in this wonderful story."

ABOUT THE AUTHOR

Elyse Douglas

Elyse Douglas is the pen name for the husband and wife writing team of Elyse Parmentier and Douglas Pennington.

Some of Elyse Douglas' novels include: "The Other Side of Summer," "Time Stranger," "The Christmas Eve Series," "Time Zone" and "The Summer Diary." They live in New York City.

www.elysedouglas.com

PRAISE FOR AUTHOR

"The Christmas Eve Series is gripping ... time travel, history, and a love story that doesn't end!"

- STORYBOOK REVIEWS

"The Lost Mata Hari Ring" is hard to put down! It is pitch-perfect and hits all the right notes. It is the best book I have read in a while! 5 Stars!"

- BOUND4ESCAPE BLOG AND REVIEWS

"Speakeasy" is a frolicky, jazzy blast that will have you eagerly turning pages into the wee hours of the night!"

- BOOKSHELF REVIEWS

"The Christmas Town" is a wonderful time travel novel. It is a beautifully written story, and it draws you in from the first page and fully engages you up until the very last. A delightful read during any time of the year."

- BAUMAN BOOK REVIEWS

"I highly recommend 'Daring Summer'! Whatever you do, do not start reading it if you have somewhere to go that day! It is impossible to put down! 5 out of 5 stars!"

- TEDDY ROSE BOOK REVIEWS

BOOKS BY THIS AUTHOR

Time Zone

In 2015, Pilot Mary McLane Carson struggles with a left engine fire. Her airplane plunges through a strange flash of light, crash-landing into a Kansas field. She wakes up, alone, in December 1942, being cared for by the handsome Dr. Thomas Fleming.

Speakeasy Book Series

One minute, singer Roxie Raines is in a 2019 West Village nightclub and the next, she's traveled back in time to New York's raucous Roaring Twenties!

Enjoy the wild ride with flappers, gangsters and speakeasies!

Time Visitor

In 1944 a Squadron of Navy Planes Disappears off the Florida Coast. One Lands in 2005... In Ohio.

The Christmas Eve Letter 5-Book Series

In an antique shop, Eve finds an old lantern with a dusty letter hidden inside. It's dated 1885, and her name is written on it. The series begins...